MOMENT OF DEATH

Motionless I stood staring at the most dangerous man in the world—transfixed, held totally immovable by his piercing gaze.

There was no sound in the room, just my awareness of sickening sensations akin to the visions of a drowning man; I was awaiting, with untold horror, the moment of my death.

Dr. Fu Manchu did not move, and my duty was plain—to rid the world of this insidious demon. I plunged for my automatic. . . .

"Stand still!" he hissed. "Don't stir. Slowly—very slowly—move your head to the left." I obeyed, moving my head inch by inch. In that position, glancing out of the corner of my eye, I became again stricken motionless. . . .

The blade of a huge, curved knife was being held less than an inch from my neck!

ZEBRA HAS IT ALL!

EAGLES (1500, $3.95)
by Lewis Orde
Never forgetting his bitter childhood as an orphan, Roland Eagles survived by instinct alone. From the horrors of London under siege to the splendors of New York high society, he would ruthlessly take what he desired—in business, and in bed—never foreseeing how easily his triumphs could turn into tragedy.

THE MOGHUL (1455, $3.95)
by Thomas Hoover
Captain Brian Hawksworth, emissary of King James, sailed to India vowing to make his mark on that dark and foreboding land. Fighting with heroism, loving with passion, he found India leaving its mark on himself as well—two cultures clashing in his own soul.

THE LAST OF DAYS (1485, $3.95)
by Moris Farhi
Though he claimed to be God's messenger, if his plan succeeded he'd create a hell on earth. Driven by voices, hidden by an army of fanatic followers, protected by the possession of a nuclear weapon, he had to be stopped before fulfilling the awesome prophecy of . . . THE LAST OF DAYS.

THE PEKING MANDATE (1502, $3.95)
by Peter Siris
The Russians, having incited a civil war in China, are secretly draining China's massive oil reserves. Caught between the ruthless agents of the KGB and the relentless assassins of the Red Guard, only one man, an untrained and untried American financier, has a chance to stop them!

PAY THE PRICE (1234, $3.95)
by Igor Cassini
Christina was every woman's envy and every man's dream. And she was compulsively driven to making it—to the top of the modeling world and to the most powerful peaks of success, where an empire was hers for the taking, if she was willing to PAY THE PRICE.

Available wherever paperbacks are sold, or order direct from the Publisher. Send cover price plus 50¢ per copy for mailing and handling to Zebra Books, Dept. 1617, 475 Park Avenue South, New York, N.Y. 10016. DO NOT SEND CASH.

SAX ROHMER'S
The Drums of FU MANCHU

ZEBRA BOOKS
KENSINGTON PUBLISHING CORP.

ZEBRA BOOKS

are published by

Kensington Publishing Corp.
475 Park Avenue South
New York, NY 10016

First printing: June 1985

Printed in the United States of America

CONTENTS

THE DRUMS OF
FU MANCHU

Chapter 1

MYSTERY COMES TO BAYSWATER

"Damn it! There *is* someone here!"

I sprang up irritably, jerked the curtains aside and stared down into Bayswater Road. My bell, "Bart Kerrigan" inscribed above it on a plate outside in the street, was sometimes rung wantonly by late revellers. The bell was out of order and I had tried to ignore its faint tinkling. But now, staring down, I saw someone looking up at me as I stood in the lighted room: a man wearing a Burberry and a soft hat, a man who signalled urgently with his arms, indicating: "Come down!"

Shooting the bolt open so that I should not be locked out, I ran downstairs. A light in the glazed arcade which led to the front door refused to function. Groping my way I threw the door open.

The man in the Burberry almost upset me as he leapt in.

"Who the devil are *you?*"

The door was closed quietly and the intruder spoke, his back to it as he faced me.

"It's not a holdup," came in coldly incisive tones. "I just *had* to get in. Thanks, Kerrigan, but you were a long time coming down."

"Good heavens!" I stepped forward in the darkness and extended my hand. "Nayland Smith! Can I believe it?"

"Absolutely! I was desperate. Is your bell out of order?"

"Yes."

"I thought so. Don't turn the light up."

"I can't; the fuse is blown."

"Good. I gather that I interrupted you, but I had an excellent reason. Come on."

As we hurried up the semi-dark staircase, I found my brain in some confusion. And when we entered my flat:

"Leave your dining room in darkness," snapped Nayland Smith. "I want to look out of the window."

Breathless, between astonishment and the race up the stairs, I stood behind him as he stared out of the dining-room window. Two men were loitering near the front door—and glancing up toward my lighted study.

"Only just in time!" said Nayland Smith. "I tricked them—but you see how wonderfully they are informed. Evidently they know every possible spot in which I might take cover. Unpleasantly near thing, Kerrigan."

In the lighted study I gazed at my visitor. Hat removed, Nayland Smith revealed a head of virile curling hair, more grey than black. Stripping off his Burberry, he faced me. His clean-cut features, burned by a recent visit to the tropics, looked almost haggardly thin, but the fire in his eyes, the tense nervous vitality of the man must have struck a spark of animosity or of friendship in any but a soul dead.

He stared at me analytically.

"You look well, Kerrigan. You have passed twenty-seven, but you are lean as a hare, clean-cut and obviously fit as a flea. The last time I saw you was in Addis-Ababa. You were sending articles to the *Orbit* and I was sending reports to the Foreign Office. Well, what is it now?"

He stared down at the littered writing desk. I moved towards the dining room.

"Drinks? Good!" he snapped. "But you must find them in the dark."

"I understand."

When presently I returned with a decanter and syphon:

"Look here," I said, "I was never happier to see a man in my life. But bring me up to date: what's the meaning of all this?"

Nayland Smith dropped a page which he had been reading and began reflectively to stuff coarse-cut mixture into his briar.

"You are writing a book about Abyssinia, I see."

"Yes."

"You are not on the staff of the *Orbit*, are you?"

"No. I am in the fortunate position of picking and choosing my jobs. I did the series on Abyssinia for them because I know that part of Africa pretty well. Now, I am doing a book on present conditions."

As I poured out drinks:

"Excuse me," said Nayland Smith, "I just want to make sure."

He walked into the darkened dining room, carefully closing the door behind him. When he returned:

"May I use your phone?"

"Certainly."

I handed him a drink of which he took a sip, then, raising the telephone receiver, he dialled a number rapidly, and:

"Yes!" His speech was curiously staccato. "Put me through to Chief Inspector Wessex' office. Sir Denis Nayland Smith speaking. Hurry!"

There was an interval. I watched my visitor fascinatedly. In my considerable experience of men, I had never known one who lived at such high pressure.

"Is that Inspector Wessex? . . . Good. I have a job for you, Inspector. Instruct Paddington Police Station to send a party in a fast car. They will find two men — dark-skinned foreigners — hanging about near the corner of Porchester Terrace. They are to arrest them — never mind the charge — and lock them up. I will deal with them later. Can I leave this to you?"

Presumably the invisible chief inspector agreed to take charge of the matter, for Nayland Smith hung up the receiver.

"I have brought you your biggest story, Kerrigan. I know you can afford to await my word before publishing. I may add" — tapping the loose manuscript on the desk — "that you have missed the real truth about Abyssinia, but I can rectify that." He began in his restless way to pace up and down the carpet. "Without mentioning any names, a prominent cabinet minister resigned quite recently. Do you recall it?"

"Certainly."

"He was a wise man. Do you know why he retired?"

"There are several versions of the story."

"He has a fine brain — and he retired because he recognised that there was in the world one *first-class* brain. He retired to review his ideas on the immediate destiny of civilisation."

"What do you mean?"

12

"The thing most desired, Kerrigan, by all women, by all sensible men, in this life, is *peace.* Wars are made by few but fought by many. The greatest intellect in the world today has decided that there must be *peace!* It has become my business to try to save the lives of certain prominent persons who are blind enough to believe that they can make war. I was en route for Sir Malcolm Locke's house, which is not five minutes' drive away, when I realised that a small Daimler was following me. I remembered, fortunately, that your flat was here, and trusted to luck that you would be at home. I worked an old trick. Fey, my man, slowed up around a corner just before the following car had turned it. I stepped out and cut through a mews. Fey drove on. But my two followers evidently detected the trick. I saw them coming back just before you opened the door! They know I am in one of two buildings. What I don't want them to know is where I am going. Hello —!"

The sound of a speeding automobile suddenly braked came up from Bayswater Road.

"Into the dining room!"

I dashed in behind Nayland Smith. We stared down. A police car stood outside. There were few pedestrians and there was comparatively little traffic. It was the lull before eleven o'clock, the lull which precedes the storm of returning theatre and picture goers. A queer scene was being enacted on the pavement almost directly below my windows.

Two men (except that they were dark fellows I could discern no more from my viewpoint) were struggling and protesting volubly amid a group of uniformed constables. Beyond, on the park side, I saw now a small car standing—it looked like a Daimler. A constable on patrol joined the party, and the police driver pointed in the direction of the Daimler. The expostulating prisoners were hustled in, the police car was driven off and the constable in the determined but leisurely way of his kind paced stolidly across the road.

"All clear!" said Nayland Smith. "Come along! I want you with me!"

"But, Sir Malcolm Locke? In what way can he be—?"

"He's a cousin of the home secretary. As a matter of fact, he's abroad. It isn't Locke I want to see, but a guest who is staying at his house. I must get to him, Kerrigan, without a moment's delay!"

"A guest?"

"Say, rather, someone who is hiding there."

"Hiding?"

"I can't mention his name—yet. But he returned secretly from Africa. He is the driving power behind one of Europe's dictators. By consent of the British Foreign Office, he came, also secretly, to London. Can you imagine why?"

"No."

"To see *me!*"

Chapter 2

SIR MALCOLM'S GUEST

Fey, that expressionless, leather-faced valet-chauffeur of Nayland Smith's, was standing at the door beside the Rolls, rug over arm, as though nothing unusual had occurred; and as we proceeded towards Sir Malcolm's house, Smith, smoking furiously, fell into a silence which I did not care to interrupt.

I count myself psychic, for this is a Celtic heritage, yet on this short journey nothing told me that, although as correspondent for the *Orbit* I had had a not uneventful life, I was about to become mixed up in a drama the outcome of which meant nothing less than the destruction of what we are pleased to call Civilisation. And in averting Armageddon, by the oddest paradox I was to find myself opposed to the one man who, alone, could save Europe from destruction.

Sir Malcolm Locke's house presented an unexpectedly festive appearance as we approached. Nearly every window in the large building was illuminated, a number of cars were drawn up and a considerable group of people had congregated outside the front door.

"Hello!" muttered Nayland Smith. He knocked out his pipe in the ash tray and dropped the briar into a pocket of his Burberry. "This is very odd."

Before Fey had pulled in Smith was out and dashing

up the steps. I followed and reached him just as the door was opened by a butler. The man's face wore a horrified expression: a constable was hurrying up behind us.

"Sir Malcolm is not at home, sir."

"I am not here to see Sir Malcolm, but his guest. My name is Nayland Smith. My business is official."

"I'm sorry, sir," said the butler, with a swift change of manner. "I didn't recognise you."

The door opened straight into a lofty hallway, from the further end of which a crescent staircase led to upper floors. As the butler closed the door I immediately became conscious of a curiously vibrant atmosphere. I had experienced it before, in places taken by assault or bombed. It is caused, I think, by the vibrations of frightened minds. Several servants were peering down from a dark landing above but the hallway itself was brightly lighted. At this moment, a door on the right opened and a clean-shaven, heavily built man with jet-black, close-cropped hair came out. He glanced in our direction.

"Good evening, Inspector," said Nayland Smith. "What's this? What are *you* doing here?"

"Thank God you've arrived, sir!" The inspector stopped dead in his stride. "I was beginning to fear something was wrong."

"This is Mr. Bart Kerrigan—Chief Inspector Leighton of the Special Branch."

Nayland Smith's loud, rather harsh tones evidently having penetrated to the room beyond, again the door opened, and I saw with astonishment Sir James Clare, the home secretary, come out.

"Here at last, Smith," was his greeting. "I heard your

16

voice." Sir James spoke in a clear but nearly toneless manner which betrayed his legal training. "I don't know your friend"—staring at me through the thick pebbles of his spectacles. "This unhappy business, of course, is tremendously confidential."

Nayland Smith made a rapid introduction.

"Mr. Kerrigan is acting for no newspaper or agency. You may take his discretion for granted. You say this unhappy business, Sir James? May I ask—"

Sir James Clare raised his hand to check the speaker. He turned to Inspector Leighton.

"See if there is any news about the telephone call, Inspector," he directed, and as the inspector hurried away: "Suppose, gentlemen, you come in here for a moment."

We followed him back into the apartment from which he had come. It was a large library, a lofty room, every available foot of the wall occupied by bookcases. Beside a mahogany table upon which, also, were many books and a number of documents, he sat down in an armchair, indicating that we should sit in two others. Smith was far too restless for inaction, but grunting irritably he threw himself down into one of the padded chairs.

"Chief Inspector Leighton of the Special Branch," said Sir James, "is naturally acquainted with the identity of Sir Malcolm's guest. But no one else in the house has been informed, with the exception of Mr. Bascombe, Sir Malcolm's private secretary. In the circumstances I think perhaps we had better talk in here. Am I to take it that you are unaware of what occurred tonight?"

"On your instructions," said Smith, speaking with a

17

sort of smothered irritability, "I flew from Berlin this evening. I was on my way here, and I can only suppose that the purpose of my return was known. A deliberate attempt was made tonight to wreck my car as I crossed Bond Street, by the driver of a lorry. Only Fey's skill and the fact that at so late an hour there were no pedestrians averted disaster. He drove right on to the pavement and along it for some little distance."

"Did you apprehend the driver of this lorry?"

"I did not stop to do so, although I recognised the fact that it was a planned attack. Then, when we reached Marble Arch, I realised that two men were following in a Daimler. I managed to throw them off the track, with Mr. Kerrigan's assistance — and here I am. What has happened?"

"General Quinto is dead!"

Chapter 3

THE GREEN DEATH

This news, coupled with the identity of the hidden guest, shocked me inexpressibly. General Quinto! Chief of Staff to Signor Monaghani; one of the most formidable figures in political Europe! The man who would command Monaghani's forces in the event of war; the first soldier in his country, almost certain successor to the dictator! But if I was shocked, the effect upon Nayland Smith was electrical.

He sprang up with clenched fists and glared at Sir James Clare.

"Good God, Sir James! You are not telling me that he has been —"

The home secretary shook his head. His legal calm remained unruffled.

"That question, Smith, I am not yet in a position to answer. But you know now why I am here; why Inspector Leighton is here." He stood up. "I shall be glad, gentlemen, if you will follow me to the study which had been placed at the disposal of the general, and in which he died."

A door at the further end of the library was thrown open and I entered a small study, intimately furnished. There was a writing desk near a curtained window, which showed evidence of someone's recent activities. But my attention was immediately focussed upon a settee in an arched recess upon which lay the body of a man. One glance was sufficient—for I had seen him many times in Africa.

It was General Quinto. But his normally sallow aquiline features displayed an agonised surprise and had acquired a sort of ghastly greenish hue. I cannot better describe what I mean than by likening the effect to that produced by green limelight.

A man whose features I could not distinguish was kneeling beside the body, which he appeared to be closely examining. A second man looked down at him; and as we entered the first stood up and turned.

It was Lord Moreton, the king's physician.

Introductions revealed that the other was Dr. Sims, the divisional police surgeon.

"This is a very strange business," said the famous consultant, removing his spectacles and placing them in a pocket of his dress waistcoat. "Do you know"—he looked from face to face, with a sort of naïve astonishment—"I have no idea what killed this man!"

"This is really terrible," declared Sir James Clare. "Personal considerations apart, his death here in London under such circumstances cannot fail to set ugly rumours afloat. I take it that you mean, Lord Moreton, that you are not prepared to give a certificate of death from natural causes?"

"Honestly," the physician replied, staring intently at him, "I am not. I am by no means satisfied that he did die from natural causes."

"I am perfectly sure that he didn't," the police surgeon declared.

Nayland Smith, who had been staring down at the body of the dead soldier, now began sniffing the air suspicously.

"I observe, Sir Denis," said Lord Moreton, "that you have detected a faint but peculiar odour in the atmosphere?"

"I have. Had you noticed it?"

"At the very moment that I entered the room. I cannot identify it; it is something outside my experience. It grows less perceptible — or I am becoming used to it."

I, too, had detected this strange but not unpleasant odour. Now, apparently guided by his sense of smell, Nayland Smith began to approach the writing desk. Here he paused, sniffing vigorously. At this moment the door opened and Inspector Leighton came in.

"I see you are trying to trace the smell, sir. I thought it was stronger by the writing desk than elsewhere, but I could find nothing to account for it."

"You have searched thoroughly?" Smith snapped.

"Absolutely, sir. I think I may say I have searched every inch of the room."

Nayland Smith stood by the desk tugging at the lobe of his ear, a mannerism which indicated perplexity, as I knew; then:

"Do these gentlemen know the identity of the victim?" he asked the minister.

"Yes."

"In that case, who actually saw General Quinto last alive?"

"Mr. Bascombe, Sir Malcolm's private secretary."

"Very well. I have reasons for wishing that Mr. Kerrigan should be in a position to confirm anything that I may discover in this matter. Where was the body found?"

"Where it lies now."

"By whom?"

"By Mr. Bascombe. He phoned the news to me."

Smith glanced at Inspector Leighton.

"The body has been disturbed in no way, Inspector?"

"In no way."

"In that case I should like a private interview with Mr. Bascombe. I wish Mr. Kerrigan to remain. Perhaps, Lord Moreton and Doctor Sims, you would be good enough to wait in the library with Sir James and the Inspector. . . ."

2

Mr. Bascombe was a tall fair man, approaching middle age. He carried himself with a slight stoop, although I learned that he was a Cambridge rowing Blue. His manner was gentle to the point of diffidence. As he entered the study he glanced in a horrified way at the body on the settee.

"Good evening, Mr. Bascombe," said Nayland Smith, who was standing before the writing table, "I thought it better that I should see you privately. I gather from Inspector Leighton that General Quinto, who arrived here yesterday morning at eleven o'clock, was to all intents and purposes hiding in these rooms."

"That is so, Sir Denis. The door behind you, there, opens into a bedroom, and a bathroom adjoins it. Sir Malcolm, who is a very late worker, sometimes slept there in order to avoid disturbing Lady Locke."

"And since his arrival, the general has never left those apartments?"

"No."

"He was a very old friend of Sir Malcolm's?"

"Yes, a lifelong friend, I understand. He and Lady Locke are in the south of France, but are expected back tomorrow morning."

"No member of the staff is aware of the identity of the visitor?"

"No. He had never stayed here during the time of Greaves, the butler — that is, during the last three years — and he was a stranger to all the other servants."

"By what name was he known here?"

"Mr. Victor."

"Who looked after him?"

"Greaves."

"No one else?"

"No one, except myself and Greaves, entered these rooms."

"The general expected me tonight, of course?"

"Yes. He was very excited when you did not appear."

"How has he occupied himself since his arrival?"

"Writing almost continuously, when he was not pacing up and down the library, or glancing out of the windows into the square."

"What was he writing?"

"I don't know. He tore up every shred of it. Late this evening he had a fire lighted in the library and burnt up everything."

"Extraordinary! Did he seem very apprehensive?"

"Very. Had I not known his reputation, I should have said, in fact, that he was panic-stricken. This frame of mind seemed to date from his receipt of a letter delivered by a district messenger at noon yesterday."

"Where is the letter?"

"I have reason to believe that the general locked it in a dispatch box which he brought with him."

"Did he comment upon the letter?"

"No."

"In what name was it addressed?"

"Mr. Victor."

Nayland Smith began to pace the carpet, and every time he passed the settee where that grim body lay, the right arm hanging down so that half-closed fingers touched the floor, his shadow, moving across the ghastly, greenish face, created an impression that the features worked and twitched and became still again.

"Did he make many telephone calls?"

"Quite a number."

"From the instrument on the desk there?"

"Yes—it is an extension from the hallway."

"Have you a record of those whom he called?"

"Of some. Inspector Leighton has already made that inquiry. There were two long conversations with Rome, several calls to Sir James Clare and some talks with his own embassy."

"But others you have been unable to check?"

"The inspector is at work on that now, I understand, Sir Denis. There was—er—a lady."

"Indeed? Any incoming calls?"

"Very few."

"I remember—the inspector told me he was trying to trace them. Any visitors?"

"Sir James Clare yesterday morning, Count Bruzzi at noon today—and, oh yes, a lady last night."

"What! A lady?"

"Yes."

"What was her name?"

"I have no idea, Sir Denis. She came just after dusk in a car which waited outside, and sent a sealed note in by Greaves. I may say that at the request of the general I was almost continuously at work in the library, so that no one could gain access without my permission. This note was handed to me."

"Was anything written on the envelope?"

"Yes: 'Personal—for Mr. Victor.' I took it to him. He was then seated at the desk writing. He seemed delighted. He evidently recognised the handwriting. Having read the message, he instructed me to admit the visitor."

"Describe her," said Nayland Smith.

"Tall and slender, with fine eyes, very long and narrow—definitely not an Englishwoman. She had graceful and languid manners, and remarkable composure. Her hair was jet black and closely waved to her head. She wore jade earrings and was wrapped up in what I assumed to be a very expensive fur coat."

"H'm!" murmured Nayland Smith, "can't place her unless"—and a startled expression momentarily crossed his brown features—"the dead are living again!"

"She remained in the study with the general for close upon an hour. Their voices sounded animated, but of course I actually overheard nothing of their words. Then the door was opened and they both came out. I rang for Greaves, the general conducted his visitor as far as the end of the library and Greaves saw her down to her car."

"What occurred then? Did the general seem to be disturbed in any way? Unusually happy or unusually sad?"

"He was smiling when he returned to the study, which he did immediately, going in and closing the door."

"And today, Count Bruzzi?"

"Count Bruzzi lunched with him. There have been no other visitors."

"Phone calls?"

"One at half past seven. It was immediately after this that General Quinto came out and told me that you were expected, Sir Denis, between ten and eleven, and were to be shown immediately jnto the study."

"Yes. I was recalled from Berlin for this interview which now cannot take place. This brings us, Mr. Bascombe, to the ghastly business of tonight."

"The general and I dined alone in the library, Greaves waiting."

"Did you both eat the same dishes and drink the same wine?"

"We did. Your suspicions are natural, Sir Denis, but such a solution of the mystery is impossible. It was a plain and typically English dinner — a shoulder of lamb with mint sauce, peas and new potatoes. Greaves carved and served. Followed by apple tart and cream of which we both partook, then cheese and young radishes. We shared a bottle of claret. That was our simple meal."

Nayland Smith had begun to walk up and down again. Mr. Bascombe continued:

"I went out for an hour after dinner. During my absence General Quinto received a telephone call and afterwards complained to Greaves that there was some-thing wrong with the extension to the study — that he had found difficulty in making himself audible. Greaves informed him that the post office was aware of this defect and that an engineer was actually coming along at the moment to endeavour to rectify it. As a matter of fact the man was here when I returned."

"Where was the general?"

"Reading in the library, outside. The man assured me that the instrument was now in order, made a test call and General Quinto returned to the study and closed the door. I remained in the library."

"What time was that?"

"As nearly as I can remember, a quarter to ten."

"Yes, go on."

"I sat at the library table writing personal letters, when I heard Greaves in the hall outside putting a call through to the general in the study. I heard General Quinto answer it, dimly at first, then more clearly. He seemed to be shouting into the receiver. Presently he came out in a state of some excitement—he was, I may add, a very irascible man. He said: 'That fool has made the instrument worse. The lady to whom I was speaking could not hear a word.'

"Realising that it was too late to expect the post office to send anyone again tonight, I went into the study and tested the instrument myself."

"But," snapped Nayland Smith, "did you observe anything unusual in the atmosphere of the room?"

"Yes—a curious odour, which still lingers here as a matter of fact."

"Good! Go on."

"I put a call through to a friend in Chelsea and was unable to detect anything the matter with the line."

"It was perfectly clear?"

"Perfectly. I suggested to the general that possibly the fault was with his friend's instrument and not with ours. I then returned to the library. He was in an extraordinarily excited condition—kept glancing at his watch and inquiring why *you* had not arrived. Some ten minutes later he threw the door open and came out again. He said: 'Listen!'

"I stood up and we both remained quite silent for a moment.

" 'Did you hear it?' he asked.

" 'Hear what, General?' I replied.

" 'Someone beating a drum!' "

"Stop!" snapped Smith. "Those were his exact words?"

"His exact words . . . 'Surely you can hear it?' he said. 'An Arab drum—what they call a darabukkeh. Listen again.'

"I listened, but on my word of honour could hear nothing whatever. I assured the general of this. His face was inflamed and he remained very excited. He went in and slammed the door—but I had scarcely seated myself before he was out again.

" 'Mr. Bascombe,' he shouted (as you probably know he spoke perfect English), 'someone is trying to frighten me! But by heavens they won't! Come into the study. Perhaps you will hear it there!'

"I went into the study with him, now seriously concerned. He grasped my arm—his hand was trembling. 'Listen!' he said, 'it's coming nearer—the beating of a drum—'

"Again I listened for some time. Finally: 'I'm sorry, General,' I had to say, 'but I can hear nothing whatever beyond the usual sounds of distant traffic.'

28

"The incident had greatly disturbed me. I didn't like the look of the general. This talk of drums was unpleasant and uncanny. He asked again what on earth had happened to you, Sir Denis, but declined my suggestion of a game of cards, so that again I left him and returned to the library. I heard him walking about for a time and then his footsteps ceased. Once I, heard him cry out: 'Stop those drums!' Then I heard no more."

"Had he referred to the curious odour?"

"He said: 'Someone wearing a filthy perfume has been in this room.' At about twenty to eleven, as he had become quite silent, I rapped on the door, opened it and went in." He turned shudderingly in the direction of the settee: "I found him as you see him."

"Was he dead?"

"So far as I was able to judge, he was."

Chapter 4

THE GIRL OUTSIDE

To that expression of agonised surprise upon the dead man's face was now added, almost momentarily, a deepening of the greenish tinge. A fingerprint expert and a photographer from Scotland Yard had come and gone. After a longish interview, Nayland Smith had released Lord Moreton and Dr. Sims. He put a call through on the desk telephone which General Quinto had found defective. Smith found it in perfect order. He examined the adjoining bedroom and the bathroom beyond and pointed out that it was just possible, although there was no evidence to confirm the theory, that someone might have entered through the bathroom window during the time that the general was alone in the study.

"I don't think that's how it was done," he said, "but it is a possibility. This dispatch box must be opened, and if Mr. Bascombe can't find the key we must force it. In the meantime, Kerrigan, you have a nose for news. I have observed that quite a number of people remain outside the house. Slip out the back way, go around the join the crowd. Ask stupid questions and study every one of them. It would not surprise me to learn that there is someone there waiting to hear of the success or failure of tonight's plot."

"Then you are satisfied that General Quinto was—

murdered?"

"Entirely satisfied, Kerrigan."

When presently I came out into the square I found that Lord Moreton's car had gone. Smith's, that of the home secretary and a Yard car were still standing there. Ten or twelve people were hanging about, attracted by that almost psychic awareness of tragedy which ahead of radio or newspaper in some mysterious way creeps through.

I examined them all carefully and selected several for conversation. Apart from the fact that they had heard that "something had happened," I gathered little news of value.

Then standing apart from the main group, I saw a girl.

This was a dark night but suddenly the house door was opened to admit someone who had driven up in a taxi. In the light from the doorway, I had a glimpse of her face. She was dressed like a working girl, wearing a light raincoat which, however, did not disguise the lines of her slim, trim figure. She wore a brown beret. But her face, as the light shone fully upon it, was so really lovely—a word which rarely can be applied—that I was astonished. In the shadows she looked like a brunette; in the swift light I saw red glints in her tightly waved hair beneath the beret, exquisitely modelled features, lips parted in what I can only describe as an expectant smile. She turned and stared at the departing taxi as I strolled in her direction.

"Any idea what's going on here?" I asked casually.

She raised her eyes in a startled way (they were wonderful eyes of a most unusual colour; they set me thinking of amethysts) keeping her hands tucked in the pockets of her coat.

"Someone told me"—she spoke broken English—"that something terrible had happened in this house."

"Really! I couldn't make out what the crowd was about. So that's it! Who's the owner of the house? Do you know?"

"Someone told me Sir Malcolm Locke."

"Oh yes—he writes books, doesn't he?"

"I don't know. They told me Sir Malcolm Locke."

She glanced up again and smiled. She had a most adorable, provocative smile. I could not place her, but I thought that with that face and figure she might be a mannequin or perhaps a show girl in a cabaret.

"Do you know Sir Malcolm Locke?" she asked, suddenly growing serious.

"No"—her change of manner had quite startled me—"except by name."

"May I speak truly to you? You look"—she hesitated—"sensible." There was a caressing note in her voice. "I know someone who is in that house. Do you understand?"

Nayland Smith had made the right move. Here was a spy of the enemy. Whatever my personal predilection, this charming young lady should be in the hands of Detective Inspector Leighton without delay.

"That's very interesting. Who is it?"

"Just someone I know. You see"—she laid her hand on my arm, and inclined ever so slightly towards me—"I saw you come out of the side entrance! You know—and so, if you please, tell me. What has happened in that house?"

Satisfied that I should not let her out of my sight: "A gentleman known as Mr. Victor has died."

32

"He is dead?"

"Yes."

Her slim fingers closed on my arm with a surprisingly strong grip.

"Thank you." Dark lashes were raised; she flashed up at me an enigmatical glance. "Good night!"

"Just a moment!" I grasped her wrist. "Please don't run away so quickly."

At which she lifted her voice:

"Let me go! How dare you! Let me go!"

Two men detached themselves from the group of loiterers and dashed in our direction. But the behaviour of my beautiful captive, who was struggling violently, was certainly remarkable. Pressing her lips very close to my ear:

"Please let me go!" she whispered. "They will kill you. Let me go! It's no use!"

I released her and turned to meet the attack of two of the most ferocious-looking ruffians I had ever encountered. They were of Mongolian type with an incredible shoulder span in proportion to their height. I had noticed them in the group about the door but had not seen their faces. Viewed from the rear with their glossy black hair might have been a pair of waiters from some neighbouring hotel. Seen face to face they were altogether more formidable.

The first on the scene feinted and then by a trick, which fortunately I knew, tried to kick me off my feet. I stepped back. The second was upon me. Other loiterers were surrounding us now and I knew that I was on the unpopular side. But I threw discretion to the winds. Until I could turn my face from these two enemies I had no means of knowing what had become of the girl. I led off with a straight left against my second opponent.

He ducked it perfectly. The first sprang behind me and seized my ankles. The house door was thrown open and Inspector Leighton raced down the steps. Fey came up at the double, so did the driver of the police car. The attack ceased. I spun around, and saw the black-haired men sprinting for the corner.

"After that pair," cried Leighton gruffly. "Don't lose 'em!"

The police driver and Fey set out.

" 'E was maulin' 'er about!" growled one of the loiterers. "They was in the right. I 'eard 'er cry out."

But the girl with the amethyst eyes had vanished. . . .

Chapter 5

THREE NOTICES

"She has got clear away," said Nayland Smith, "thanks to her bodyguard."

We stood in the library, Smith, myself, Mr. Bascombe and Inspector Leighton. Sir James Clare was seated in an armchair watching us. Now he spoke:

"I understand, Smith, why General Quinto came from Africa to the house of his old friend, secretly, and asked me to recall you for a conference. This is a very deep-laid scheme. You are the only man who might have saved him—"

"But I failed."

Nayland Smith spoke bitterly. He turned and stared at me.

"It appears, Kerrigan, that your charming acquaintance who so unfortunately has escaped—I am not blaming you—differs in certain details from Mr. Bascombe's recollections of the general's visitor. However, it remains to be seen if they are one and the same."

"You see," the judicial voice of the home secretary broke in, "it is obviously impossible to hush this thing up. A post-mortem examination is unavoidable. We don't know what it will reveal. The fact that a very distinguished man, of totally different political ideas from our own, dies here in London under such circumstances is calculated to produce international

35

results. It's deplorable — it's horrible. I cannot see my course clearly."

"Your course, Sir James," snapped Nayland Smith, "is to go home. I will call you early in the morning." He turned. "Mr. Bascombe, decline all information to the press."

"What about the dead man, sir?" Inspector Leighton interpolated.

"Remove the body when the loiterers have dispersed. Report to me in the morning, Inspector."

It was long past midnight when I found myself in Sir Denis' rooms in Whitehall. I had not been there for some time, and from my chair I stared across at an unusually elaborate radio set with a television equipment.

"Haven't much leisure for amusement, myself," said Smith, noting the direction of my glance. "Television I had installed purely to amuse Fey! He is a pearl above price, and owing to my mode of life is often alone here for days and nights."

Standing up, I began to examine the instrument. At which moment Fey came in.

"Excuse me, sir," he said, "electrician from firm requests no one touch until calls again, sir."

Fey's telegraphic speech had always amused me. I nodded and sat down, watching him prepare drinks. When he went out:

"Our return journey was quite uneventful," I remarked. "Why?"

"Perfectly simple," Smith replied, sipping his whisky and soda and beginning to load his pipe. "My presence tonight threatened to interfere with the plot, Kerrigan. The plot succeeded. I am no longer of immediate interest."

"I don't understand in the least, Smith. Have you any theory as to what caused General Quinto's death?"

"At the moment, quite frankly, not the slightest. That indefinable perfume is of course a clue, but at present a useless clue. The autopsy may reveal something more. I await the result with interest."

"Assuming it to be murder, what baffles me is the purpose of the thing. The general's idea that he could hear drums rather suggests a guilty conscience in connection with some action of his in Africa—a private feud of some kind."

"Reasonable," snapped Smith, lighting his pipe and smiling grimly. "Nevertheless, wrong."

"You mean"—I stared at him—"that although you don't know *how*—you do know *why* General Quinto was murdered?"

He nodded, dropping the match in an ash tray.

"You know of course, Kerrigan, that Quinto was the right-hand man of Pietro Monaghani. His counsels might have meant an international war."

"It hangs on a hair I agree, and I suppose that Quinto, as Monaghani's chief adviser, might have precipitated a war—"

"Yes—undoubtedly. But what you don't know (nor did I until tonight) is this: General Quinto had left Africa on a mission to Spain. If he had gone I doubt if any power on earth could have preserved international peace! One man intervened."

"What man?"

"If you can imagine Satan incarnate—a deathless spirit of evil dwelling in an ageless body—a cold intelligence armed with knowledge so far undreamed

37

of by science — you have a slight picture of Doctor Fu Manchu."

In my ignorance I think I laughed.

"A name to me — a bogey to scare children. I had never supposed such a person to exist."

"Scotland Yard held the same opinion at one time, Kerrigan. But you will remember the recent suicide of a distinguished Japanese diplomat. The sudden death of Germany's foremost chemist, Erich Schaffer, was front-page news a week ago. Now — General Quinto."

"Surely you don't mean —"

"Yes, Kerrigan, the work of one man! Others thought him dead, but I have evidence to show that he is still alive, If I had lacked such evidence — I should have it now. I forced the general's dispatch box, we failed to find the key. It contained three sheets of note paper — nothing else. Here they are." He handed them to me. "Read them in the order in which I have given them to you."

I looked at the top sheet. It was embossed with a hieroglyphic which I took to be Chinese. The letter, which was undated, was not typed, but written in a squat, square hand. This was the letter:

FIRST NOTICE

The Council of Seven of the Si-Fan has decided that at all costs another international war must be averted. There are only fifteen men in the world who could bring it about. You are one of them. Therefore, these are the Council's instructions: You will not enter Spain but will resign your commission immediately, and retire to your villa in Capri.

I looked up.

"What ever does this mean?"

"I take it to mean," Smith replied, "that the first notice which you have read was received by General Quinto in Africa. I knew him, and he knew — as every man called upon to administer African or Asiatic people knows — that the Si-Fan cannot be ignored. The Chinese Tongs are powerful, and there is a widespread belief in the influence of the Jesuits; but the Si-Fan is the most formidable secret society in the world: fully twenty-five per cent of the coloured races belong to it. However, he did not resign his commission. He secured leave of absence and proceeded to London to consult *me*. Somewhere on the way he received the second notice. Read it, Kerrigan."

I turned to the second page which bore the same hieroglyphic and a message in that heavy, definite handwriting. This was the message:

SECOND NOTICE
The Council of Seven of the Si-Fan would draw your attention to the fact that you have not resigned your commission. Failing your doing so, a third and final notice will be sent to you.

PRESIDENT OF THE SEVEN

I turned to the last page; it was headed *Third Notice* and read as follows:

You have twenty-four hours.

PRESIDENT OF THE SEVEN

"You see, Kerrigan," said Nayland Smith, "it was this third notice"—which must have reached him by district messenger at Sir Malcolm's house—"which produced that state of panic to which Bascombe referred. The Council of Seven have determined to avert war. Their aim must enlist the sympathy of any sane man. But there are fourteen other men now living, perhaps misguided, whose lives are in danger. I have made a list of some of those whose removal in my opinion would bring at least temporary peace to the world. But it's my job at the moment to protect them!"

"Have you any idea of the identity of this Council of Seven?"

"The members are changed from time to time."

"But the president?"

"The president is Doctor Fu Manchu! I would give much to know where Doctor Fu Manchu is tonight—"

And almost before the last syllable was spoken a voice replied:

"No doubt you would like a word with me, Sir Denis . . ."

For once in all the years that I knew him, Smith's iron self-possession broke down. It was then he came to his feet as though a pistol shot and not a human voice had sounded. A touch of pallor showed under the prominent cheekbones. Fists clenched, a man amazed beyond reason, he stared around.

I, too, was staring—at the television screen.

It had become illuminated. It was occupied by an immobile face—a wonderful face—a face that might have served as model for that of the fallen angel. Long, narrow eyes seemed to be watching me. They held my gaze hypnotically.

A murmur, wholly unlike Smith's normal tones, reached my ears . . . it seemed to come from a great distance.

"Good God! *Fu Manchu!*"

Chapter 6

SATAN INCARNATE

I can never forget those moments of silence which followed the appearance of that wonderful evil face upon the screen.

The utterly mysterious nature of the happening had me by the throat, transcending as it did anything which I could have imagined. I was prepared to believe Dr. Fu Manchu a wizard—a reincarnation of some ancient sorcerer; Apollonius of Tyana reborn with the fires of hell in his eyes.

"If you will be so good, Sir Denis"—the voice was sibilant, unemotional, the thin lips barely moved—"as to switch your lights off, you will find it easier to follow me. Just touch the red button on the right of the screen and I shall know that you have complied."

That Nayland Smith did so was a fact merely divined from an added clarity in that image of the Chinese doctor, for I was unaware of any movement, indeed, of any presence other than that of Fu Manchu.

The image moved back, and I saw now that the speaker was seated in a carved chair.

"This interesting device," the precise, slightly hissing voice continued, "is yet in its infancy. If I intruded at a fortunate moment, this was an accident—for I am unable to hear you. Credit for this small contribution belongs to one of the few first-class mechanical brains which the West has produced in recent years."

I felt a grip upon my shoulders. Nayland Smith stood beside me.

"He was at work upon the principle at the time of his reported death! . . . He has since improved upon it in my laboratories."

Only by a tightening of Smith's grip did I realise the fact that this, to me, incomprehensible statement held a hidden meaning.

"I find it useful as a means of communication with my associates, Sir Denis. I hope to perfect it. Do not waste your time trying to trace the mechanic who installed it. My purpose in speaking to you was this: You have recently learned the distressing details concerning the death of General Quinto. Probably you know that he complained of a sound of drums just before the end—a characteristic symptom. . . ."

The uncanny speaker paused—bent forward—I lost consciousness of everything save of his eyes and of his voice.

"My drums, Sir Denis, will call to others before I shall have satisfied the fools in power today that I, Fu Manchu, and I alone, hold the scales in my hand. I ask you to join me now—for my enemies are your enemies. Consider my words—consider them deeply."

Smith did not stir, but I could hear his rapid breathing.

"You would not wish to see the purposeless slaughter in Spain, in China, carried into England? Think of that bloody farce called the Great War!" A vibrating guttural note had entered into the unforgettable voice. "I, who have had some opportunities of seeing you in action, Sir Denis, know that you understand the rules of boxing. Your objectives are the heart and the point of the jaw: you strike to paralyse brain and blood supply. That is how *I* fight. I strike at those who cause, at those who direct, at those who aid war — at the brain and at the heart, not at the arms, the shoulders — the deluded masses who suffer and die in order that arrogant fools may be gratified, that profiteers may grow fat. Consider my words. . . ."

Dr. Fu Manchu's eyes now were opened widely. They beckoned, they called to me. . . .

"Steady, Kerrigan."

Darkness. The screen was blank.

A long time seemed to elapse before Nayland Smith spoke, before he stirred, then:

"I have seen that man being swept to the verge of Niagara Falls!" he said, speaking hoarsely out of the darkness. "I prayed that he had met a just fate. The body of his companion — a maddened slave of his will — was found."

"But not Fu Manchu! How could he have escaped?"

Smith moved — switched up the light. I saw how the incident had affected him, and it gave me courage; for the magnetism of those eyes, of that voice, had made me feel a weakling.

"One day, Kerrigan, perhaps I shall know."

He pressed a bell. Fey came in.

"This television apparatus is not to be used, not to be touched by anyone, Fey."

Fey went out.

I took up my glass, which remained half filled.

"This has staggered me," I confessed. "The man is more than human. But one thing I *must* know: what did he mean when he spoke of someone — I can guess to whom he referred—who died recently but who, since his death, has been at work in Fu Manchu's laboratories?"

Smith turned on his way to the buffet; his eyes glittered like steel.

"Were you ever in Haiti?"

"No."

"Then possibly you have never come across the ghastly tradition of the *zombie*?"

"Never."

"A human corpse, Kerrigan, taken from the grave and by means of sorcery set to work in the cane fields. Perhaps a Negro superstition, but Doctor Fu Manchu has put it into practice."

"What!"

"I have seen men long dead and buried labouring in his workshops!"

He squirted soda water into a tumbler.

"You were moved, naturally, by the words and by the manner of, intellectually, the greatest man alive. But forget his sophistry, forget his voice—above all, forget his eyes. Doctor Fu Manchu is Satan incarnate."

Chapter 7

"INSPECTOR GALLAHO REPORTS"

In the days that followed I thought many times about those words, and one night I dreamed of beating drums and woke in a nameless panic. The morning that followed was lowering and gloomy. A fine drizzling rain made London wretched.

When I stood up and looked out of the window across Hyde Park I found the prospect in keeping with my reflections. I had been working on the extraordinary facts in connection with the death of General Quinto and trying to make credible reading of the occurrence in Nayland Smith's apartment later the same night. All that I had ever heard or imagined about Dr. Fu Manchu had been brought into sharp focus. I had sometimes laughed at the Germanic idea of a superman; now I knew that such a demigod, and a demigod of evil, actually lived.

I read over what I had written. It appeared to me as a critic that I had laid undue stress upon the haunting figure of the girl with the amethyst eyes. But whenever my thoughts turned, and they turned often enough, to the episodes of that night those wonderful eyes somehow came to the front of the picture.

London and the Home Counties were being combed by the police for the mysterious broadcasting station controlled by Dr. Fu Manchu. A post-mortem examination of the general's body had added little to our knowledge of the cause of death. Inquiries had failed also to establish the identity of the general's woman friend who had called upon him on the preceding day.

The figure of this unknown woman tortured my imagination. Could it be, could it possibly be the girl to whom I had spoken out in the square?

I ordered coffee, and when it came I was too restless to sit down. I walked about the room carrying the cup in my hand. Then I heard the doorbell and heard Mrs. Merton, my daily help, going down. Two minutes later Nayland Smith came in, his lean features wearing that expression of eagerness which characterised him when he was hot on a trail, his grey eyes very bright. He nodded, and before I could speak:

"Thanks! A cup of coffee would be just the thing," he said.

Peeling off his damp raincoat and dropping it on the floor, he threw his hat on top of it, stepped to my desk and began to read through my manuscript. Mrs. Merton bringing another cup, I poured his coffee out and set it on the desk. He looked up.

"Perhaps a little undue emphasis on amethyst eyes," he said slyly.

I felt myself flushing.

"You may be right, Smith," I admitted. "In fact I thought the same myself. But you see, you haven't met her — I have. I may as well be honest. Yes! She did make a deep impression upon me."

"I am only joking, Kerrigan. I have even known the symptoms." He spoke those words rather wistfully.

"But this is very sudden!"

"I agree!" and I laughed. "I know what you think, but truly, there was some irresistible appeal about her."

"If, as I suspect, she is a servant of Doctor Fu Manchu, there would be. He rarely makes mistakes."

I crossed to the window.

"Somehow I can't believe it."

"You mean you don't want to?" As I turned he dropped the manuscript on the desk. "Well, Kerrigan, one thing life has taught me — never to interfere in such matters. You must deal with it in your own way."

"Is there any news?"

He snapped his fingers irritably.

"None. The man who came to Sir Malcolm Locke's house to adjust the telephone did not come from the post office, but unfortunately he can't be traced. The fellow who came to my flat to fix the television set did not come from the firm who supplied it — but he also cannot be traced! And so, you see —"

He paused suddenly as my phone bell began to ring. I took up the receiver.

"Hello — yes? . . . He is here." I turned to Smith. "Inspector Gallaho wants you."

He stepped eagerly forward.

"Hello! Gallaho? Yes — I told Fey to tell you I was coming on here. What's that! — What?" His voice rose on a high note of excitement. "Good God! What do you say? Yes — details when I see you. What time does the train leave? Good! Coming now."

He replaced the receiver and turned. His face had grown very stern. Here was a sudden change of mood.

"What is it?"

"Fu Manchu has struck again. We have just twenty

48

minutes to catch the train. Come on!"

"But where are we going?"

"To a remote corner of the Essex marshes."

Chapter 8

IN THE ESSEX MARSHES

A depressing drizzle was still falling when amid semi-gloom I found myself stepping out of a train at a station on one of those branch lines which intersect the map of Essex. A densely wooded slope arose on the north. It seemed in some way to bear down oppressively on the little station, as though at any moment it might slip forward and crush it.

"Gallaho is a good man to have in charge," said Nayland Smith. "A stoat on a scent and every whit as tenacious."

The chief detective inspector was there awaiting us—a thickset, clean-shaven man of florid colouring and truculent expression, buttoned up in a blue overcoat and having a rather wide-brimmed bowler hat, very wet, jammed tightly upon his head. With him was a uniformed officer who was introduced as Inspector Derbyshire of the Essex Constabulary. Greetings over:

"This is an ugly business," said Gallaho, speaking through clenched teeth.

"So I gather," said Nayland Smith rapidly. "We can talk on the way. I'm afraid you'll have to ride in front with the driver, Kerrigan."

Gallaho nodded and presently, in a police car which stood outside the station, we were on our way. It was a longish drive, mostly through narrow, muddy lanes. At last, on the outskirts of a village through which ran a little stream, we pulled up. A constable was standing outside a barnlike structure, separated by a small meadow, from the nearest cottage. He was a sinister-looking man who harmonised with his surroundings and whose jet-black eyebrows joined in the middle to form one continuous whole. He saluted as we stepped down, unlocked the barn door and led the way in. In spite of the disheartening weather a group of idlers hung about staring vacantly at the gloomy building.

"Not a pleasant sight, sir," Inspector Derbyshire warned us as he removed a sheet from something which lay upon a trestle table.

It was the body of a man wearing a tweed jacket and open-neck shirt, flannel trousers and thick-soled shoes: the equipment, I thought, of a hiker. All his garments—from which water dripped—were horribly stained with blood, and his face was characterised by an unnatural pallor.

I check an exclamation of horror when I realised that he had died of a wound which appeared nearly to have severed his head from his body!

"Right across the jugular," Gallaho muttered, staring down savagely at the victim of this outrage.

He began to chew vigorously, although as I learned later he used no gum; it was merely an unusual ruminatory habit.

"Good God!" Nayland Smith whispered. "Good God! No doubt of the cause of death here! Thank you, Inspector. Cover the poor fellow up. The surgeon has seen him, of course?"

"Yes. He estimated that he had been dead for six or

seven hours. But I left him just as we found him for you to see."

"He was hauled out of the river, I'm told?"

"Yes—half a mile from here. The body was jammed in under the branches of an overhanging willow."

"Who found it?"

"A gypsy called Barnett who was gathering rushes. He and his family are basketmakers."

"When was that?"

"Ten-thirty, sir," Inspector Derbyshire replied. "I got straight through to Inspector Gallaho; he arrived an hour later. Doctor Bridges saw the body at eleven."

"Why did you call Scotland Yard?"

"I recognised him at once. He had reported to me yesterday morning—"

"As I told you, sir," Gallaho's growling voice broke in, "he was a bit after your time at the Yard. But Detective Sergeant Hythe was one of my most promising juniors. He was working under me. He was down here looking for the secret radio station. B.B.C. engineers had noticed interference from time to time and they finally narrowed it down to this end of Essex."

We came out of the barn and the constable locked the door behind us. Smith turned and stared at Gallaho.

"It looks," Gallaho added, "as though poor Hythe had got too near to the heart of the mystery."

"If you'll just step across to the constable's cottage, sir, I want you to see the few things that were found on the dead man," said Inspector Derbyshire.

As we walked along the narrow village street to the modest police headquarters the group of locals detached themselves from the barn and followed us at a

52

discreet distance. Nayland Smith glanced back over his shoulder.

"No one of interest there, Kerrigan!" he snapped.

Laid out upon a table in the sitting room I saw a Colt automatic, an electric flashlamp and a Yale key.

"There wasn't another thing on him!" said Inspector Derbyshire. "Yet I know for a fact that he carried a knapsack and a stick. He was smoking a pipe, too; and he asked me for the name of a cottage where he could spend a night, quiet-like, in the neighbourhood."

Smith was staring at the exhibits.

"This key," he remarked, "is the most significant item."

"I spotted that," growled Gallaho. "It's the key of an A.A. call box — and the nearest is at the crossroads by Woldham Forges, a mile or so from here."

"Smart work," snapped Smith. "What did this important discovery suggest to you?"

"It's plain enough. He had been watching during the night (if the doctor's right, he was murdered between four and five) and he'd found out something so important that he was making for the nearest phone to get assistance."

"Anything else?"

"That the phone nearest to whatever he'd discovered was at Woldham Forges — and that he was working from some base where he must have left his other belongings."

"What did you do?"

"We've made a house-to-house search, sir," Inspector Derbyshire replied. "It isn't very difficult about here. But we can't find where he spent the night."

Nayland Smith gazed out of the window. Several

loiterers were hanging about, but the arrival of the constable now released from his duty as keeper of the morgue dispersed them.

"I shall want a big-scale map of the district," said Smith.

"At your service, sir!"

We all turned and stared. The sinister-looking constable was the speaker. But he was sinister no more. His remarkable eyebrows were raised in what I assumed to be an expression of enthusiasm. He was opening the drawer of a bureau.

"Constable Weldon," explained Inspector Derbyshire, "is an authority on this area. . . ."

Chapter 9

THE HUT BY THE CREEK

Ten minutes later I set out along a road running south by east. Nayland Smith had split up the available searchers in such a way that, the police station as centre, our lines of inquiry formed a rough star.

Sergeant Hythe's equipment certainly suggested that if he had come upon a clue and had decided to work from some point nearby while covering it, an uninhabited building, any old barn or hut, might prove to be the base selected.

Nayland Smith had some theory regarding the spot at which Hythe had been attacked and accordingly had set out for Woldham Forges.

My own instructions, based upon the encyclopaedic knowledge of the neighbourhood possessed by Constable Weldon, were simple enough. My first point was a timbered ruin, once the gatehouse of a considerable monastery long ago demolished. Half a mile beyond was an unoccupied cottage ("Haunted," Constable Weldon had said) in some state of dilapidation, but entrance could be effected through one of the broken windows. Finally, crossing a wooden bridge and bearing straight on, there was an old barn.

We had lunched hastily upon bread and cheese and onions and uncommonly flat beer. . . .

The drizzling rain had ceased, giving place to a sort

of Dutch mist which was even more unpleasant. I could see no further than five paces. My orders were so explicit, however, that I anticipated no difficulty; furthermore, I was provided with a flashlamp.

In the reedy marshes about me, wild fowl gave their queer calls. I heard a variety of notes, some of them unfamiliar, which told me that this was a bird sanctuary undisturbed for generations. Once a mallard flew croaking and flapping across my path and made me jump. The strange quality of some of those cries sounded eerily through the mist.

From a long way off, borne on a faint southerly breeze, came the sound of a steamer's whistle. I met never a soul, nor heard a sound of human presence up to the time that the ruined gatehouse loomed up in the gloom.

It was a relic of those days when great forests had stretched almost unbroken from the coast up to the portals of London, enshrined now in a perfect wilderness of shrubbery. I had no difficulty in obtaining entrance — the place was wide open. Decaying timbers supported a skeleton roof: here was poor shelter; and a brief but careful examination convinced me that no one had recently occupied it.

I stood for a moment in the gathering darkness listening to the notes of wild fowl. Once I caught myself listening for something else: the beating of a drum. . . .

Then again I set out. I followed a narrow lane for the best part of half a mile. Ruts, but not recent ruts, combined to turn its surface into a series of muddy streamlets. At length, just ahead, I saw the cottage of ghostly reputation.

Mist was growing unpleasantly like certifiable fog, but I found the broken window and scrambled in. There was no evidence that anyone had entered the building for a year or more. It was a depressing place as I saw it by the light of the flashlamp. Some biblical texts were decaying upon one wall and in another room, among a lot of litter, I found a headless doll.

I was glad to get out of that cottage.

Greater darkness had come by the time I had regained the lane, and I paused in the porch to relight my pipe, mentally reviewing the map and the sergeant's instructions. Satisfied that the way was clear in my mind, I moved on.

Very soon I found myself upon a muddy path following the banks of a stream. I was unable to tell how much water the stream held, for it was thick with rushes and weeds. But presently as I tramped along I could see that it widened out into a series of reedy pools — and right ahead of me, as though the path had led to it, I saw wooden hut.

I paused. This was not in accordance with plan. I had made a mistake and lost my way. However, the place in front of me was apparently an uninhabited building, and pushing on I examined it with curiosity.

It was a roughly constructed hut, and I saw that it possessed a sort of crude landing stage overhanging the stream. The only visible entrance from the bank was a door secured by a padlock. The padlock proved to be unfastened. Some recollection of this part of Essex provided by the garrulous sergeant flashed through my mind. At one time these shallow streams running out into the wider estuary had been celebrated for the quality of the eels which came there in certain seasons.

As I opened the door I knew that this was a former eel fisher's hut.

I shone a beam of light into the interior.

At first glance the place appeared to be empty, then I saw something. . . . A recently opened sardine tin lay upon a ledge. Near it was a bottle bearing the label of a local brewer. And as I stepped forward and so obtained a better view I discovered in an alcove on the right of the ledge part of a loaf and a packet of butter.

My heart beat faster. By sheer accident I had found what I sought, for it seemed highly improbably from the appearance of the hut that this evidence had been left by anyone but Sergeant Hythe!

And now I made another discovery.

At one end of the place was what looked like a deep cupboard. Setting my lamp on the ledge I opened the cupboard—and what I saw clinched the matter.

There was a shelf about a foot up from the floor, and on it lay an open knapsack! I saw a clasp knife, a box of bar chocolate, a small tin of biscuits and a number of odds and ends which I was too excited to notice at the time—for, most extraordinary discovery of all, I saw a queer-looking hat surmounted by a coral bead.

At this I stared fascinatedly, and then taking it up, carried it nearer to the light. Its character was unmistakable.

It was a mandarin's cap!

And as I stared all but incredulously at this thing which I found in a deserted hut on an Essex marsh, a faint movement made me acutely, coldly alert.

Someone was walking very quietly along the path outside. . . .

What sounded like the booming call of a bittern

came from over the marshes. The footsteps drew nearer. I stood still in an agony of indecision. Like a revelation the truth had come to me: We were searching for the base used by the murdered man. *Others* were searching, too. And this astounding piece of evidence which I held in my hand—this was the object of their search!

I knew from the nearness of the footsteps that retreat was impossible. Already I had selected my hiding place. What to do with the mandarin's cap was the only questionable point. I solved it quickly. I placed the cap upon the ledge littered with the remains of what had probably been poor Hythe's last meal, extinguished my flashlamp, crept into the cupboard and nearly closed the door. . . .

Chapter 10

THE MANDARIN'S CAP

Through the chink of the opening I stared out. I wondered if the fact that I had left the door open would warn whoever approached that someone was inside. However, he might not be aware that it was ordinarily fastened. Closer and closer drew the footsteps on the muddy path; then the sound gave place to the swishing of long, wet grass, and I knew that the intruder was actually at the door.

What had seemed at first to be impenetrable darkness proved now to allow of some limited vision. Framed in the grey oblong of the doorway I saw a motionless figure.

So still it was in that small building that I wondered if the sound of my breathing might be audible. The booming cry sounded again from near at hand, and I questioned it, listening intently, wondering if it might have been simulated—a signal from some watcher covering the motionless figure framed in the doorway.

During the few seconds that elapsed in this way I managed to make out certain details. The new arrival wore a long raincoat and what looked like a black cap; also I saw leggings or riding boots. So much I had discovered, peering cautiously out, when a beam from an electric torch shot through the darkness, directed straight into the hut. Its light fell upon the mandarin's cap.

"*Ah!*" I heard.

That one exclamation revealed an astounding fact: the intruder was a girl!

She stepped in and crossed to the ledge. My heart began to beat irregularly. A queer mingling of fear and hope which had claimed me at the sound of her voice, now became focussed in one huge indescribable emotion as I saw that pure profile, the clinging curls under the black cap, the outline, I thought, of a Greek goddess.

As I quietly slipped across to the open door and stood with my back to it, the girl turned in a flash — and I found myself looking into those magnificent eyes which had so strangely and persistently haunted me from the hour of that first brief meeting.

Their expression now in the light reflected from the ray of the torch, which moved unsteadily in her grasp, was compounded of fear and defiance. She was breathing rapidly, and I saw the glitter of white teeth through slightly parted lips.

Quite suddenly, it seemed, she recognised me. As I wore a soft-brimmed hat, perhaps my features were partly indistinguishable.

"You!" she whispered, "*you* again!"

"Yes," I said shortly. Now, although it had cost me an effort, I had fully mastered myself. "I again. May I ask what you are doing here?"

A hardness crept over her features; her lips set firmly. She put the torch down on the ledge beside her while I watched her intently, then:

"I might quite well ask you the same question," she replied, and her enchanting accent gave the words the value of music.

I laughed, standing squarely in the doorway and watching her.

Wisps of fog floated between us.

"I am here because a man was brutally murdered last night — and here, on the ledge beside you, is the clue to his murderer."

"What are you talking about?" she asked quietly.

"Only about what I know."

"Suppose what you say is true, what has it to do with you?"

"It is every man's business to run down a murderer."

Her wonderful eyes opened more widely; she stared at me like a bewildered child — a pose, I told myself, perfectly acted.

"But I mean — what brings you here, to this place? You are not of the police."

"No, I am not 'of the police.' My name is Bart Kerrigan; I am a journalist by profession. Now I am going to ask you what brings *you* here to this place. What is your name?."

Her expression changed again; she lowered her lashes disdainfully.

"You could never understand and it does not matter. My name — my name — would mean nothing to you. It is a name you have never heard before."

"All the more reason why I should hear it now."

Unwittingly I said the words softly, for as she stood there wrapped in the soiled raincoat, her little feet in muddy riding boots, I thought there could be no more desirable woman in the world.

"My name is Ardatha," she replied in a low voice.

"Ardatha! A charming name, but as you say one I

have never heard before. To what country does it belong?"

Suddenly she opened her eyes widely.

"Why do you keep me here talking to you?" she flashed, and clenched her hand. "I will tell you nothing. I have as much right to be here as you. Please stand away from that door and let me go."

The demand was made imperiously, but unless my vanity invented a paradox her eyes were denying the urgency of her words.

"It is the duty of every decent Christian," I said, reluctantly forcing myself to face facts, "to detain any man or any woman belonging to the black organisation of which you are a member."

"Every Christian!" she flashed back. *"I* am a Christian. I was educated in Cairo."

"Coptic?"

"Yes, Coptic."

"But you are not a Copt!"

"Did I say I was a Copt?"

"You belong to the Si-Fan."

"You don't know what you are talking about. Even if I did, what then?"

I was drifting again and I knew it. The words came almost against my will:

"Do you understand what this society stands for? Do you know that they employ stranglers, garroters, poisoners, cutthroats, that they trade in assassination?"

"Is that so?" She was watching me closely and now spoke in a quiet voice. "And your Christian rulers, your rulers of the West—yes? What do *they* do? If the Si-Fan kills a man, that man is an active enemy. But

63

when your Western murderers kill they kill men, women and children—hundreds—thousands who never harmed them—who never sought to harm anybody. My whole family—do you hear me?—my whole family, was wiped from life in one bombing raid. I alone escaped. General Quinto ordered that raid. You have seen what became of General Quinto. . . ."

I felt the platform of my argument slipping from beneath my feet. This was the sophistry of Fu Manchu! Yet I hadn't the wit to answer her. The stern face of Nayland Smith seemed to rise up before me; I read reproach in the grey eyes.

"I think we've talked long enough," I said. "If you will walk out in front of me, we will go and discuss the matter with those able to decide between us."

She was silent for a moment, seeming to be studying my considerable bulk, firmly planted between herself and freedom.

"Very well." I saw the gleam of little white teeth as she bit her lip. "I am not afraid. What I have done I am proud to have done. In any case I don't matter. But bring the notebook—it might help me if I am to be arrested."

"The notebook?"

She pointed to the open cupboard out of which I had stepped. I turned and saw in the dim light among the other objects which I have mentioned what certainly looked like a small notebook. Three steps and I had it in my hand.

But those three steps were fatal.

From behind me came a sound which I can only describe as a rush. I turned and sprang to the doorway. She was through—she must have reached it in one bound! The door was slammed in my face, dealing me a staggering blow on the forehead. I took a step back to hurl myself against it and heard the click of the padlock.

Undeterred, I dashed my weight against the closed door; but although old it was solid. The padlock held.

"Don't try to follow me!" I heard. "They will kill you if you try to follow me!"

I stood still, listening, but not the faintest sound reached my ears to inform me in which direction Ardatha had gone. Switching on my lamp I stared about the hut.

Yes, she had taken the mandarin's cap! I had shown less resource than a schoolboy! I had been tricked, outwitted by a girl not yet out of her teens, I judged. I grew hot with humiliation. How could I ever tell such a story to Nayland Smith?

The mood passed. I became cool again and began to search for some means of getting out. Barely glancing at the notebook, I thrust it into my pocket. That the girl had deliberately drawn my attention to it I did not believe. She had had no more idea than I what it was, but its presence had served her purpose. I could find nothing else of importance.

And now I set to work on the small shuttered window at the back of the ledge upon which those fragments of food remained. I soon had the shutter open, and as I had hoped, the window was unglazed. I climbed through on to a rickety landing stage and from there made my way around to the path. Here I stood stock still, listening.

One mournful boom of that strange solitary bird disturbed the oppressive silence, this and the whispering of reeds in a faint breeze. I could not recall ever to have found myself in a more desolate spot.

Fog was rapidly growing impenetrable.

Chapter 11

AT THE MONKS' ARMS

I found myself mentally reviewing the ordnance map I had seen at the policeman's cottage, listening to the discursive instructions of the sinister but well-informed Constable Weldon.

"After you leave the cottage where old Mother Abel hanged herself"—a stubby finger moved over the map—"there's a path along beside a little stream. You don't take that"—I had—"you go straight on. This other road, bearin' left, would bring you to the Monks' Arms, one of the oldest pubs in Essex. Since the by-pass was made I don't know what trade is done there. It's kept by an old prize fighter, a Jerseyman, or claims to be; Jim Pallant they call him—a mighty tough customer; Seaman Pallant was his fightin' name. The revenue officers have been watchin' him for years, but he's too clever for 'em. We've checked up on him, of course. He seems to have a clean slate in this business. . . ."

Visualising the map, I decided that the route back via the Monks' Arms was no longer than the other, and I determined to revive my drooping spirits before facing Nayland Smith. Licensed hours did not apply in my case for I was a "bona-fide traveller" within the meaning of the act.

I set out on my return journey.

At one time I thought I had lost my way again, until presently through the gloom I saw a signboard projecting above a hedge, and found myself before one of those timbered hostelries of which once there were many in this neighbourhood, but of which few remain today! I saw that the Monks' Arms stood on the bank of a stream.

I stepped into a stuffy bar. Low, age-blackened beams supported the ceiling; there were some prints of dogs and prize fighters; a full-rigged ship in a glass case. The place might have stood there when all but unbroken forest covered Essex. As a matter of fact though not so old as this, part of it actually dated back to the time of Henry VII.

There was no one in the barroom, dimly lighted by two paper-shaded lamps. In the bar I saw bottle-laden shelves, rows of mugs, beer engines. Beyond was an opening in which hung a curtain composed of strings of coloured rushes. Since no one appeared I banged upon the counter. This produced a sound of footsteps; the rush curtain was parted, and Pallant, the landlord, came out.

He was as fine a specimen of a retired prize fighter as one could hope to find, with short thick nose, slightly out of true, deep-set eyes and several battle scars. His rolled-up shirt sleeves revealed muscular forearms and he had all the appearance of being, as Constable Weldon had said, "a tough customer."

I called for a double scotch and soda.

"Traveller?"

"Yes. London."

He stared at me with his curiously unblinking deep-set brown eyes, then turned, tipped out two measures from an inverted bottle, squirted soda into the glass and set it before me. I paid, and he banged down my change on the counter. A cigarette drooping from his thick underlip he stood, arms folded, just in front of the rush curtain, watching me with that unmoving stare. I sipped my drink, and:

"Weather bad for trade?" I suggested.

He nodded but did not speak.

"I found you almost by accident. Lost my way. How far is it to the station?"

"What station?"

This was rather a poser, but:

"The nearest of course," I replied.

"Mile and a half, straight along the lane from my door."

"Thanks." I glanced at my watch. "What time does the next train leave?"

"Where for?"

"London."

"Six-eleven."

I lingered over my drink and knocking out my pipe began to refill it. The unmoving stare of those wicked little eyes was vaguely disconcerting, and as I stood there stuffing tobacco into the hot bowl, a possible explanation occurred to me: Perhaps Pallant mistook me for a revenue officer!

"Is the fishing good about here?" I asked.

"No."

"You don't cater for fishermen then?"

"I don't."

Then with a final penetrating stare he turned, swept the rush curtain aside and went out. I heard his curiously light retreating footsteps.

As I had paid for my drink he evidently took it for granted that I should depart now, and clearly was not interested in the possibility that I might order another. However, I sat for a while on a stool, lighted my pipe and finished my whiskey and soda at leisure. A moment later no doubt I should have left, but a slight, a very slight movement beyond the curtain drew my glance in that direction.

Through the strings of rushes, almost invisible, except that dim light from the bar shone upon her eyes, I saw a girl watching me. Nor was it humanly possible to mistake those eyes!

The formidable Jim Pallant was forgotten—everything was forgotten. Raising a flap in one end of the counter I stepped into the bar, crossed it and just as she turned to run along a narrow passage beyond, threw my arms around Ardatha!

"Let me go!" She struggled violently. "Let me go! I warned you, and you are mad—mad, to come here. For God's sake if you value your life, or mine, let me go!"

But I pulled her through the curtain into the dingy bar and held her firmly.

"Ardatha!" I spoke in a guarded, low voice. "God knows why you can't see what it means to be mixed up with these people, but *I* can, and I can't bear it. Listen! You have nothing, nothing in the world to fear. Come away! My friend who is in charge of the case will absolutely guarantee your safety. But please, please, come away with me now!"

She wore a silk pullover, riding breeches and the muddy boots which I remembered. Her slender body writhed in my grasp with all the agility of a captured eel.

One swift upward glance she gave me, a glance I was to remember many, many times, waking and sleeping. Then with a sudden unexpected movement she buried her wicked little teeth in my hand!

Pained and startled I momentarily released her. The reed curtain crackled as she turned and ran. I heard her pattering footsteps on an uncarpeted stair.

Clenching my fist I stood there undetermined what to do—until, realising that an uncommonly dangerous man for whom I might not prove to be a match was somewhere in the house, for once I chose discretion.

I was crossing to the barroom door when, heralded only by a crash of the curtain and a dull thud, Pallant vaulted *over* the counter behind me, twisted my right arm into the small of my back and locked the other in a hold which I knew myself powerless to break!

"I know your sort!" he growled in my ear. "Anyone that tries games with my guests goes the same way!"

"Don't be a fool!" I cried angrily as he hustled me out of the building. "I have met her before—"

"Well—she don't want to meet you again, and she ain't likely to!"

Down the three worn steps he ran me, and across the misty courtyard to the gate. He was heavier, and undoubtedly more powerful than I, and ignominiously I was rushed into the lane.

"I've broke a man's neck for less," Pallant remarked.

I said nothing. The tone was very menacing.

"For two pins," he continued, "I'd chuck you in the river."

However, the gateway reached, he suddenly released his hold. Seizing me from behind by both shoulders, he gave me a shove which sent me reeling for three or four yards.

"Get to hell out of here!" he roared.

At the end of that tottering run I pulled myself up. What prompted the lunacy I really cannot say, except perhaps that a Rugby Blue doesn't enjoy being hustled out of the game in just that way.

I came about in one jump, ran in and tackled him low!

It was on any count a mad thing to do, but he wasn't expecting it. He went down beautifully, I half on top of him — but I was first up. As I stood there breathing heavily I was weighing my chances. And looking at the bull neck and span of shoulders, an uncomfortable conviction came that if Seaman Pallant decided to fight it out I was probably booked for a first-class hiding.

However, he did not move.

I watched him second after second, standing poised with clenched fists; I thought it was a trick. Still he did not move. Very cautiously, for I knew the man to be old in ringcraft, I approached and bent over him. And then I saw why he lay there.

A pool of blood was forming under his head. He had pitched on to the jagged edge of the gatepost — and was quite insensible!

For a long minute I waited, trying to find out if accidentally I had killed him. But satisfied that he was merely stunned, those counsels of insanity which I count to be hereditary, which are responsible for some of the tightest corners in which I have ever found myself, now prevailed.

Ardatha's dangerous bodyguard was out of the way.

I might as well take advantage of the fact.

Turning, I ran back into the barroom, raised the flap, crossed the bar, and gently moving the rush curtain, stood again in the narrow passage. On my extreme right was a closed door; on the left, lighted by another of the paper-covered hanging lamps, I saw an uncarpeted staircase. I had heard Ardatha's footsteps going up those stairs, and now, treading softly, I began to mount.

That reek of stale spirits and tobacco smoke which characterised the bar was equally perceptible here. Two doors opened on a landing. I judged that on my left to communicate with a room overlooking the front of the Monks' Arms, and I recalled that as I returned from my encounter with Pallant I had seen no light in any of the windows on this side of the house. Therefore, creeping forward on tiptoe, I tried the handle of the other door.

It turned quite easily and a dim light shone out as I pushed the door open.

The room was scantily furnished: an ancient mahogany chest of drawers faced me as I entered and I saw some chairs of the same wood upholstered with horsehair. A lamp on an oval table afforded the only light, and at the far end of the room, which had a sloping ceiling, there was a couch or divan set under a curtained window.

Upon this a man was reclining, propped upon one elbow and watching me as I stood in the doorway. . . .

He wore a long black overcoat having an astrakhan collar, and upon his head a Russian cap, also of astrakhan. One slender hand with extraordinarily long fingernails rested upon an outstretched knee; his chin was cupped in the other. He did not stir a muscle as I entered, but simply lay there watching me.

A physical chill of a kind which sometimes precedes an attack of malaria rose from the base of my spine and stole upwards. I seemed to become incapable of movement. That majestic, evil face fascinated me in a way I cannot hope to make clear. Those long, narrow, emerald-green eyes commanded, claimed, absorbed me. I had never experienced a sensation in my life resembling that which held me nailed to the floor as I watched the man who reclined upon the divan.

For this was the substance of that dreadful shadow I had seen on the screen in Nayland Smith's room . . . it was Dr. Fu Manchu!

Chapter 12

DR. FU MANCHU'S BODYGUARD

Motionless I stood there staring at the most dangerous man in the world.

In that moment of realisation it was a strange fact that no idea of attacking him, of attempting to arrest him, crossed my mind. The complete unexpectedness of his appearance, a *danse macabre* which even in that sordid little room seemed to move behind him like a diabolical ballet devised by an insane artist, stupefied me.

The windows were closed and there was no sound, for how many seconds I cannot say. I believe that during those seconds my sensations were akin to the visions of a drowning man; I must in some way have accepted this as death.

I seemed to see and to hear Nayland Smith seeking for me, urgently calling my name. The whole pageant of my history joined and intermingled with a phantom army, invisible but menacing, which was the aura of Dr. Fu Manchu. Dominating all was the taunting face of Ardatha, an unspoken appeal upon her lips; and the thought, like a stab of the spirit, that unquestionably Ardatha was the woman associated with the assassination of General Quinto, the willing accomplice of this Chinese monster, and a party to the murder of Sergeant Hythe.

Dr. Fu Manchu did not move; the gaze of his unnatural green eyes never left my face. That bony hand with its long, highly polished nails lay so motionless upon the pile of the black coat that it might have been an ivory carving.

Then after those moments of stupefaction the spell broke. My duty was plain, my duty to Nayland Smith, to humanity at large. As quick resolve claimed my mind Dr. Fu Manchu spoke:

"Useless, Mr. Kerrigan." His thin lips barely parted. "I am well protected; in fact I was expecting you."

He bluffed wonderfully, I told myself; I plunged for my automatic.

"Stand still!" he hissed; "don't stir, you fool!"

And so tremendous was the authority in that sibilant voice, in the swiftly opened magnetic eyes, that even as my hand closed upon the weapon I hesitated.

"Now, slowly—very slowly, I beg of you, Mr. Kerrigan—move your head to the left. You will see from what I have saved you!"

Strange it may sound, strange it appears to me now, but I obeyed, moving my head inch by inch. In that position, glancing out of the corner of my eye, I became again stricken motionless.

The blade of a huge curved knife resembling a sickle was being held motionless by someone who stood behind me, a hair's breadth removed from my neck! I could see the thumb and two fingers of a muscular-brown hand which clutched the hilt. One backward sweep of such a blade would all but sever a man's head from his body. In that instant I knew how Sergeant Hythe had died.

"Yes"—Dr. Fu Manchu's voice was soft again; and

slowly, inch by inch, I turned as he began to speak—"that was how he died, Mr. Kerrigan: your doubts are set at rest."

Even before the astounding fact that he had replied to an unspoken thought had properly penetrated, he continued:

"I regret the episode. It has seriously disarranged my plans: it was unnecessary and clumsily done—due to overzealousness on the part of one of my body-guards. These fellows are difficult to handle. They are *Thugs,* members of a religious brotherhood specialising in murder—but long ago stamped out by the British authorities as any textbook will tell you. Nevertheless I find them useful."

I was breathing hard and holding myself so tensely that every muscle in my body seemed to be quivering. Dr. Fu Manchu did not stir, his eyes were half closed again, but their contemplative gaze was terrifying.

"I can only suppose," I said, and the sound of my own voice muffled in the little room quite startled me, "that much learning has made you mad. What have you or your cause—if you have a cause—to gain by this indiscriminate murder? Let me draw your attention to the state of China, to which country I believe you belong. There is room there for your particular kind of activity."

This speech had enabled me somewhat to regain control of myself, but in the silence that followed I wondered how it would be accepted.

"My particular activities, Mr. Kerrigan, are at the moment directed to the correction of certain undesirable menaces to China. You are thinking of the armies who clash and vainly stagger to and fro in my country.

I assure you that the real danger to China lies not within her borders, but outside. The surgeon seeks below the surface. Muscles are useless without nerves and brain. My concern is with nerves and brain. However, these details cannot interest you, as I fear you will not be in a position to impart them to Sir Denis Nayland Smith. Had your talents been outstanding I might have employed you—but they are not; therefore I have no use for you."

Following those softly spoken words came a high, guttural order.

A cloth was whipped over my mouth and secured before I fully realised what had happened. In less time than it takes to write of it I was lashed wrist and ankle by some invisible expert stationed behind me! The curved blade of the knife I could see out of the corner of my left eye.

Dr. Fu Manchu never stirred a muscle.

I longed to cry out but could not. Another guttural order—and the blade disappeared. He who had held the knife stepped forward, and I saw a thickset, yellow-faced man dressed in an ill-fitting blue suit. Immediately I recognised him for one of the pair who had attacked me on the night that I first saw and spoke to Ardatha. Although short of stature he was immensely powerful, and without ceremony he stooped, hoisted me upon his shoulder and carried me like a sack from the room!

My last impression was one of that dreadful, motionless figure upon the settee. . . .

Down the stairs I was borne, helpless as a trussed chicken. Considering my weight it was an astonishing feat on the part of the man who performed it. Past the rush curtain of the bar we went and along the passage. Dread of my impending death was almost swamped by loathing of the blood-lustful creature who carried me. Another of Dr. Fu Manchu's evil-faced thugs held a door open, and a damp smell, the ringing sound of footsteps on stove paving, told me that I was being taken down into the cellars. Something like a scream arose to my lips—but I stifled it, for I knew not for the first time since I had met the Chinese doctor stark terror's icy hand.

From those cellars I should never come out alive.

Chapter 13

IN THE WINE CELLARS

The cellars of the Monks' Arms were surprisingly equipped. They reminded me of those of a well-known speak-easy in New York which I had once explored. Beyond the cellar proper, the contents of which looked innocent enough, other cellars, altogether more extensive, lay concealed. By means of manipulating hidden locks seemingly solid walls could be opened.

In the light of a hurricane lamp carried by one of the Thugs, I saw casks of brandy and bins of French wines which certainly were never intended for the clientèle of the Monks' Arms. As Sergeant Weldon had more than hinted, this ancient inn was a smugglers' base. Its subterranean ramifications suggested that at some time the building above had been larger.

At what I judged to be the end of the labyrinth, I was carried up several well-worn steps into a long, rectangular room. I noticed a stout door set in the thickness of the wall, and then I was dumped unceremoniously upon the paving stones. The place contained nothing but lumber: broken fishing tackle, nets, empty casks, old furniture and similar odds and ends. Among these was the dismantled frame of a heavy iron bedstead. Hauling out what had been the headpiece — it had cross bars strong enough for a prison window — the two yellow men laid it on the floor and stretched me upon it.

From first to last they worked in silence.

Deftly they lashed me to the rusty bars until even slight movement became almost impossible and the pain was all I could endure. At first their purpose remained mysterious, then with a new pang of terror I recognised it. . . .

Dr. Fu Manchu was determined that a second body should not be found in the neighbourhood of the Monks' Arms. Secured to the heavy iron framework I was to be taken out and thrown into the river!

When at last the two had completed their task and one, standing up, raised the lantern from the floor, the horror of the fate which I felt was upon me reached such a climax that again I stifled a desire to scream for help. A sound, faint but just discernible, which came through a grating up in one corner of the wall, told me that the stream beside which the inn was built passed directly outside the door.

Perhaps I had little cause for it, but when the yellow men turned, and he carrying the lantern leading, went back by the way they had come, I experienced such a revulsion from despair to almost exultant optimism that I cannot hope to describe it.

I was still alive! My absence could not fail to result in a search party being sent out. My chances might be poor but my position was no longer desperate!

Why had I been left there?

Dr. Fu Manchu's words allowed no room for doubt regarding his intention. Why then this delay? And — an even greater mystery — what had brought him to the Monks' Arms and why did he linger? Overriding my own peril, topping everything, was the maddening knowledge that if I could only communicate what I knew to Nayland Smith, it might alter the immediate history of the world.

Audacity is an outstanding characteristic of all great criminals, and that Dr. Fu Manchu should calmly recline in that room upstairs while the district all about him was being combed for the murderer of Sergeant Hythe, illustrated the fact that he possessed it in full measure. The clue was perhaps to be found in his words that something had seriously disarranged his plans. I wondered feverishly if happy chance would lead Nayland Smith to the inn. Even so, and the thought made me groan, he would probably go away again never suspecting what the place contained!

Now came an answer to one of my questions — an answer which sent a new chill through my veins.

Dimly I heard the sound of oars. I knew that a boat was being pulled along the creek in the direction of the oak door close to which my head rested.

Of course I was to be transported to some spot where the water was deep, and thrown in there!

I listened eagerly, fearfully, to the creak of the nearing oars; and when I knew that the invisible boat had reached those steps which I divined to be beyond the door, I gave myself up for lost. But my calculations were at fault.

The boat passed on.

I could tell from the sound that an oar had been reversed and was being used as a punt pole. The swish of the rushes against the side of the craft was clearly discernible. I doubted if the little stream was navigable far above that point, but as those ominous sounds died away I knew at least that I had had a second reprieve.

Breathing was difficult because of the bandage over my mouth, and my heart was beating madly. Through the grating a sound reached me—that bumping and scraping which tells of someone entering or leaving a boat. Then I knew that poling had recommenced, but never once did I hear a human voice.

The boat was coming back. I heard the faint rattle of an oar set in a rowlock, the drip of water from the blade; but until the rower had crept past outside the oak door I doubt if I breathed again.

What did it all mean?

Someone, I reasoned, had been brought from the inn and was being rowed downstream to the larger river of which it was a tributary.

Dr. Fu Manchu!

Yes, it must be. The monstrous Chinaman, having lain within the grasp of the law, almost under the very nose of Nayland Smith, was escaping!

I tugged impotently at my lashings, but the pain I suffered soon checked my struggles. In fact this, with the damp silence of the cellar and the difficulty which I experienced in breathing, now threatened to overcome me. Clenching my teeth, I fought against the weakness and lay still.

How long I lay it is impossible to say. Those moments of mental and physical agony seemed to stretch out each into an eternity, and then . . .

I heard the boat returning.

This time there could be no doubt. Dr. Fu Manchu had been smuggled away—doubtless to some larger craft which awaited him—and they were returning to deal with *me*.

Yes, I was right. I heard the boat grating against the

stone steps, a stumbling movement and a key being inserted in the lock above and behind me. The door, which opened outward, was flung back. A draught of keen air swept into the cellar.

Shadowy, looking like great apes, the yellow men entered. One at my head and one at my feet, they lifted the iron framework to which I was lashed. I have an idea that I muttered a sort of prayer, but of this I cannot be certain, for there came an interruption so unexpected, so overwhelming, that I must have given way to my mental and physical agony. I remember little more.

A series of loud splashes, as though a number of swimmers had plunged into the water — the bumping and rolling of a boat — a rush of footsteps — a glare of light . . .

Finally, a voice — the voice of Nayland Smith:

"In you go, Gallaho! Don't hesitate to shoot!"

Chapter 14

THE MONKS' ARMS (CONCLUDED)

"All right, Kerrigan? Feeling better?"

I stared around me. I was lying on a sofa in a stuffy little sitting room which a smell of stale beer and tobacco smoke told me to be somewhere at the back of the bar of the Monks' Arms. I sat up and finished what remained of a glass of brandy which Smith was holding to my lips.

"Gad!" I muttered, "every muscle in my body will be stiff for twenty-four hours. It was mostly the pain that did it, Smith."

"Don't apologize," he returned drily, and looking at his blanched face as he stood beside me, I could read a deep anger in his eyes. "We were only just in time."

"Doctor Fu Manchu?"

He snapped his fingers irritably.

"A motor launch had crept up in the mist and his yellow demons got him aboard, only a matter of minutes before our arrival. Take it easy, Kerrigan; you can tell us your story later. I found this in your pocket, so I gather that you had succeeded where we failed." He held up the little notebook which I had found in the eel fisher's hut. "It tells the story of poor Hythe's last hours. It was traces of oil on the water that gave him the clue. He selected a hiding place which evidently you found, and watched from some point near by. He saw the motor craft arrive. It was met by a boat which belongs to the inn. Someone was rowed ashore. He seems to have waded or swum out to the deserted motor launch, and apparently he made a curious discovery—"

"He did." I stood up gingerly, to test my leg muscles. "He found a mandarin's cap."

"Good for you, Kerrigan. So he reports in his notes. He took this back to his hiding place as some evidence in case his quarry should escape him. His last entry says that the boat could only have been making for the Monks' Arms. The rest we have to surmise, but I think it is fairly easy."

He dropped the notebook back into his pocket.

"I assume that he crept up to the inn to learn the identity of the new arrival or arrivals. Having satisfied himself in some way, he then set out across country for the A.A. call box. Unfortunately he had been seen— and someone was following him. At a stone bridge which spans the stream the follower overtook him. Yes—I have found the bloodstains. As he received the fatal stoke he toppled over the parapet. A slow current carried his body down to the point at which it was found."

He ceased speaking and stood staring at me in a curious way. I was seated on the sofa, rubbing my aching leg muscles.

"There's one thing, Smith," I said, "for which I owe thanks to heaven. Whatever brought you to my rescue in the nick of time?"

"I was about to mention that," he snapped. "Someone called up the police (I had just returned from my visit to the scene of the crime) begging us to set out without a moment's delay—not for the inn itself, but for a stone boathouse which lies twenty yards further down the creek. We had come provided to break the door in, but as luck would have it, Constable Weldon, who was leading us, detected the sound made by those Thugs in the boat. You know the rest."

He continued to stare at me and I at him.

"Was it a man's voice?"

"No: a woman—a young woman."

A medley of emotions had me silent for a moment, and then:

"Did you find anyone here?"

"My party, with Gallaho, found the pair of Thugs, as you know. Inspector Derbyshire, who entered from the front, discovered the man Pallant bathing a deep cut in his forehead. There's a fellow who combines the duties of stablelad and bartender, but he's off duty. . . . There was no one else."

"I am glad—although perhaps I shouldn't be."

After ten minutes' rest I was fit to move again.

Apart from the fact that the secret cellars were packed with contraband, nothing of value bearing upon the matter which had brought the police there was discovered in the Monks' Arms. Both yellow men remained imperturbably dumb. The ex-pugilist, under a gruelling examination by Chief Detective Inspector Gallaho, pleaded guilty to smuggling but denied all knowledge of the identity or activities of his Chinese guest. He said that from time to time this person whom he knew as Mr. Chang, stayed at the inn, usually accompanied by two coloured servants, and sometimes by a lady. He flatly denied all knowledge of the tragedy, and finally:

"Take him away," Gallaho growled, "we'll find enough evidence later. Book him in on a charge of smuggling."

Chapter 15

THE SI-FAN

Many hours had elapsed, hours of bitter disappointment, before Nayland Smith and I found ourselves at his flat in Whitehall.

Fey had nothing to report. Smith glanced significantly at the television set which in some unaccountable manner Dr. Fu Manchu had converted to his private uses.

"No sir." Fey shook his head.

When he had gone out:

"It seems almost incredible," said Smith, beginning to pace up and down the carpet, "that this man whom I held in the hollow of my hand has slipped away! Every point of egress was watched, every officer afloat and ashore notified for miles around."

"Perhaps he doubled back?"

Nayland Smith began to tug at the lobe of his left ear.

"Impossible to predict his movements. I am beginning to wonder if it is time I retired from the unequal contest. It is many years since Doctor Fu Manchu first crossed my path. It was in a swampy district of Burma and I was nearly counted out in the first round." He suddenly pulled up his sleeve and rolled back his shirt cuff, revealing a wicked-looking wound upon the forearm. "A primitive weapon, but a deadly one. An

89

arrow, steeped in snake's venom."

He rolled his sleeve down again.

"You should never be alone, Smith. You need a bodyguard."

"I assure you I rarely go about alone. Why do you suppose I drag six feet of newspaper correspondent about with me? You are my bodyguard, Kerrigan! But Fu Manchu's methods are of a kind from which no bodyguard could protect me. I am saved by my utter futility. I believe he is laughing at me."

"He has small cause for laughter. Although you have failed to destroy him you have foiled him all along."

Nayland Smith's grim face relaxed in a smile.

"Then I can't account for it. He must enjoy the sport, or I shouldn't be alive!"

"Do you think he was making for the open sea?"

"I have a strong suspicion that he was. It has occurred to me that this mysterious radio plant which he controls may be on some vessel."

"Such a vessel would require a pretty tall mast."

"Not at all. Fu Manchu is probably half a century ahead of what we call modern radio. However, I can do no more. We can hang the Thugs, no doubt, but like Fu Manchu, what we want to do is to strike at the 'nerves and brain.' "

He dropped into an armchair and began to load his pipe; then, looking up, he stared across at me.

"Judging from what you told me in the train," he said, "I gather that your feelings about this girl Ardatha remain the same. Am I right?"

I felt acutely uncomfortable under the piercing scrutiny, but I replied:

"Yes, I am afraid you are, Smith. You see, although

90

a criminal, she doesn't realise that she is a criminal. In any case she has certainly saved my life. No one else could have given the warning."

Nayland Smith nodded, proceeded with the filling of his pipe and lighted it carefully.

"A cunning scheme," he muttered, standing up and walking about again. "Dictatorships with their ruthless methods have brought in crowds of willing recruits. Don't you see it, Kerrigan? There are thousands, perhaps hundreds of thousands, living today, embittered by injustice, willing, eager, to enter into a blood feud against those who have destroyed husbands, children, families, wrecked their homes. The Si-Fan, always powerful, working for a dimly seen end, an end never appreciated by the West, today has become a mighty instrument of vengeance — and that flaming sword, Kerrigan, is firmly held by Doctor Fu Manchu."

He stared from the window awhile, and I watched the grim outline of his features.

"One thing, and it looks as though the clue had eluded me," he said suddenly, "is this: What was Fu Manchu doing in Essex? Assuming, as the radio experts believe, that this mysterious interference came from somewhere in that area, even that it came from a vessel lying off the Essex shore — we still come back to the same point. What was Fu Manchu doing there?"

He turned and stared at me fixedly.

"That problem is worrying me badly," he added.

Frankly, it had not occurred to me before, but so stated I saw the significance of the thing. I was considering it while Nayland Smith resumed his restless promenade, when, preceded by a gentle rap, Fey opened the door and entered.

"Chief Detective Inspector Gallaho."

Hot on the words came Gallaho, wrenching his tightly fitting bowler from his close-cropped skull and leaving a mark like a scar around his brow.

"Yes?" snapped Smith and took a step forward. "What is it? You have news?"

"News, yes!" the detective answered bitterly — "but has it come too late?"

He pulled out his pocket case and withdrew a slip of paper which he tossed on to the desk in front of Smith. As Smith picked it up I sprang to my feet and hurried forward. Over his shoulder I read — it was written in pencil, in plain block letters — the following:

FINAL NOTICE

The Council of Seven of the Si-Fan grants you twelve hours in which to carry out its orders.

PRESIDENT OF THE COUNCIL

Nayland Smith's expression had something wild in it as he turned to Gallaho.

"To whom was this sent?" he snapped.

"Doctor Martin Jasper."

Smith's expression changed; his face became almost blank.

"Who the devil is Doctor Martin Jasper?"

"I have looked him up, sir. He has a row of degrees; he's a research man and for some time was technical director of the great Caxton armament factory up in the north."

"Armament factory? I begin to understand. Where does he live?"

"That's the significant thing, sir. It may account for the presence of Doctor Fu Manchu where we found him—or rather, where we lost him. This Doctor Martin Jasper lives at a house called Great Oaks just on the Suffolk border, not ten miles, as the crow flies, from the Monks' Arms."

Chapter 16

GREAT OAKS

It was a cross-country journey and the night was misty and moonless; but although unknown to us by name clearly enough Dr. Martin Jasper was someone of importance in the eyes of the Si-Fan.

Smith attacked the matter with feverish energy.

A special train was chartered. The railway officials were given twenty-five minutes in which to clear the line. Arrangements were made for a car to meet us at our journey's end. And at about that hour when after-theatre throngs are congesting the West End thorough-fares, we set out in the big Rolls, Fey at the wheel.

Nayland Smith's special powers (which enabled him to ignore traffic regulations) and the wizard driving of Fey, resulted in a dash through London's crowded streets which even I, who had known so many thrills, found exciting.

Smith uttered scarcely a word either to myself or to Gallaho, until arriving at the terminus he was assured by a flustered stationmaster that the special was ready to start. Once on board and whirling through that dark night, he turned to the inspector.

"Now, Gallaho, the full facts!"

"Well sir"—Gallaho steadied himself against the arm rest, for the solitary coach was rocking madly—"I have very little to add." He pulled out his notebook. "This is what I jotted down during the telephone conversation."

"The local police are not in charge then?" Smith snapped.

"No sir, and I took the step of requesting that they shouldn't be notified."

"Good."

"It was a Mr. Bailey, the doctor's private secretary, who called up the Yard."

"When?"

"At ten-seventeen—so we've wasted no time! This was what he told me." He consulted his notes. "The doctor, who is engaged upon experiments of great importance in his private laboratory, had alarmed his secretary by his behaviour—that is in the last week or so. He seemed to be in deadly fear of something or someone, so Mr. Bailey told me. But whatever was bothering him he kept it to himself. It came to a head though last Wednesday. Something reduced Doctor Jasper to such a state of utter panic that he abandoned work in his laboratory and for hours walked up and down his study. Today he was even worse. In fact Mr. Bailey said he looked positively ill. But somewhere around noon as the result, it seems, of a long telephone conversation—"

"With whom?"

"Mr. Bailey didn't know—but as a result, the doctor resumed work, although apparently on the verge of a nervous breakdown. He worked right on up till to-night, refusing to break off for dinner. His behaviour so alarmed his secretary that Mr. Bailey took the liberty of searching the study to see if he could find any evidence pointing to the cause of it."

"And he found—"

"The original of the message I showed you."

"No other message?"

"No other."

"Anything else?"

"Nothing that he could in any way connect with the remarkable behaviour of his employer. He went to the laboratory, which is separate from the house, but Doctor Jasper refused to unlock the door and said that on no account was he to be disturbed. Very wisely, Mr. Bailey called up Scotland Yard, and that's about all I know."

Onward we raced through the black night, at one point passing very near to the scene of my last meeting with Ardatha. Within me I fought desperately to solve the mystery of those enigmatic eyes. Even when she looked at me with scorn, mocked me, fought with me, they seemed to mirror a second Ardatha, submerged, all but hidden perhaps from herself—a frightened soul who appealed, appealed for help—protection.

The whistle shrieked wildly. We went through stations at nightmare speed. Once we roared past a sidetracked express. I had a fleeting glimpse of lighted windows, staring faces.

A useful-looking Daimler met us at the station where we were received with some ceremony by the stationmaster. But brushing all inquiries aside, Smith climbed into the car followed by myself and Gallaho, and we set out for Great Oaks. Once on the way Smith glanced at his watch.

"I take it you don't know, Gallaho, at what time the original of this message was received?"

"No, Mr. Bailey couldn't tell me."

Then having followed a high and badly kept yew

hedge for some distance, the car was turned in between twin stone pillars and began to mount a drive which ascended slightly through a grove of magnificent oaks. I saw the house ahead. A low-pitched, irregular building, the characteristics of Great Oaks were difficult to discern, but the place was evidently of considerable age.

"Hullo!" muttered Smith; "what's this? Some new development?"

Light streamed out into the porch and I could see that the front door was open.

As our car swung around and was pulled up before the steps two men ran down. They evidently had been awaiting us.

Smith sprang out to meet them. Gallaho and I followed. One of the pair was plainly a butler; the other, a youngish, dark-haired man with a short military moustache, whom I assumed normally to be of healthy colouring but who looked pale in the reflected light, stepped forward and introduced himself.

"My name is Horace Bailey," he said in an agitated voice. "Do you come from Scotland Yard?"

"We do," said Gallaho. "I'm Detective Inspector Gallaho—this is Sir Denis Nayland Smith, and Mr. Kerrigan."

"Thank God you're here!" cried Bailey, and glanced aside at the butler, who nodded sympathetically.

Both faces, I saw as we all entered Great Oaks, were stamped by an expression of horrified amazement.

"I have a foreboding," said Smith, glancing about the entrance hall in which we found ourselves, "that I come too late."

Mr. Bailey slowly inclined his head and something

like a groan came from the butler.

"Good God, Kerrigan! A second score to the enemy!"

He dropped down on a leather-covered couch set in a recess over which hung a trophy of antlers. For a moment his amazing vitality, his electrical energy, seemed to have deserted him, and I saw a man totally overcome. As I stepped towards him he looked up haggardly.

"The facts, Mr. Bailey, if you please." He spoke more slowly than I remembered ever to have heard him speak. "When did it happen? Where? How?"

2

"I discovered the tragedy not five minutes ago." Bailey spoke and looked as a man distraught. "You must understand that Doctor Jasper has been locked in his laboratory since noon and at last I determined to face any rebuff in order to induce him to rest. I beg, gentlemen, that you will return there with me now! Hale, the chauffeur, and Bordon, the doctor's mechanic, are trying to cut out the lock of the door!"

"What do you mean?" I asked.

The overstrung man, waving us to follow, already was leading the way along a passage communicating with the rear of the house.

"When I reached the laboratory," he cried back, now beginning to run, "through the grille in the door I saw the doctor lying face downwards . . . I immediately returned for assistance. . . . It was hearing the approach of your car that brought me to the porch to meet you."

A somewhat straggling party, we followed the hurrying figure through a dim garden and along a path which zigzagged, sloping slightly upwards to a coppice of beech trees. He knew the way, but we did not. Inspector Gallaho, stumbling and growling, produced a flashlamp for our guidance.

The laboratory was some two hundred yards removed from the house, a squat brick building with a number of high-set windows, screened and iron-barred. The entrance was on the further side, and as we approached I heard a sound of hammering and wrenching. Onto a gravel path and around the corner we ran, and there, where light shone out through a grille in a heavy door, I saw two men at work with chisels, hammers and crowbars.

"Are you nearly through?" Bailey panted.

"Another two minutes should do it, sir."

"Surely there is more than one key!" Smith snapped.

"I regret to say there is only one. Doctor Jasper always held it."

We crowded together to look through the thick glass behind the grille.

I saw a long, narrow workroom, well lighted. It resembled less a laboratory than a machine shop, but I noticed chemical impedimenta, mostly unfamiliar. That which claimed and held my attention was the figure of a short, thick-set man wearing a white linen coat. He lay face downward, arms outstretched, some two paces from the door. Owing to his position, it was impossible to obtain more than a glimpse of the back of his head. But there was something grimly significant in the slump of the body.

The workmen carried on unceasingly. I thought I had heard few more mournful sounds than those of the blows of the hammer and splintering of stout wood as they struggled to force a way into the locked laboratory.

"This is ghastly," Smith muttered, "ghastly! He may not be dead. Have you sent for a doctor?"

"I am myself a qualified physician," Bailey replied, "and following Inspector Gallaho's advice, I have not notified the local police."

"Good," said Gallaho.

"I am still far from understanding the circumstances," snapped Nayland Smith, with the irritability of frustration. "You say that Doctor Jasper has been locked in his laboratory all day?"

"Yes. His ways have become increasingly strange for some time past. Something—I can only guess what—evidently occurred which threw him into a state of nervous tension some ten days or a fortnight ago. Then again, last Wednesday to be exact, he seemed to grow worse. I have come to the conclusion, Sir Denis, that he had received two of these notices. The third—I dictated its contents to the inspector over the telephone—must actually have come by the second post this morning."

"Are you certain of this?"

"All his mail passes through my hands, and I now recall that there was one letter marked 'Personal & Private' which naturally I did not open, delivered at eleven forty-five this morning."

"Eleven forty-five?"

"Yes."

I saw Smith raise his wrist watch to the light shining

out from the grille.

"Two minutes short of midnight," he murmured. "The message gave him twelve hours. We are thirteen minutes too late."

"But do you realise, Sir Denis," the secretary cried, "that he is alone, and locked in? This door is of two-inch teak set in an iron frame. To batter it down would be impossible—hence this damnable delay! How can the question of foul play arise?"

"I fear it does," Smith returned sternly. "From what you have told me I am disposed to believe that the ultimate result of these threats was to inspire Doctor Jasper to complete his experiments within the period granted him."

"Good heavens!" I murmured, "you are right, Smith!"

The chauffeur and the mechanic laboured on the door feverishly, their hammer blows and the splintering of tough wood punctuating our conversation.

"He doesn't move," muttered Gallaho, looking through the grille.

"Might I ask, Mr. Bailey," Smith went on, "if you assisted Doctor Jasper in his experiments?"

"Sometimes, Sir Denis, in certain places."

"What was the nature of the present experiment?"

There was a perceptible pause before the secretary replied.

"To the best of my belief—for I was not fully informed in the matter—it was a modified method of charging rifles—"

"Or, one presumes, machine guns?"

"Or machine guns, as you say. An entirely new principle which he termed 'the vacuum charger.' "

"Which increased the velocity of the bullet?"

"Enormously."

"And, in consequence, increased the range?"

"Certainly. My employer, of course, is not a medical man, but a doctor of physics."

"Quite," snapped Smith. "Were the doctor's experiments subsidised by the British government?"

"No. He was working independently."

"For whom?"

"I fear, in the circumstances, the question is rather an awkward one."

"Yet I must request an answer."

"Well—a gentleman known to us as Mr. Osaki."

"Osaki?"

"Yes."

"You see, Kerrigan"—Smith turned to me—"here comes the Asiatic element! No description of Mr. Osaki (an assumed name) is necessary. Descriptions of any one of Osaki's countrymen sound identical. This Asiatic gentleman was a frequent visitor, Mr. Bailey?"

"Oh yes."

"Was he a technician?"

"Undoubtedly. He sometimes lunched with the doctor and spent many hours with him in the laboratory. But I know for a fact that at other times he would visit the laboratory without coming through the house."

"What do you mean exactly?"

"There is a lane some twenty yards beyond here and a gate. Osaki sometimes visited the doctor when he was working, entering by way of the gate. I have seen him in the laboratory, so this I can state with certainty."

"When was he here last?"

"To the best of my knowledge, yesterday evening.

He spent nearly two hours with Doctor Jasper."

"Trying, no doubt, to set his mind at rest about the second notice from the Si-Fan. Then this morning the third and final notice arrives. But Mr. Osaki, anxious about results, phones at noon—"

"Binns, the butler, thinks the caller this morning was Osaki—"

"Undoubtedly urging him to new efforts," jerked Smith. "You understand, Kerrigan?"

"For heaven's sake are you nearly through?" cried Bailey to the workmen.

"Very nearly, sir. It's a mighty tough job," the chauffeur replied.

To the accompaniment of renewed hammering and wrenching:

"There are two other points," said Bailey, his voice shaking nervously, "which I should mention, as they may have a bearing on the tragedy. First, at approximately half past eleven, Binns, who was in his pantry at the back of the house, came to me and reported that he had heard the sound of three shots, apparently coming from the lane. I attached little importance to the matter at the time, being preoccupied about the doctor, and assuming that poachers were at work. The second incident, which points to the fact that Doctor Jasper was alive after seven-thirty, is this:

"A phone call came which Binns answered. The speaker was a woman—"

"Ah!" Smith murmured.

"She declined to give her name but said that the matter was urgent and requested to be put through to the laboratory. Binns called the doctor, asking if the line should be connected. He was told, yes, and the call was put through. Shortly afterwards, determined at all costs to induce the doctor to return to the house, I came here and found him as you see him."

A splintering crash announced that the end of the task of forcing the door was drawing near.

"Had the doctor any other regular visitors?" jerked Smith.

"None. There was one lady whom I gathered to be a friend, although he had never spoken of her — Mrs. Milton. She lunched here three days ago and was shown over the laboratory."

"Describe Mrs. Milton."

"It would be difficult to describe her, Sir Denis. A woman of great beauty of an exotic type, tall and slender, with raven black hair — "

"Ivory skin," Smith went on rapidly, "notably long slender hands, and unmistakable eyes, of a quite unusual colour, nearly jade green — "

"Good heavens!" cried Bailey, "you know her?"

"I begin to believe," said Nayland Smith, and there was a curious change of quality in his voice, "that I *do* know her. Kerrigan" — he turned to me — "we have heard of this lady before?"

"You mean the woman who visited General Quinto?"

"Not a doubt about it! I absolve Ardatha: this is a *zombie* — a corpse moving among the living! This woman is a harbinger of death and we must find her."

"You don't suggest," cried Bailey, "that Mrs. Milton is in any way associated — "

"I suggest nothing," snapped Smith.

A resounding crash and a wrenching of metal told us that the lock had been driven through. A moment later and the door was flung open.

I clenched my fists and for a moment stood stock still.

An unforgettable, unmistakable, but wholly indescribable odour crept to my nostrils.

"Kerrigan!" cried Smith in a stifled voice and sprang into the laboratory—"you smell it, Kerrigan? He's gone the same way!"

Bailey had hurried forward and now was bending over the prone body. In the stuffy atmosphere of this place where many queer smells mingled, that of the strange deathly odour which I must always associate with the murder of General Quinto predominated to an appalling degree.

"Get those blinds up! Throw the windows open!"

Hale, the chauffeur, ran in and began to carry out the order, as Smith and Bailey bent and turned the body over. . . .

Then I saw Bailey spring swiftly upright. I saw him stare around him like a man stricken with sudden madness. In a voice that sounded like a smothered scream:

"This isn't Doctor Jasper," he cried; "it's *Osaki!*"

Chapter 17

IN THE LABORATORY

"The green death! The green death again!" said Nayland Smith.

"Whatever is it?" There was awe in my voice. "It's ghastly! In heaven's name what is it?"

We had laid the dead man on a sort of day bed with which the laboratory was equipped, and under the dark Asiatic skin already that ghastly greenish tinge was beginning to manifest itself.

The place was very quiet. In spite of the fact of all windows being opened that indescribable sweetish smell—a smell, strange though it may sound, of which I had dreamed, and which to the end of my life I must always associate with the assassination of General Quinto—hung heavily in the air.

Somewhere in a dark background beyond the shattered door the chauffeur and mechanic were talking in low voices.

Mr. Bailey had gone back to the house with Inspector Gallaho. There was hope that the phone call which had immediately preceded the death of Osaki might yet be traced.

The extension to the laboratory proved to be in perfect order, but the butler was in so nervous a condition that Gallaho had lost patience and had gone to the main instrument.

"This," said Smith, turning aside and staring down at a row of objects which lay upon a small table, "is in many ways the most mysterious feature."

The things lying there were those which had been in the dead man's possession. There was a notebook containing a number of notes in code which it would probably take some time to decipher, a wad of paper money, a cigarette case, a railway ticket, a watch, an ivory amulet and a bunch of keys on a chain.

But (and this it was to which Nayland Smith referred) there were two keys—Yales—unattached, which has been found in the pocket of the white coat which Osaki had been wearing.

"We know," Smith continued, "that both these keys are keys of the laboratory, and Mr. Bailey was quite emphatic on the point that Doctor Jasper possessed only one. What is the inference, Kerrigan?"

I sniffed the air suspiciously and then stared at the speaker.

"I assume the inference to be that the dead man also possessed a key of the laboratory."

"Exactly."

"This being the case, why should *two* be found in his possession?"

"My theory is this: Doctor Jasper, for some reason which we have yet to learn, hurried out of the laboratory just before Osaki's appearance, and—a point which I think indicates great nervous disturbance—left his key in the door. Osaki, approaching, duplicate key in hand, discovered this. Finding the laboratory to be empty, he put on a white jacket—intending to work, presumably—and dropped the key in the pocket in order to draw Doctor Jasper's attention to this carelessness when the doctor returned."

"No doubt you are right, Smith!"

"You are possibly wondering, Kerrigan, why Osaki, finding himself being overcome by the symptoms of the Green Death, of which we know one to be an impression of beating drums, did not run out and hurry to the house."

"I confess the point had occurred to me."

"Here, I think, is the answer. We know from the case of General Quinto that the impression of beating drums is very real. May we not assume that Osaki, knowing as he certainly did know that imminent danger overhung Doctor Jasper and himself, believed the menace to come from the outside—believed the drumming to be real and deliberately remained in this place?"

"The theory certainly covers the facts, but always it brings us back to—"

"What?"

"The mystery of how a man . . ."

"A man locked in alone," Smith snapped, "can nevertheless be murdered and no clue left to show what means has been employed! Yes!" the word sounded almost like a groan. "The second mystery, of course, is the extraordinary behaviour of Doctor Jasper. . . ."

He paused.

From somewhere outside came the sound of running footsteps, a sudden murmur of voices, then—I thought Hale, the chauffeur, was the speaker:

"Thank God you're alive, sir!"

A man burst into the laboratory, a short, thick-set, dark man, hair dishevelled and his face showing every evidence of the fact that he had not shaved for some time. His eyes were wild—his lips were twitching; he stood with clenched hands looking about him. Then his pale face seemed to grow a shade paler. Those staring eyes became focused upon the body lying on the sofa.

"Good God!" he muttered, and then addressing Smith:

"Who are you? What has happened?"

"Doctor Martin Jasper, I presume?"

"Yes, yes! But who are you? What does this mean?"

"My name is Nayland Smith; this is Mr. Bart Kerrigan. What it means, Doctor Jasper, is that your associate Mr. Osaki has died in your place!"

Chapter 18

DR. MARTIN JASPER

"You are indeed a fortunate man to be alive." Nayland Smith gazed sternly at the physicist. "You have been preparing a deadly weapon of warfare — not for the protection of your own country, but for the use of a belligerent nation."

"I am entitled," said Dr. Jasper, shakily wiping his wet brow, "to act independently if I choose to do so."

"You see the consequences. As he lies, so *you* might be lying. No, Doctor Jasper. You had received three notices, I believe, from the Si-Fan."

Dr. Jasper's twitching nervousness became even more manifest.

"I had — but how do you know?"

"It happens to be my business to know. The Si-Fan, sir, cannot be ignored."

"I know! I know!"

The doctor suddenly dropped on to a chair beside one of the benches and buried his dishevelled head in his hands.

"I have been playing with fire, but Osaki, who urged me to it, is the sufferer!"

He was very near to the end of his resources; this was plain enough, but:

"I am going to suggest," said Nayland Smith, speaking in a quiet voice, "that you retire and sleep, for if ever a man needed rest, you do. But first I regret duty demands that I ask a few questions."

Dr. Jasper, save for the twitching of his hands, did not stir.

"What were the Si-Fan's orders?"

"That I deliver to them the completed plans and a model of my vacuum charger."

"This invention, I take it, gives a great advantage to those employing it?"

"Yes." His voice was little more than a whisper. "It increases the present range of a rifle rather more than fifty per cent."

"To whom were you to deliver these plans and model?"

"To a woman who would be waiting in a car by the R.A.C. call box at the corner of the London Road."

"A woman!"

"Yes. A time was stated at which the woman would be waiting at this point. Failing my compliance, I was told that on receipt of a third and final notice at any hour during the twelve which would be allotted to me, if I cared to go to this call box, I should be met there by a representative."

"Yes?" Smith urged gently. "Go on."

The speaker's voice grew lower and lower.

"I showed these notes to Osaki."

"Where are they now?"

"He took them all. He urged me, always he urged me, to ignore them. By tonight I thought that my experiments would be completed, that I should have revolutionized the subject. He was to meet me here in the laboratory, and we both fully anticipated that the charger would be an accomplished fact."

"He had a key of the laboratory?"

"Yes."

Nayland Smith nodded to me.

"Just before half past eleven an awful dread possessed me. I thought that the price which I should receive for this invention would be useless to a dead man. Just before Osaki was due I took my plans, my model — everything, slipped on a light coat, in the pockets of which I placed all the fruits of my experiments, and ran — I do not exaggerate — ran to the appointed spot."

"What did you find? By whom were you met?" Smith snapped.

"There was a car drawn up on the north side of the road. A woman was just stepping into it — "

"Describe her."

"She is beautiful — dark — slender. I know her as Mrs. Milton. I know now she is a spy!"

"Quite enough. What happened?"

"She seemed to be much disturbed as I hurried up. Her eyes — she has remarkable eyes — opened almost with a look of horror."

"What did she do — what did she say?"

"She said: 'Doctor Jasper, are you here to meet me?' I was utterly dumbfounded. I knew in that awful moment what a fool I had been! But I replied that I was."

"What did she say then?"

"She enumerated the items which I had been ordered to deliver up — took them from me one by one . . . and returned to the car. Her parting words were, 'You have been wise.' "

"Then your invention, complete and practical, is now in the hands of the Si-Fan?"

"It is!" groaned Dr. Jasper.

"Some deadly thing," said Nayland Smith bitterly, "was placed in the laboratory during the time that your key remained in the door—for in your nervous state you forgot to remove it. A few moments later Osaki entered. Someone who was watching mistook Osaki for you. The shots heard by the butler were a signal to that call box. The phone call is the clue! It was Osaki who took it. . . ."

Inspector Gallaho dashed into the laboratory.

"I have traced the call," he said huskily—"the local police are of some use after all! It's a box about half a mile from here, on the London Road."

"I know," said Smith wearily.

"You know, sir!" growled Gallaho, then suddenly noticing Dr. Martin Jasper: "Who the devil have we here?"

The doctor raised his haggard face from his hands.

"Someone who has no right to be alive," he replied.

Gallaho began chewing phantom gum.

"I said the local police were of some use," he went on truculently, staring at Nayland Smith. "What I mean is this: They have the woman who made the call."

"What!"

Smith became electrified; his entire expression changed.

"Yes. I roused everybody, had every car challenged, and luckily got a description of the one we wanted from a passing A.A. scout who had seen it standing near the box. The village constable at Greystones very cleverly spotted the right one. The woman is now at police headquarters there, sir! I suggest we proceed to Greystones at once."

Chapter 19

CONSTABLE ISLES'S STATEMENT

When presently Smith, Gallaho and I set out in the police car for Greystones, we had succeeded in learning a little more about the mysterious Mrs. Milton. A police inspector and the police surgeon we had left behind at Great Oaks; but as Nayland Smith said, what expert opinion had failed to learn in regard to the death of General Quinto local talent could not hope to find out.

Mrs. Milton, Dr. Jasper had told us before he finally collapsed (for the ordeal through which he had passed had entirely sapped his nervous energy), was a chance acquaintance. The doctor, during one of his rare constitutionals in the neighbouring lanes, had found her beside a broken-down car and had succeeded in restarting the engine. Quite obviously he had been attracted. They had exchanged cards and he had invited her to lunch and to look over his laboratory.

His description of Mrs. Milton tallied exactly with that of the woman who had visited General Quinto on the night before his murder!

My excitement as we sped towards Greystones grew ever greater. With my own eyes I was about to see this harbinger of death employed by Dr. Fu Manchu, finally to convince myself that she was not Ardatha.

But indeed little doubt on this point remained.

"Unless I am greatly mistaken," said Nayland Smith, "you are going to meet for the first time, Kerrigan, an example of a dead woman moving among the living, influencing, fascinating them. I won't tell you, Inspector Gallaho"—he turned to the Scotland Yard officer—"whom I suspect this woman to be. But she is someone you have met before."

"Now that I know Doctor Fu Manchu is concerned in this case," the inspector growled in his husky voice, "nothing would surprise me."

We passed along the main street of a village in which all the houses and cottages were in darkness and pulled up before one over which, dimly, I could see a tablet which indicated that this was the local police headquarters. As we stepped out:

"Strange," murmured Nayland Smith, looking about him—"there's no car here and only one light upstairs."

"I don't like this," said Gallaho savagely, marching up the path and pressing a bell beside the door.

There was some delay which we all suffered badly. Then a window opened above and I saw a woman looking out.

"What do you want?" she called: it was a meek voice.

"I want Constable Isles," said Gallaho violently. "This is Detective Inspector Gallaho of Scotland Yard. I spoke to the constable twenty minutes ago, and now I'm here to see him."

"Oh!" said the owner of the meek voice, "I'll come down."

A minute later she opened the door. I saw that she wore a dressing gown and looked much disturbed.

"Where's the woman," snapped Nayland Smith, "whom the constable was detaining?"

"She's gone, sir."

"What!"

"Yes. I suppose he must have been satisfied to have let her go. My husband has had a very hard day, and he's fast asleep in the parlour. I didn't like to disturb him."

2

"What is the meaning of this?"

Nayland Smith spoke as angrily as he ever spoke to a woman. Accompanied by the hastily attired Mrs. Isles, we stood in a little sitting room. A heavily built man who wore a tweed suit was lying on a couch, apparently plunged in deep sleep. Chief Detective Inspector Gallaho chewed ominously and glared at the woman.

"I think it's just that he's overtired, sir," she said. She was a plump, dark-eyed, hesitant sort of a creature, and our invasion seemed to have terrified her. "He has had a very heavy day."

"That is not the point," said Smith rapidly. "Inspector Gallaho here sent out a description of a car seen by an A.A. man near a call box on the London Road. All officers, on or off duty, were notified to look out for it and to stop it if sighted. Your husband telephoned to Great Oaks twenty minutes ago saying that he had intercepted this car and that the driver, a woman, was here in his custody. Where is she? What has occurred?"

"I don't really know, sir. He was just going to bed when the phone rang, and then he got up, dressed, and went out. I heard a car stop outside, and then I heard him bring someone in. When the car drove away again and he didn't come up I went to look for him and found him asleep here. When he's like that I never disturb him, because he's a bad sleeper."

"He's drugged," snapped Smith irritably.

"Oh no!" the woman whispered.

Drugged he was, for it took us nearly ten minutes to revive him. When ultimately Constable Isles sat up and stared about I thought that I had rarely seen a more bewildered man. Smith had been sniffing suspiciously and had examined the stubs of two cigarettes in an ash tray.

"Hello, Constable," he said, "what's the meaning of this? Asleep on duty, I'm afraid."

Constable Isles sat up, then stood up, clenched his fists and stared at all of us like a man demented.

"I don't know what's happened," he muttered thickly. "I don't know!"

He looked again from face to face.

"I'm Chief Detective Inspector Gallaho. Perhaps you know what's happened *now!* You reported to me less than half an hour ago. Where's the car? Where's the prisoner?"

The wretched man steadied himself, outstretched hand against the wall.

"By God, sir!" he said, and made a visible attempt to pull himself together. "A terrible thing has happened to me!"

"You mean a terrible thing is going to happen to you," growled Gallaho.

"Leave this to me." Nayland Smith rested his hand on Isles's shoulder and gently forced him down on to the couch again. "Don't bother about it too much. I think I know what occurred, and it has occurred to others before. When the general order came you dressed and went out to watch the road. Is that so?"

"Yes sir."

"You saw what looked like the car described, coming along this way. You stopped it. How did you stop it?"

"I stood in the road and signalled to the driver to pull up."

"I see. Describe the driver."

"A woman, sir, young—" The speaker clutched his head. Obviously he was in a state of mental confusion. "A very dark young woman; she was angry at first and glared at me as though she was in half a mind to drive on."

"Do you remember her eyes?"

"I'm not likely to forget them, sir—they were bright green. She almost frightened me. But I told her I was a police officer and that there was a query about her car. She took it quietly after that, left the car at the gate out there and came in. That was when I telephoned to the number I had been given and reported that I had found the wanted car."

"What happened after that?"

"Well sir, I could see she was a foreigner, good looking in her way, although"—glancing at his buxom wife—"a bit on the thin side from my point of view. And she was so nice and seemed so anxious not to want to wake the missus, that I felt half sorry for her."

"What did she say to you? What did she talk about?"

"To tell you the truth, sir," he stared pathetically at Nayland Smith, "I can't really remember. But while we were waiting she asked me to have a cigarette."

"Did you do so?"

"Yes. I lighted it and one for her at the same time, and we went on talking. The reason I remember her eyes, is because that's the last thing I do remember—" He swallowed noisily. "Although there was nothing, I give you my word, there was nothing to give me the tip in time, I know now that that cigarette was drugged. I hope, sir"—turning to Gallaho—"that I haven't failed in my duty."

"Forget it," snapped Nayland Smith. "Men far senior to you have failed in the same way where this particular woman has been concerned."

Chapter 20

A MODERN VAMPIRE

"There are certain features about this case, Kerrigan," said Nayland Smith, "which I have so far hesitated to mention to you."

Alone in the police car we were returning to London. The night remained mistily gloomy, and I was concerned with my own private thoughts.

"You mean perhaps in regard to the woman known as Mrs. Milton?"

"Yes!" He pulled out his pipe and began to load it. "She is a phenomenon."

"You referred to her, I remember, as a *zombie*."

"I did. A dead woman moving among the living. Yes, unless I am greatly mistaken, Kerrigan, Mrs. Milton is a modern example of the vampire."

"Ghastly idea!"

"Ghastly, if you like. But there is very little doubt in my mind that Mrs. Milton is the woman who was concerned—although as it seemed at the time, remotely—in the death of General Quinto. Those descriptions which we have had unmistakably tally. Stress this point in your notes, Kerrigan. For there is a bridge here between life and death."

Tucked into one corner of the car as it raced through the night, I turned and stared at my companion.

"You think you know her?"

"There is little room for error in the matter. The facts we learned from Constable Isles go to confirm my opinion. That so simple a character should fall victim to this woman is not surprising. She is as dangerous to humanity at large as Ardatha is dangerous to you."

I did not reply, for he seemed to have divined that indeed I had been thinking about Ardatha. Of one thing I was sure: Ardatha was not the harbinger of death employed by Dr. Fu Manchu in the assassination of General Quinto and in that of Osaki.

Chief Detective Inspector Gallaho had been left in charge of the inquiry in Suffolk. Among his duties was that of obtaining a statement from Dr. Martin Jasper regarding the exact character of the vacuum charger and the identity of the man known as Osaki. That he, with local assistance, would come upon a clue to the mystery of the Green Death was unlikely, since London experts had failed in an earlier case.

Nayland Smith had worked himself to a standstill in the laboratory. The mystery of why Osaki, locked in there alone, should have died remained a mystery. I began to feel drowsy but became widely awake again when Nayland Smith, striking a match to light his pipe, spoke again.

"Whoever was watching that laboratory, Kerrigan, must have been prepared with some second means of dealing with Doctor Jasper."

"Why?"

"Well, they could not have known that he would open the door. They must have assumed when he *did* open the door that he was returning to the house and would come back."

"Why should they suppose that he would come back?"

"Obviously they knew of his appointment with Osaki."

"Why not have just removed the model and the plans?"

"They knew that neither model nor plans were of any avail if their inventor still defied the Si-Fan. Doctor Fu Manchu's object, Kerrigan, was not to steal the plans of the vacuum charger, but to prevent those plans falling into the hands of that Power represented by Mr. Osaki. I am convinced that Osaki's death was an accident, but it probably suited the Si-Fan."

In the bumping of the car over a badly paved road I seemed to hear the beating of drums.

Chapter 21

THE RED BUTTON

"Sir Denis evidently detained, sir. Expect any moment."

It was the evening of the following day and I had called at Smith's flat in Whitehall by appointment. I looked at the expressionless face of the speaker.

"That's all right, Fey. I'll come in and wait."

As I crossed the lobby and entered the sitting room which contained the big radio and that television set upon which miraculously once Dr. Fu Manchu had manifested himself, I heard the phone ringing. Staring at the apparatus, I took out a cigarette. I could detect Fey's monosyllables in the lobby. A few moments later he entered.

"Going out, sir," he reported. "Whisky-soda? Buffet at disposal. Sir Denis at Yard with Inspector Gallaho. Will be here inside ten minutes."

He prepared a drink for me and went out.

I sipped my whisky and soda and inspected some of the pictures and photographs which the room contained. The pictures were landscapes, almost exclusively Oriental. A fine photograph of a handsome grey-haired man I was able to identify as that of Dr. Petrie, Nayland Smith's old friend who had been associated with him in those early phases of his battle with Fu Manchu, of which I knew so little. Another, a grimly humorous, square-jawed, moustached face, I was unable to place, but I learned later that it represented Superintendent Weymouth, once of the Criminal Investigation Department, but now attached to the Cairo police.

There were others, not so characteristic. And on a small easel on top of a bookcase I came across a water color of an ethereally beautiful woman. Upon it was written:

"To our best and dearest friend from Karamaneh."

I stared out of a window across the embankment to where old Father Thames moved timelessly on. A reluctant moon, veiled from moment to moment, sometimes gleamed upon the water. For many years, as Nayland Smith had told me, the Thames had been Dr. Fu Manchu's highway. His earliest base had been at Limehouse in the Chinese quarter. London River had served his purpose well.

Nothing passed along the stream as I watched and my thoughts wandered to that Essex creek on the banks of which stood the Monks' Arms. How hopelessly they wandered there!

Ardatha!—a strange name and a strange character. To me, lover of freedom, it was appalling to think that in those enigmatical amethyst eyes I had lost myself—had seen my philosophy crumble, had read the doom of many a cherished principle. Almost certainly she was evil; for how, otherwise, could she be a member of so evil a thing as the Si-Fan?

I tried to cease contemplating that bewitching image. Crossing to an armchair, I was about to sit down when I heard the phone bell in the lobby. I set my glass on a table and went out to answer the call.

"Hello," said a voice, "can I speak to Sir Denis Nayland Smith?"

"Sir Denis is out. But can I take a message?"

The speaker was a man who used good but not perfect English—a foreigner of some kind.

"Thank you. I will call again."

I returned to the armchair and lighted a cigarette.

What was the mystery of the Green Death? Where medical analysis had failed, where Nayland Smith had failed, what hope had I of solving it? It was an appalling exhibition of that power possessed by the awful man I had met out on the Essex marshes. A monster had been reborn—and I had stood face to face with him.

Closing my eyes I lay back in the chair . . .

"If you will be good enough to lower the light, Mr. Kerrigan"—the voice was unmistakable—"and sit closer to the screen. There is something important to yourself and to Sir Denis which I have to communicate."

I sprang up—I could not have sprung up more suddenly if a bomb had exploded at my feet. The screen was illuminated, as once before I had seen it illuminated . . . And there looking out at me was Dr. Fu Manchu!

Perhaps for a decimal moment I doubted what course to take; and then (I think almost anyone would have done the same) I extinguished the light.

The switches were remote from the television

screen; and I confess, as I turned and stood in darkness before that wonderful evil face which apparently regarded me, I was touched by swift fear. In fact I had to tell myself that this was not the *real* Dr. Fu Manchu but merely his image before I summoned up the courage enough to approach and to watch.

"Will you please touch the red button on the right of the screen," the sibilant voice went on, "merely to indicate that you have observed my wishes."

I touched the red button. My heart was beating much too rapidly; but sitting down on an ottoman, I compelled myself to study that wonderful face.

It might have been the face of an emperor. I found myself thinking of Zenghis Khan. Intellectually, the brow was phenomenal, the dignity of the lined features might have belonged to a Pharaoh, but the soul of the great Chinese doctor lay in his eyes. Never had I seen before, and never have I seen since, such power in a man's eyes as lay in those of Dr. Fu Manchu.

Then he spoke, and his voice, too, was unforgettable. One hearing its alternate sibilants and gutturals must have remembered every intonation to the end of his days.

"I regret, Mr. Kerrigan," he said, "that you are still alive. Your rescue meant that an old and useful base is now destroyed. I suspect that some member of the Si-Fan has failed me in this matter. If so, there will be retribution."

His words chilled me coldly.

Ardatha!

She had defied me, jeered at me, fought with me,

but in the end she had saved me. It was a strange romance, but I knew that on my side it was real. Ardatha was my woman, and if I lost her I should have lost all that made life worth-while. I think, except for that unreadable expression which seemed to tell me that her words did not mean all they conveyed, I had had but little hope, in spite of my masculine vanity, until I had realised that she had risked everything to rescue me from the cellars of the Monks' Arms.

I was watching the image of those strange eyes as this thought flashed through my mind.

Good God! Did he suspect Ardatha?

"In the absence of Sir Denis"—the words seemed to reach me indistinctly—"I must request *you*, Mr. Kerrigan, to take my message. It is very simple. It is this: Sir Denis has fought with me for many years. I have come to respect him as one respects an honourable enemy, but forces difficult to control now demand that I should act swiftly. Listen, and I will explain what I mean to do."

That forceful voice died away unaccountably. My brain suggested that the instrument, operated by an unknown principle, had failed. But then conscious thought petered out altogether, I suppose. The eyes regarding me from the screen, although the image was colourless, seemed, aided by memory, to become *green*. . . . Then they merged together and became one contemplative eye. That eye grew enormous—it dominated the picture—it became a green lake—and a remorseless urge impelled me to plunge into its depths. . . .

I stood up, or so I thought, from the ottoman on

which I had been seated and walked forward into the lake.

Miraculously I did not sink. Stepping across a glittering green expanse, I found myself upon solid land. Here I paused, and the voice of Dr. Fu Manchu spoke:

"Look! — this is China."

I saw a swamp, a vast morass wherein no human thing could dwell, a limitless and vile corruption. . . . I saw guns buried in the mud; in pools I saw floating corpses: the foetid air was full of carrion, and all about me I heard wailing and lamentations. So desolate was the scene that I turned my head aside until the Voice spoke again.

"Look! It is Spain."

I saw a waste which once had been a beautiful village: the shell of an old church; ruins of a house upon whose scarred walls bougainvillea bloomed gaily. People, among them women and children, were searching in the ruins. I wondered for what they were searching. But out of the darkness the Voice came again:

"Look! This is London."

From my magic carpet I looked down upon Whitehall. Almost that spectacle conquered the magic of the Voice. I fought against mirage, but the mood of rebellion passed. . . . I saw the cenotaph partly demolished. I heard crashes all around me, muted but awful. Where I thought familiar buildings should be there were gaping caverns. Strange figures, antlike as I looked down upon them, ran in all directions.

"*Your* world!" said the Voice. "Come, now, into

mine. . . ."

And Ardatha was beside me!

It was a rose garden, the scent of the flowers intoxicating. Below where the roses grew I saw steps leading down to a marble pool upon the cool surface of which lotus blossoms floated. Bees droned amid the roses, and gaily plumaged birds darted from tree to tree. An exquisite sense of well being overcame me. I turned to Ardatha — and her lips were irresistible.

"Why did you ever doubt what I told you?" she whispered.

"Only because I was a fool."

I lost myself in a kiss which realised all the raptures of which I had ever dreamed. . . .

Ardatha melted from my arms. . . . I sought her, called her name — "Ardatha! Ardatha!" But the rose garden had vanished: I was in darkness — alone, helpless, though none constrained me. . . .

Flat on the carpet of Nayland Smith's apartment, as I had fallen back from the ottoman, I lay! — fully alive to my environment, but unable to speak — to move!

Chapter 22

LIVING DEATH

The screen, the magical screen, was black. Faint light came through the windows. Something — some damnable thing — had happened. I had gone mad — or been bewitched. That power, suspected but now experienced, of the dreadful Chinese doctor had swept me up.

With what purpose?

There seemed to be nothing different about the room — but how long had I been unaware of what was going on? Most accursed thing of all, I could think, but I couldn't move! I lay there flat on my back, helpless as one dead. My keen mental activity in this condition was a double agony.

As I lay I could see right into the lobby — and now I became aware of the fact that I was not alone!

A small, dark man had opened the outer door quietly, glanced in my direction, and then set down a small handbag which he had seemed to carry with great care. He wore thick-rimmed glasses. He opened the bag, and I saw him doing something to the telephone.

I tried to command nerve and muscle — I tried to move. It was futile.

My body was dead: my brain alone lived. . . .

I saw the man go. Even in that moment of mental

torment I must watch passively, for I could not close my eyes!

Here I lay at the point from which my journeys to China, to Spain, to an enchanted rose garden had begun, and so lying, unable to move a muscle, again I heard a key inserted in the door. . . . The door opened and Nayland Smith dashed into the room. He looked down at me.

"Good God!" he exclaimed, and bent over me.

My eyes remained fixed: they continued to stare towards the lobby.

"Kerrigan! Kerrigan! Speak, old man! What's happened?"

Speak! I could not stir. . . .

He placed his ear to my chest, tested my pulse, stood up and seemed to hesitate for a moment. I heard and partly saw him going from room to room, searching. Then he came back and again fully into view. He stared down at me critically. He had switched up all the lights as he had entered. He walked across to the lobby, and I knew that he was about to take up the telephone!

His intentions were obvious. He was going to call a doctor.

A scream of the spirit implored me to awake, to warn him not to touch that telephone. This was the supreme moment of torture. . . .

I heard the faint tinkling of the bell as Nayland Smith raised the receiver.

2

I became obsessed with the horrible idea that Dr. Fu

Manchu had in some way induced a state of catalepsy! I should be buried alive! But not even the terror caused by this ghastly possibility would make me forget that small, sinister, figure engaged in doing something to the telephone.

That it was something which meant death, every instinct told me.

Yet I lay there, myself already in a state of living death!

Smith stood, the receiver in his hand, and I could see and hear him dialling a number.

But it was not to be. . . .

A crashing explosion shook the entire building! It shattered several panes of glass in one window, and it accomplished that which my own brain had failed to accomplish. It provided a shock against which the will of Dr. Fu Manchu was powerless.

I experienced a sensation exactly as that of some tiny but tough thread which had held the cells of my brain immured in inertia being snapped. It was a terrifying sensation — but its terrors were forgotten in the instant when I realised that I was my own master again!

"Smith!" I cried, and my voice had a queer, hysterical ring — "Smith! *Don't touch that telephone!*"

Perhaps the warning was unnecessary. He had replaced the receiver on the hook and was staring blankly across the apartment in the direction of the shattered window.

"Kerrigan!"

He sprang forward as I scrambled to my feet.

"I can't explain yet," I muttered (the back of my head began to ache madly) "except that you must not touch that telephone."

He grabbed me by the shoulders, stared into my eyes.

"Thank God you're all right, Kerrigan! I can't tell you what I feared—but will tell you later. Somewhere down the river there has been a catastrophe."

"It has saved us from a catastrophe far greater."

Smith turned, threw a window open (I saw now that he had been deeply moved) and craned out. Away downstream black smoke was rising over a sullen red glow.

Police whistles shrieked and I heard the distant clangour of a fire engine . . . Later we learned—and the tragedy was front-page news in the morning—of that disastrous explosion on a munition barge in which twelve lives were lost. At the moment, I remember, we were less concerned with the cause of the explosion than with its effect.

Smith turned from the window and stared at me fixedly.

"How did you get in, Kerrigan? Where is Fey?"

"Fey let me in, then he was called up by Inspector Gallaho from Scotland Yard to meet you there."

"I have not been there—and I have reason to know that Gallaho is not in London. However, go on."

"Fey evidently had no doubt that Gallaho was the speaker. He gave me a drink, told me that you would return directly he, Fey, reached Scotland Yard, and went out."

"What happened then?"

"Then the incredible happened."

"You are sure that you feel perfectly restored?"

"Certain."

Smith pushed me down into an armchair and crossed to the buffet.

"Go on," he said quietly.

"The television screen lighted up. Doctor Fu Manchu appeared."

"What!"

He turned, his hand on a syphon and his expression very grim.

"Yes! You wondered for what purpose he had caused the thing to be installed here, Smith. I can give you an example of *one* use he made of it! Perhaps I am particularly susceptible to the influence of this man. I think you believe I am, for you observed on a former occasion that I was behaving strangely as I watched those awful eyes. Well this time I succumbed altogether. I had a series of extraordinary visions, almost certainly emanations from the brain of Doctor Fu Manchu. And then I became fully conscious but quite incapable of movement!"

"That was your condition when I returned," Smith snapped.

He crossed to me with a tumbler in his hand.

"I had been in that condition for some time before your return. A man admitted himself to the lobby with a key."

"Describe him."

"A small man with straight black hair, who wore what seemed to be powerful spectacles. He carried a bag which he handled with great care. He proceeded to make some adjustment to the mouthpiece of the telephone, and then with a glance in my direction—I was lying on the floor as you found me—he went out again as quietly as he had come."

"Clearly," said Smith, staring into the lobby, "your unexpected appearance presented a problem. They did not know you were coming. It had been arranged for Fey to be lured away by this unknown mimic who can evidently imitate Gallaho's voice; but you, the unexpected intruder, had to be dealt with in a different manner. I am wondering about two things now, Kerrigan. Do you feel fit to investigate?"

"Perfectly."

"First: how long you would have remained in that state in which I found you, failing the unforeseen explosion which shocked you into consciousness; and second: what the small man with the black hair did to the telephone."

"For heaven's sake be careful!"

He crossed to the lobby and very gently raised the instrument. I stood beside him. Apart from a splitting headache I felt perfectly normal. He tipped up the mouthpiece and stared curiously into it.

"You are sure it was the mouthpiece that he adjusted?"

"Quite sure."

And now he turned it round to the light which was streaming through the doorway of the sitting room.

We both saw something.

A bead, quite colorless and no larger than a small pea, adhered to the instrument just below the point where a speaker's lips would come. . . .

"Good God!" Nayland Smith whispered. "Kerrigan! You understand!"

I nodded. I could not find my voice — for the appalling truth had come to me.

"Anyone speaking loudly would burst this bubble

and inhale its contents! God knows what it contains—but we know at last how General Quinto and Osaki died!"

"The Green Death!"

"Undoubtedly. It was a subtle brain, Kerrigan, which foresaw that finding you unconscious, I should immediately call a doctor, that my voice would be agitated. The usual routine, as you must see now, was for someone to call the victim and complain that his voice was not audible, thus causing him to speak close to the receiver and to speak loudly."

Very gently he replaced the instrument.

At this moment the door was partly opened and Fey came in. He glanced from face to face.

"Glad, sir! Frightened! Something funny going on!"

"Very funny, Fey. I suppose when you got to the Yard you found that the summons did not come from there?"

"Yes sir."

The phone bell rang. Fey stepped forward.

"Stop! On no account are you to touch the telephone, Fey, until further orders."

"Very good sir."

Chapter 23

TREMORS UNDER EUROPE

"Doctor Fu Manchu evidently is losing his sense of humour," said Nayland Smith with a smile.

It was noon of the following day, and he stood in my room. He was seated at the desk and was reading my notes. Now he laid them down and began to fill his pipe.

"What do you mean, Smith?"

"I mean that two things—your unexpected appearance, and that explosion on the powder barge—together saved my life. By the way, here is an addition to your notes."

"What is it?"

"The home office analyst's report. You know the difficulty we had to remove the mouthpiece of the telephone without breaking the bubble. However, it was done, and you will see what Doctor O'Donnell says."

I took up the report from the home office consultant. It was not his official report but one he had sent privately to Nayland Smith.

"The construction of the small globe or bubble," I read, "is peculiarly delicate. Examination of the fragments suggests that it is composed of some kind of glass and is probably blown by an instrument which at the same time fills the interior with gas.

The effect of breaking the bubble, however, is to leave no trace whatever, apart from a fragment of powder which normally would be indiscernible. It was attached to the mouthpiece by a minute speck of gum, and I should imagine the operation required great dexterity. As to its contents:

"My full report may be consulted, but briefly I may say that the composition of the gas which this bubble contained is unknown to me. It belongs to none of the groups with which I am familiar. It is the most concentrated poison in gaseous form which I have ever encountered. In addition to the other experiments (see report) I smelled this gas — but for a moment. The result was extraordinary. It induced a violent increase of blood pressure, followed by a drumming in my ears which created such an illusion of being external that for a time I was persuaded someone was beating a drum in the neighbourhood. . . ."

As I laid the letter on the table:

"Have you considered," Nayland Smith asked, "what revolutionary contributions Doctor Fu Manchu could make to science, particularly to medicine, if he worked for heaven and not for hell?"

"Yes, it's a damnable thought."

"The greatest genius living — perhaps as great as has ever been born — toiling for the destruction of humanity!"

"Yet, at the moment, he seems to be working for its preservation."

"But only *seems*, Kerrigan. Its preservation for his own purposes — yes! I strongly suspect, however, that his recent attempt upon me was dictated by an

139

uncanny knowledge of my movements."

"What do you mean?"

"I am being shadowed day and night. There have been other episodes which I have not even bothered to mention."

"You alarm me!"

"Fortunately for myself, the doctor has his hands full in other directions. If he once concentrated upon me I believe I should give up hope. You see, he knows that I am watching his next move, and with devilish cunning, so far, he has headed me off."

"His next move . . ." I stared questioningly.

"Yes. In his war against dictators. At the moment it is concentrated upon one of them — and the greatest."

"You don't mean — "

"I mean Rudolf Adlon! In view of the way in which he is guarded and of the many attempts by enemies to reach him which have failed, it seems perhaps absurd that I should be anxious because one more man has entered his lists."

"But that man is Doctor Fu Manchu!"

"Not a doubt about it, Kerrigan. Yet, officially, my hands are tied."

"Why?"

"Adlon has refused to see me, and I cannot very well force myself upon him."

"Have you definite evidence that Adlon has been threatened?"

Nayland Smith lighted his pipe and nodded shortly.

"I am in the difficult position of having to keep an eye on a number of notable people — many of them, quite frankly, not friends of Great Britain. With a view to doing my best to protect them, the legitimate functions of the secret service up to a certain extent have been switched into this channel, and I had information three days ago that Adlon had received the first notice from the Si-Fan!"

"Good heavens! What did you do?"

"I immediately advised him that whatever he might think to the contrary, he was in imminent peril of his life. I suggested a conference."

"And he refused to see you?"

"Exactly. Whatever is pending—and rest assured it will affect the fate of the world—it is clearly a matter of some urgency, for I am informed that a *second notice* has reached Adlon."

"What do you make of it? What is he planning?"

Nayland Smith stood up, irritably snapping his fingers.

"I don't know, nor can I find out. Furthermore, for any evidence to the contrary, there might be no such person as Doctor Fu Manchu in the world. Do you think it conceivable that such a personality is moving about among us—as undoubtedly he is—and yet not one clue fall into the hands of a veritable army of searchers?"

I watched him for some time as he paced nervously up and down the carpet, then:

"Having met Doctor Fu Manchu," I replied slowly, "I am prepared to believe anything about him. What is bothering me at the moment, Smith, is this: On you own admission he knows that you are trying to protect Adlon."

Nayland Smith sighed wearily.

"He knows every move I make, Kerrigan. Almost, I believe, those which I am likely to make but upon which I have not yet decided."

"In other words your own danger is as great, if not greater, than that of the chancellor."

He smiled wryly.

"Since one evening in Burma, many years ago — an evening of which I bear cherished memories, for it was then that I first set eyes on Doctor Fu Manchu — I have gone in hourly peril of assassination. Yet, here I am — thanks to the doctor's sense of humour! You see" — he began to walk up and down again — "I doubt if ever before have I had the entire power of the Si-Fan directed against me. And so this time, I am wondering . . ."

Chapter 24

A CAR IN HYDE PARK

An unavoidable business appointment called me away that afternoon. My personal inclination was never to let Nayland Smith out of my sight although heaven knows what I thought I could do to protect him. But as he never went about alone and rarely failed to notify me of any move in the game in order that I might be present, we parted with an understanding to meet at dinner.

My business took me to Westminster. Fully an hour had passed, I suppose, when I began to drive back, and I found myself in the thick of the afternoon traffic. As I made to cross towards Hyde Park I was held up. Streams of vehicles coming from four different directions were heading for the gate. I resigned myself and lighted a cigarette.

Idly I inspected a quantity of luggage strapped on the rack of a big saloon car. It was proceeding very slowly out of the Park in that pent-up crawling line of traffic and had just passed my off-side window. There were new labels over many old ones, but from my position at the wheel I could read none of them, except that clearly enough this was the baggage of a world traveller, for I recognised the characteristic hotel designs of Mount Lavinia in Colombo, Shepheard's in Cairo and others East and West which I knew.

The constable on the gate had apparently become rooted just in front of me with outstretched arm. Curious for a glimpse of these travellers who were presumably bound for Victoria Station, I leaned back and stared out at the occupants of the car. A moment I glanced—and then turned swiftly away.

A chauffeur whose face I could not see was driving. There were two passengers. One was a darkly beautiful woman. She was smoking a cigarette, and I could not fail to note her long ivory hand, her slender, highly burnished fingernails. In fact, except for their smooth beauty, those hands reminded me of the hands of Dr. Fu Manchu. But it was that one glimpse of her companion which had urged me to turn aside, praying that I had not been recognised. . . .

It was Ardatha!

Useless to deny that my heart had leapt at sight of her. She wore a smart little hat crushed down on her coppery curls, and some kind of fur-collared coat. I had seen no more, had noticed no more. I had eyes for nothing but that bewitching face. And now, as I stared at the broad, immovable back of the constable, I was thinking rapidly and hoping that he would remain stationary long enough for me to rearrange my plans.

Somehow, I must follow that car!

Once at Victoria it should not be difficult for a man with newspaper training to learn the destination of the travellers. If I failed to do so I could never face Nayland Smith again with a clear conscience. But here was a problem. I must enter the

144

Park now for I was jammed in the traffic stream, and the car which contained Ardatha was leaving or waiting to leave! It meant a detour and I had to plan quickly. I must bear left, leave by the next gate (I prayed I might not be held up there) and make my way to Victoria across Knightsbridge.

This plan was no sooner formed than the constable moved and waved me on.

I proceeded as fast as I dared in the direction of the next gate — and I was lucky. Oncoming traffic was being let out, that from the opposite direction being held.

Last but one, I got through.

I was lucky on the rest of the way, too, and having hastily disposed of my car I went racing into the station. I knew that (a) I must take care not to be seen; that (b) I must find out what trains were about to depart and swiftly make up my mind for which I wanted a platform ticket.

A Continental boat train was due to leave in five minutes.

This struck me as being quite the likeliest bet. The next departure, seven minutes later, was for Brighton, and somehow I felt disposed to wash this out as a possibility. Turning up the collar of my topcoat and pulling my hat well forward, I took a platform ticket and strolled among departing passengers and friends, porters, refreshment wagons and news vendors.

I glanced at the luggage van, but doubted if I should recognise the particular baggage I had seen upon the tail of the car. Then, time being short, I walked along the platform. I could see no sign of the two women, and I began to wonder if I had made a mistake. I started back again, scrutinising all the compartments and staring into the Pullman cars.

But never a glimpse did I obtain of Ardatha or her companion. I was almost in despair and was standing looking right and left when a conversation taking place nearby arrested my attention.

"I've got an old lady going through to Venice. I noticed you had a party of two for Venice, so I wondered if you could arrange to give them adjoining places in the car. They might strike up an acquaintance—see what I mean?"

"You mean the two good-lookers—the red head and the dark one—in D? Yes, they're booked to Venice but I don't know if they're going direct. Where's your passenger?"

"D. Number eleven. Do what you can, Jack."

"Right-o!"

I glanced quickly at the speakers. One was a Cook's man and the other the chief Pullman attendant. It was perhaps a forlorn hope, but I had known equally unlikely things to come off. I turned back and went to look at coach D.

One glance was enough!

Ardatha was seated in a corner reading. Her companion was standing up and placing something upon the rack, for I had a momentary impression of a tall, slender, almost serpentine figure. I turned away quickly and hurried back to the barrier.

The beautiful dark mystery was undoubtedly the woman associated with the death of General Quinto—with the death of Osaki! The woman who had drugged Constable Isles and who had escaped

146

with the model and plans of the vacuum charger! Although perhaps not blood guilty, Ardatha was her accomplice. It was an unhappy, a wildly disturbing thought. Yet, I must confess, so profound was my dread of the Chinese doctor, that I rejoiced to know she lived! His words about retribution had haunted me. . . . But one thing I must do and do quickly:

I must advise Nayland Smith.

Here were two known accomplices of Dr. Fu Manchu. My duty to my friend—to the world—demanded that steps should be taken to apprehend them at Folkestone. There was no room for sentiment; my conscience pointed the straight road to duty.

Chapter 25

"THE BRAIN IS DR. FU MANCHU"

"Dinner's off, Kerrigan! We shall have to get what we can on the way."

"What!"

"Accident has thrown the first clue of many weary days and nights in your way, Kerrigan, and you handled it very cleverly."

"Thank you."

"My latest information, just to hand, explains why Doctor Fu Manchu's attention has become directed upon Rudolf Adlon. Adlon is on his way to Venice for a secret meeting with his brother dictator, Monaghani!"

"But that's impossible, Smith!" I exclaimed. I was still figuratively breathless from my dash to Victoria. "It's in the evening papers that Adlon is reviewing troops tomorrow morning."

Smith was pacing up and down in an old silk dressing gown and smoking his pipe. He paused, turned, and stared at me with raised eyebrows. His glance was challenging.

"I thought it was common knowledge, Kerrigan," he said quietly, "that Adlon has a double."

"A double!"

"Certainly. I assumed you knew; almost everybody else knows. Stalin of Russia has three."

"Three doubles?"

"Three. He knows that he is likely to be assassinated at almost any moment and in this way the odds are three to one in his favour. On such occasions as that which you have mentioned, when the director of his country stands rigidly at the salute for forty minutes or so while troops march by with mechanical accuracy, it is not Rudolf Adlon the First who stands in that painful position. Oh no, Kerrigan: It is Rudolf Adlon the Second! The Second will be there tomorrow, but the First, the original, the real Rudolf Adlon, is already on his way to Venice."

"Then you think that the fact of these two women proceeding to Venice means—"

"It means that Doctor Fu Manchu is in Venice, or shortly will be! Throughout his career he has used the weapon of feminine beauty, and many times that weapon has proved to be double-edged. However, we know what to look for."

"Surely you will take steps to have them arrested at Folkestone?"

"Not at all."

"Why?"

He smiled, paused.

"Do you recall Fu Manchu's words on striking at the heart, the brain? Very well. The heart is the Council of Seven—the brain is Doctor Fu Manchu. It is at the brain I mean to strike, therefore we are leaving for Venice immediately."

He had pressed the bell and now the door opened and Fey came in.

"Advise Wing Commander Roxburgh that I shall want the plane to leave for Venice in an hour. He is to notify Paris and Rome and to arrange for a night landing."

"Very good, sir."

"Stand by with the car."

Fey went out.

"You are sure, Kerrigan, you are sure"—Nayland Smith spoke excitedly—"that you were not recognised?"

"Sure as it is possible to be. Ardatha was reading. I am practically certain that she could not have seen me. The other woman doesn't know me."

Nayland Smith laughed aloud and then stared in an amused way.

"You have much to learn yet," he said, "about Doctor Fu Manchu."

Chapter 26

VENICE

Of those peculiar powers possessed by Nayland Smith, I mean the facilities with which he was accredited, I had a glimpse on this journey. And if confirmation had been needed of the gravity of the menace represented by Dr. Fu Manchu and the Council of Seven, I should have recognised from the way in which his lightest wishes were respected that this was a very grave menace indeed.

We had travelled by a Royal Air Force plane which had performed the journey in little more than half the time of the commercial service!

As we entered the sitting room allotted to us in the Venice hotel, we found Colonel Correnti, chief of police, waiting.

Smith, dismissing an obsequious manager with a smile and wave of the hand, turned to the police officer.

He presented me.

"You may speak with complete confidence in Mr. Kerrigan's presence. Has Rudolf Adlon arrived?"

"Yes."

Smith dropped into an armchair. He had not yet removed hat or Burberry, and groping in a pocket of the latter he produced that dilapidated pouch in which normally he carried about half a pound of tobacco. He began to load his pipe.

"This is a great responsibility for you?"

"A dreadful responsibility!" The colonel nodded. "The greater because Signor Monaghani is expected on Tuesday morning.

"Also incognito?"

"Alas, yes! It is these visits of which so few are aware which make my life a misery. Our task is far heavier than that of Geneva. Venice is the favourite rendezvous of some of the greatest figures in European politics. Always they come incognito, but not always for political reason! Why should Venice be selected? Why should this dreadful onus be placed upon *me*?"

His Latin indignation was profound.

"Where is the chancellor staying?"

"At the Palazzo da Rosa, as guest of the baron. He has stayed there before. They are old friends."

"Are there any other of Herr Adlon's friends in Venice at present?"

"But yes! James Brownlow Wilton is here. He leases the Palazzo Brioni on the Grand Canal, at no great distance from this hotel. His yacht Silver Heels is in the lagoon."

"Will he be entertaining Herr Adlon?"

"I believe there is to be a small private luncheon party, either at the Palazzo or on board the yacht."

Nayland Smith crushed tobacco into the big cracked bowl of his pipe. Only once he glanced at me. But I knew what he had in mind and thrilled with anticipation, then:

"You have arranged to have agents on board, Colonel?"

"Certainly. This was my duty."

"I appreciate that. No doubt you can arrange for Mr. Kerrigan and myself to be present?"

For a moment Colonel Correnti was taken aback. He looked from face to face in astonishment.

"Of course." He endeavoured to speak easily. "It could be arranged."

Nayland Smith stood up and smiled.

"Let it be arranged," he said. "I have an appointment to meet Sir George Herbert who is accompanying me to see Herr Adlon. I shall be free in an hour. If you will be good enough to return then we can make all necessary plans. . . ."

During the next hour I was left to my own devices. That Dr. Fu Manchu, if not there in person certainly had agents in Venice, had made me so intensely nervous that I only let Nayland Smith leave the hotel when I realised that a bodyguard in the form of two plainclothes police accompanied him.

I tried to distract myself by strolling about these unique streets.

This was comparatively new territory. I had been there but once before and only for a few hours. Night had long fallen, touching Venice with its magic. Lights glittered on the Grand Canal, shone from windows in those age-old palaces, and a quarter moon completed the picture.

Somewhere, I thought, as I peered into the faces of passers-by, Ardatha might be near to me. Smith was of opinion that they would have flown from Paris, avoiding Croydon as at Croydon they were likely to be recognised. Assuming a fast plane to have been awaiting them, they were probably in Venice now.

Automatically, it seemed, and in common with

everyone else, I presently drifted towards St. Mark's. Despite the late hour it seemed that all Venice took the air. Had my mind been not a boiling cauldron but normally at peace I must have enjoyed the restfulness of my surroundings.

But feverishly I was thinking, "Ardatha is here! At any moment she may become involved in a world tragedy from which I shall be helpless to extricate her."

One who, whatever his faults, however right or wrong his policy, was yet the idol of a great country, stood in peril of sudden death. Perhaps only one man could save him — Nayland Smith! And upon that man's head, also, a price had been set by the dreadful Chinese doctor.

I found it impossible to relax. I recalled Smith's words: "Do as you please, Kerrigan, but for heaven's sake don't show yourself."

It was impossible, this walking in shadow, distrusting the moonlight, avoiding all places where people congregated, and slinking about like a criminal who feared arrest. I went back to the hotel.

The lounge appeared to be deserted, but I glanced sharply about me before crossing it, making my way to the suite reserved for Smith and myself.

I found the sitting room in darkness, but an odour of tobacco smoke brought me up sharply as I was about to cross the threshold.

"Hello!" I called, "is anyone there?"

"*I* am here," came Smith's voice out of the darkness.

He stood up and switched on the light, and I saw that his pipe was between his teeth. Even before he spoke his grim expression told me all there was to know.

"Have you seen him?"

He nodded.

"What was his attitude?"

"His attitude, you will be able to judge for yourself when you see him on Silver Heels tomorrow. He has gone so far, has risen so high, that I fear he believes himself to be immortal!"

"Megalomania?"

"Hardly that perhaps, but he sets himself above counsel. He admitted reluctantly that he had received the Si-Fan notices—two at least. He merely shrugged his shoulders when I suggested that a third had come to hand."

He was walking up and down the room now tugging at the lobe of his left ear.

"If Adlon is to be saved, he must be saved against himself. If I had the power, Kerrigan, I would kidnap him and transport him from Venice tonight!"

2

"I count upon you, Colonel," said Nayland Smith as the chief of police rose to go. "My friend and I will be present on Silver Heels tomorrow. I *must* have an opportunity of inspecting Mr. Brownlow Wilton's guests and of seeing in which of them Rudolf Adlon is interested."

When we were alone:

"Have the police obtained any clue?" I asked.

Smith shook his head irritably.

"Very rarely indeed does the doctor leave clues. And this is a major move in his game. I don't know if

Monaghani is marked down, but Adlon admits that *he* is. We have yet to see if Monaghani arrives. But for tonight, I suppose my work is done. Have you any plans?"

"None."

"I wish I could find Ardatha for you," he said softly, and went out. "Good night."

As the door closed and I heard him walking along to his room I dropped down on to a settee and lighted a cigarette. How I wished that *I* could find her! I had never supposed love to come in this fashion. Quite easily I could count the minutes—had often done so—that I had been in Ardatha's company. Collectively they amounted to less than an hour. Yet of all the women I had known, she was the one to whom my thoughts persistently turned.

I tried to tell myself that this was an obsession born of the mystery in which I had met her—an infatuation which would pass—but always the effort failed. No, she haunted me. I knew every expression of her piquant face, every intonation of her voice; I heard her talking to me a thousand times during the day—I dreamed of her, I suspected, throughout the night.

That Nayland Smith was tired I could not doubt; I was tired myself. Yet, although it was long past midnight, any idea of sleep I knew to be out of the question. Outside, divided from the window only by a narrow quay, the Grand Canal lapped its ancient walls. Occasionally, anomalous motorboats passed; at other times I heard the drip of an oar as some ghostly gondola crept upon its way. Once the creaking of a boat, as a belated guest returned to the hotel, reminded me—terrifyingly—of the cellars under the

Monks' Arms where I had so nearly come to an end.

I rang for a waiter and ordered a drink to be brought to my room; then, extinguishing the lights of the sitting room, I went along the corridor intending to turn in.

However, when my drink arrived and I had lighted another cigarette, I was overcome with recklessness. Crossing to the window I threw open the shutters and looked down upon the oily glittering waters of the canal.

Venice! The picture city, painted in blood and passion. In some way it seemed fitting that Fu Manchu should descend upon Venice; fitting, too, that Ardatha should be there. The moon had disappeared; mysterious lights danced far away upon the water, beckoning me back to the days of the doges.

From my window I looked down upon a shadowy courtyard, a corner of the platform upon which the hotel (itself an old palace) was built. It could be approached from the steps which led up to the main door, but so far as I could make out in the darkness it formed a sort of cul-de-sac. My window ledge was no more than four feet from the stone paving.

And now, in the shadows, I detected someone moving . . .

I drew back. My hand flew to a pocket in which, always, since I had met Dr. Fu Manchu, an automatic rested. Then a voice spoke—a soft voice:

"Please help me up. I must talk to you."

It was Ardatha!

Chapter 27

ARDATHA

She sat in a deep, cushioned divan, a Renaissance reproduction, watching me with a half smile.

"You look frightened," she said. "Do I frighten you?"

"No, Ardatha, it isn't that you frighten me, although I admit your appearance was somewhat of a shock."

She wore a simple frock and a coat having a fur-trimmed collar, which I recognised as that which I had seen in the car near Hyde Park corner. She had a scarf tied over her hair, and I thought that her eyes were mocking me.

"I am mad to have done this," she went on, "and now I am wondering—"

I tried to conquer a thumping heart, to speak normally.

"You are wondering if I am worth it," I suggested, and forced myself to move in her direction.

Frankly, I was terrified as I never could have believed myself to be terrified of a woman. My own wild longing had awakened some sort of response in Ardatha! I had called to her and she had come! But as the lover of a girl so complex and mysterious I had little faith in Bart Kerrigan.

Tonight it was my part to claim her—or to lose her forever. Her eyes as well as her words told me that the choice was mine.

I offered her a cigarette and lighted it, then sat down beside her. My impulse was to grab her—hold her—never let her go again. But I took a firm grip upon these primitive urges, and then:

"I saw you at Victoria," she said.

"What! How could you have seen me?"

"I have eyes and I can see with them."

She lay back among the cushions, and turning, smiled up at me.

"I had no idea you had seen me."

"That is why I am here tonight." Suddenly, seriously: "You must go back! I tell you, you must go back. I came here tonight to tell you this."

"Is that all you came for, Ardatha?"

"Yes. Do not suppose it means what you are thinking. I like you very much, but do not make the mistake of believing that I love easily."

She spoke with a quiet imperiousness of manner which checked me. My emotions pulled me in various directions. In the first place, this beautiful girl of the amethyst eyes, who, whatever she did, whatever she said, allured, maddened me, was a criminal. In the second place, unless the glance of those eyes be wildly misleading, she wanted me to make love to her. But in the third place, although she said her nocturnal visit had been prompted by friendship, what was her real motive? I clasped my knees tightly and stared aside at her.

"I am glad you are a man who thinks," she said softly, "for between us there is much to think about."

"There is only one thing I am thinking about—that I want you. You are never out of my mind. Day and night I am unhappy because I know you are involved in a conspiracy of horror and murder in which you, the real *you*, have no part. If I thought lightly of you and merely desired you, then as you say I should not have thought. I should have my arms around you now, kissing you, as I want to kiss you. But you see, Ardatha, you mean a lot more than that. Although I know so little about you, yet—"

"*Ssh!*"

Swiftly she grasped my arm—and I seized her hand and held it. But the warning had been urgent, and I listened.

We both sat silent for a while. My gaze was set upon a strange ring which she wore. The clasp of her fingers gave me a thrill which passionate kisses of another woman could never have aroused.

Somewhere out there in the shadows I had detected the sound of a dull thud—of soft footsteps.

Releasing Ardatha's hand, I would have sprung up, but:

"Don't look out!" she whispered. "No! No! Don't look out!"

I hesitated. She held me tightly.

"Why?"

"Because it is just possible—I may have been followed. Please, don't look out!"

I heard the sound of a distant voice out over the canal; splashing of water . . . nothing more. I turned to Ardatha. There was no need for words.

She slipped almost imperceptibly into my arms, and raised her lips. . . .

Chapter 28

NAYLAND SMITH'S ROOM

For a long time after Ardatha had gone—I don't know how long a time—I knelt there by my open window staring out over the canal. She had trusted herself to me. How could I detain her—how could I regard her as a criminal? Indeed I wondered if ever I should be able so to regard her again.

The fear now burning in my brain was fear solely for her safety.

Always I had found it painful to imagine her in association with the remorseless murder group controlled by Dr. Fu Manchu, but now that idea was agony. I dared not imagine what would happen if her visit to me should be discovered, if the double part which she played came to the knowledge of the Chinese doctor . . . and I could not forget that queer sound down by the waterside, those soft footsteps.

Ardatha suspected that she might have been followed. Perhaps her suspicions were well founded!

I stared out intently into misty darkness. I listened but could hear nothing save the lapping of water. From where had she come—to where had she gone? I knew little more about her than I had ever known, except that she was anxious to save me from some dreadful fate which obviously she believed to be pending.

One thing I had learned: Ardatha was of mixed

Oriental and European blood. On her father's side she descended from generations of Eastern rulers; petty chieftains from a Western standpoint, but potentates in their own land. Her murderous hatred of dictatorships was understandable. Practically the whole of her family had been wiped out by General Quinto's airmen . . .

Silence!—and in the silence another idea was born. The watcher in the night perhaps had a double purpose. Satisfied that I was fully preoccupied, he might have given some signal which meant that Nayland Smith was alone!

Most ghastly idea of all—this may have been the real purpose of Ardatha's visit!

I tried in retrospect to analyse every expression in the amethyst eyes; and I found it hard, in fact impossible, to believe treachery to be hidden there. I thought of her parting kiss. My heart even now beat faster when I recalled it. Surely it could not have been a Judas kiss?

No sound could I detect anywhere about me. The Grand Canal was deserted, the moon partly veiled; but my thoughts had made me restlessly uneasy. I must make sure that Nayland Smith was safe.

Quietly opening my door I walked along and switched up the light in the sitting room.

It presented exactly the same appearance as when I had left it. I moved on to Smith's closed door. I listened intently but could hear nothing. However, he was a deep, silent sleeper, and I was not satisfied. Very gently I moved the handle. The door was unlocked. Inch by inch I opened it, until at last, having made hardly any sound, I could creep in.

The room was in darkness, save for a dim reflection through the slats of the shutters. Yet I was afraid to switch on the light, for I had no wish to disturb him. I crept slowly forward in the direction of the bed, and my eyes growing accustomed to the semidarkness, by the time that I reached it a startling fact had become evident:

The bed was empty! It had never been slept in!

I switched on the bedside lamp and stared about me distractedly.

He had not undressed!

I crossed to the shuttered window. The shutters were not fastened but just lightly closed. I pushed them open and stared out. I could see across to the landing stage. The ledge was not more than four feet above the pavement, as was the case in my own room. Why, I asked myself desperately, had he of all men, he, marked down as Enemy Number One by Dr. Fu Manchu, exposed himself to such a risk?

And where was he?

I pressed the night porter's bell, crossed to the sitting room and threw the door open. In less than a minute, I suppose, the porter appeared.

"Can you tell me," I asked, "if Sir Denis Nayland Smith has gone out tonight?"

"No sir, he has not gone out."

The man looked surprised—in fact, startled.

"But I suppose he could have gone out without being seen?"

"No sir. After midnight, except on special occasions, the door is locked. I open it for anyone returning late."

"And do you remain in the lobby?"

"Yes sir."

"Did anyone return late tonight?"

"No sir. There are few people in the hotel at the moment and all were in before eleven o'clock."

"When you came on duty?"

"When I came on duty, yes sir."

"You mean that it is quite impossible for Sir Denis to have gone out without your seeing him?"

"Quite impossible, sir."

Although his room exhibited no evidence whatever of a struggle, one explanation, a ghastly one, alone presented itself to my mind.

He had been overcome, carried out by way of the window and so to the landing stage! Those movements in the night were explained. My lovely companion's coolness under circumstances calculated to terrify a normal girl assumed a different aspect. . . .

My friend, the best friend I should ever have, had been fighting for his life while I clung to the lips of Ardatha!

Chapter 29

VENICE CLAIMS A VICTIM

A police officer was an almost unendurably long time in reaching the hotel. When at last he arrived, a captain of Carabinieri, he brought two detectives with him. His English was defective but fortunately for me one of the men spoke it well.

When I had made the facts clear and a search of the room had taken place:

"I fear, sir," said the English-speaking detective, "that your suspicions are confirmed. I am satisfied that your friend did not leave by the front door of the hotel. As he evidently did not go to bed, however, there is a possibility, is there not, that he left of his own free will?"

"Yes." I grasped gladly at this straw. "There is! Why had I not thought of that?"

There was a brief conference in Italian between the three, and then:

"It has been suggested," the detective went on, "that if Sir Denis Nayland Smith, for whom a bodyguard had been arranged by order of Colonel Correnti, had decided to go out for any reason, he would probably have awakened you."

"I was not asleep," I said shortly.

Where did my duty lie? Should I confess that Ardatha had been with me?

"It makes it all the more strange. You were perhaps reading or writing?"

"No. I was thinking and staring out of the window."

"Did you hear any suspicious sounds?"

"Yes. What I took to be footsteps and a faint scuffling. But I heard no more."

"It is all the more curious," the man went on, "because we have two officers on duty, one in a gondola moored near the steps, and the other at the back of the hotel. Before coming here I personally interviewed both these officers and neither had seen anything suspicious."

The mystery grew deeper.

"My own room was lighted," I said. "Are my windows visible from the point of view of the man in the gondola?"

"We will go and see."

We moved along to my room. My feelings as I looked at the divan upon which Ardatha had lain in my arms I find myself unable to describe. . . . One of the detectives glanced out of the window and reported that owing to the wall of that little courtyard to which I have referred, this window would be outside the viewpoint of the man in the gondola.

"But the window of Sir Denis' room—this he could see."

Another idea came.

"The sitting room!"

"It is possible. Let us look."

We looked—and solely because, I suppose, no one had attached any importance to the sitting room, it now immediately became evident that one shutter was open.

It had not been open when I had parted from Smith that night!

"You see!" exclaimed the detective, "here is the story: He was overcome, perhaps drugged, in his room, carried in here and lowered out through that window!"

"But" — I was thinking now of Ardatha — "how could the kidnappers have got him away without attracting the notice of one of your men?"

Another consultation took place. All three were becoming wildly excited.

"I must explain" — a half-dressed and bewildered manager had joined us — "that passing under the window of your own room, Mr. Kerrigan, it is possible — there is a gate there — to reach the bridge over the Rio Banieli — the small canal."

"But you say" — I turned to the detective — "that you had a man on duty at the rear of the hotel?"

"True, but here is dense shadow at this hour of the night. It would be possible — just possible — for one to reach and cross that bridge unnoticed."

In my mind I was reconstructing the tragedy of the night. I saw Nayland Smith, drugged, helpless, being carried (probably on the shoulder of one of Dr. Fu Manchu's Thugs) right below my window as I lay there intoxicated by the beauty of Ardatha. I felt myself choked with rage and mortification.

"But it is simply incredible," I cried, "that such a crime can be committed here in Venice! We must find Sir Denis! We must find him!"

"It is understood, sir, that we must find him. This is very bad for the Venice police, because you are under our special protection. The chief has been notified and will shortly be here. It is a tragedy—yes: I regret it deeply."

Overcome by a sense of the futility of it all, the hopelessness of outwitting that criminal genius who played with human lives as a chess player with pieces, I turned and walked back to the sitting room. I stared dumbly at the open window through which my poor friend had disappeared, probably forever.

The police left the suite, in deference, I think, to my evident sorrow, and I found myself alone.

The girl to whom I had lost my heart, my reason, was a modern Delilah. Her part had been to lull my suspicions, to detain me there—if need be with kisses—while the dreadful master of the Si-Fan removed an enemy from his path.

My thoughts tortured me—I clenched my teeth; I felt my brain reeling. In every way that a man could fail, I had failed. I had succumbed to the wiles of a professional vampire and had given over my friend to death.

There were perhaps issues greater than my personal sorrow. The life of Rudolf Adlon hung upon a hair. Nayland Smith was gone!

Venice, the city of the doges, had claimed one more victim.

2

Dawn was creeping gloriously over the city when the first, the only clue, came to hand.

A Carabinieri patrol returning at four o'clock was subjected, in common with all others who had been on duty that night, to a close examination. He remembered (a fact which normally he would not have reported) that a girl, smartly dressed and wearing a scarf over her hair, had hurried past him at a point not far from the hotel. He had paid little attention to her, except that he remembered she was pretty, but his description of her dress strongly suggested Ardatha!

Twenty yards behind and, as he recalled, seeming deliberately to keep in the shadow, he had noticed a man: an Englishman, he was confident, tall, wearing a tweed suit and a soft-brimmed hat.

The time, as nearly as I could judge, would have corresponded to that at which I had parted from Ardatha. . . .

The detective's theory had been the right one. Something had drawn Smith's attention to the presence of the girl. He had not been kidnapped—he had watched and followed her. To where? What had become of him?

That sense of guilt which weighed heavily upon me became heavier than ever. I was indeed directly responsible for whatever had befallen my friend.

I was already at police headquarters when this report came in. The man was sent for and through an interpreter I questioned him. Since I knew the two people concerned more intimately than anyone present his answers to my questions removed any possibility of doubt.

The girl described was Ardatha. Nayland Smith had been following her!

Even at this stage, frantic as I was with anxiety about Smith, almost automatically I compromised with my conscience when Colonel Correnti asked me:

"Do you think this girl is someone known to Sir Denis?"

"Possibly," I replied. "He may have thought he recognised an accomplice of Doctor Fu Manchu."

When I left police headquarters to walk back to the hotel, Venice was bathed in its morning glory. But I moved through the streets and across the canals of that fairy city in a state of such utter dejection that any I passed surely pitied me.

Of Smith's plans in regard to the luncheon party on Silver Heels I had very little idea, but I had been fully prepared to go with him. I was anxious to see Rudolf Adlon in person. It seemed to me to be pointless to go alone. What he had hoped to learn I could not imagine. James Brownlow Wilton, the New York newspaper magnate, would seem to have no place in this tangled skein. It was a baffling situation and I was hopelessly worn out.

I tried to snatch a few hours' sleep, but found sleep to be impossible. Sir George Herbert called at ten o'clock, an old young man with foreign office stamped indelibly upon him. His expression was grave.

"This is a great blow, Mr. Kerrigan," he said. "I can see how it has affected you. To me, it is disastrous. These threats to Rudolf Adlon, who is here incognito as you know, are backed by an organisation which does not threaten lightly. General Quinto has been assassinated—why not Rudolf Adlon?"

"I agree. But I know nothing of Smith's plans to protect him."

"Nor do I!" He made a gesture of despair. "It had been arranged for him to go on board Mr. Wilton's yacht during today's luncheon, but what he hoped to accomplish I have no idea."

"Nor I."

I spoke the words groaningly, dropped on to a chair and stared I suppose rather wildly at Sir George.

"The Italian authorities are sparing no effort. Their responsibility is great, for more than the reputation of the chief of police is at stake. If any news should reach me I will advise you immediately, Mr. Kerrigan. I think you would be wise to rest."

Chapter 30

A WOMAN DROPS A ROSE

The human constitution is a wonderfully adjusted instrument. I had no hope, indeed no intention, of sleeping. Venice, awakened, living gaily about me. Yet, after partially undressing, within five minutes of Sir George's departure I was fast asleep.

I was awakened by Colonel Correnti. Those reflected rays through my shutters which I had not closed told me the truth.

It was sunset. I had slept for many hours.

"What news?"

Instantly I was wide awake, a cloak of sorrow already draped about me.

He shook his head.

"None, I fear."

"The luncheon party on the yacht took place, I suppose? Sir Denis feared that some attempt might be made there."

"Rudolf Adlon was present, yes. He is known on these occasions as Major Baden. My men report that nothing of an unusual nature took place. The dictator is safely back at the Palazzo da Rosa where he will be joined tomorrow by Pietro Monaghani. There is no evidence of any plot." He shrugged his shoulders. "What can I do? Officially, I am not supposed to know that the chancellor is here. Of Sir Denis no trace can be found. What can I do?"

His perplexity was no greater than mine. What, indeed, could any of us do?

I forced myself to eat a hasty meal. The solicitude of the management merely irritated me. I found myself constantly looking aside, constantly listening, for I could not believe it possible for a man so well known as Nayland Smith to vanish like a mirage.

Of Ardatha I dared not think at all.

To remain there inert was impossible. I could do nothing useful, for I had no plan, but at least I could move, walk the streets, search the cafés, stare up at the windows. With no better object than this in view, I set out.

Before St. Mark's I pulled up abruptly. The magic of sunset was draping the façade in wonderful purple shadows. I was torn between two courses. If I lost myself in this vain hunt through the streets of Venice, I might be absent when news came. In a state of indecision I stood there before the doors of that ornate, ancient church. What news could come? News that Smith was dead!

From these ideas I must run away, must keep moving. Indeed I found myself incapable of remaining still, and now a reasonable objective occurred to me. Since Rudolf Adlon was staying at the Palazzo da Rosa this certainly would be the focus of Dr. Fu Manchu's attention. Actually, of course, I was seeking some excuse for action, something to distract my mind from the ghastly contemplation of Nayland Smith's fate.

I hurried back to the hotel and learned from the hall porter that no message had been received for me. Thereupon I walked out and chartered a motorboat.

A gondola was too slow for my humour.

"Go along the Grand Canal," I directed, "and show me the Palazzo da Rosa."

We set out, and I endeavoured to compose myself and to submit without undue irritation to the informative remarks of the man who drove the motorboat. He wished to take me to the Rialto Bridge, to the villa where Richard Wagner had died, to the Palace of Gabriel d'Annunzio; but finally, with a great air of mystery, slowing his craft:

"Yonder," he said, "where I am pointing, is the Palazzo da Rosa. It is here, sir, that Signor Monaghani, himself, stays sometimes when he is in Venice. Also it is whispered, but I do not know, that the great Adlon is there."

"Stop awhile."

Dusk had fallen and light streamed from nearly all the windows of the palace. I observed much movement about the water gate, many gondolas crowded against the painted posts, there was a stir and bustle which told of some sort of entertainment taking place.

A closed motorboat, painted black, and apparently empty, passed almost silently between us and the steps.

"The police!"

We moved on. . . .

Two seagoing yachts were at anchor, and out on the lagoon we met a freshening breeze. One of the yachts belonged to an English peer, the other, Silver Heels, was Brownlow Wilton's beautiful white cruiser, built on the lines of an ocean greyhound. All seemed to be quiet on board, and I wondered if the celebrated American was being entertained at the Palazzo da Rosa.

"Where to now, sir?"

"Anywhere you like," I answered wearily.

The man seemed to understand my mood. I believe he thought I was a dejected lover whose mistress had deserted him. Indeed, he was not far wrong.

We turned into a side canal where there were ancient windows, walls and trellises draped in clematis and passion flower, a spot, as I saw at a glance, perpetuated by many painters. In the dusk it had a ghostly beauty. Here the motorboat seemed a desecration, and I wished that I had chartered a gondola. Even as the thought crossed my mind, one of those swan-like crafts, carrying the bearing of some noble family, and propelled by a splendidly uniformed gondolier, swung silently around a corner, heralded only by the curious cry of the man at the oar.

My fellow checked his engine.

"From the Palazzo da Rosa!" he said and gazed back fascinatedly.

Idly, for I was not really interested, I turned and stared back also. There was but one passenger in the gondola.

It was Rudolf Adlon!

"Stop!" I ordered sharply as the man was about to restart his engine. "I want to watch."

For I had seen something else.

On the balcony of a crumbling old mansion, once no doubt the home of a merchant prince but now falling into ruin, a woman was standing. Some trick of reflected light from across the canal made her features clearly visible. She wore a gaily-coloured shawl which left one arm and shoulder bare.

She was leaning on the rail of the balcony, staring

175

down at the passing gondola—and as I watched, eagerly, almost breathlessly, I saw that the gondolier had checked his graceful boat with that easy, sweeping movement which is quite beyond the power of an amateur oarsman. Rudolf Adlon was standing up, his eyes raised. As I watched, the woman dropped a rose to which, I was almost sure, a note was attached!

Adlon caught it deftly, kissed his fingers to the beauty on the balcony and resumed his seat. As the gondola swung on and was lost in deep shadows of a tall, old palace beyond:

"Ah!" sighed the motor launch driver—and he also kissed his fingers to the balcony—"a tryst—how beautiful!"

She who had made the assignation had disappeared. But there was no possibility of mistake. She was the woman I had seen with Ardatha—the woman whom Nayland Smith had described as "a corpse moving among the living—a harbinger of death!"

2

The chief of police hung up the telephone.

"Major Baden is in his private apartments," he said, "engaged on important official business. He has given orders that he is not to be disturbed. And so"—he shrugged his shoulders—"what can I do?"

I confess I was growing weary of those oft-repeated words.

"But I assure you," I cried excitedly, "that he is *not* in his private apartments! At least he was not there a quarter of an hour ago!"

"That is possible, Mr. Kerrigan. I have said that some of the great men who visit Venice incognito have sometimes other affairs than affairs of State. But since, in the first place, I am not supposed to know that Rudolf Adlon is at the Palazzo at all what steps can I take? I have one of my best officers on duty there and this is his report. What more can I do?"

"Nothing!" I groaned.

"In regard to protecting this minister, nothing, I fear. But the other matter—yes! This woman whom you describe is known to be an accomplice of these people who seek the life of Rudolf Adlon?"

"She is."

"Then we shall set out to find her, Mr. Kerrigan! I shall be ready in five minutes."

Complete darkness had come when we reached the canal in which I had passed the dictator, but the light of a quarter moon painted Venice with silver. I travelled now in one of those sinister-looking black boats to which my attention had been drawn earlier.

"There is the balcony," I said, "directly over us."

Colonel Correnti looked up and then stared at me quite blankly.

"I find it very difficult to believe, Mr. Kerrigan," he said. "Do not misunderstand me—I am not doubting your word. I am only doubting if you have selected the right balcony."

"There is no doubt about it," I said irritably.

"Then the matter is certainly very strange."

He glanced at the two plain-clothes police officers who accompanied us. I had met them before, one, Stocco, was he who spoke good English.

"Why?"

"Because this is the back of the old Palazzo Mori. It is the property of the Mori family, but as you see it is in a state of great dilapidation. It has not been occupied, I assure you, for many, many years. I know for a fact that it is unfurnished."

"This does not interest me," I replied, now getting angry. "What I have stated is fact. Great issues are at stake, and I suggest that we obtain a key and search this place."

He turned with a despairing gesture to his subordinates.

"Where are the keys of the Palazzo Mori?"

There was a consultation, in which the man who drove the motor launch took part.

"The Mori family, alas, is ruined," said Correnti, "and its remaining members are spread all over the world. I do not know where. The keys of the palazzo are with the lawyer Borgese, and it would be difficult, I fear, to find him tonight."

"Also a waste of time," I replied, for I knew what Nayland Smith would have done in the circumstances. "From the balustrade of the steps there to that lower iron balcony is an easy matter for an active man. We are all active men, I take it? Even from here one can see that the latchet of the window is broken. Here is our way in. Why do we hesitate?"

The chief of police seemed to have doubts, but recognising, I suppose, what a terrible responsibility rested upon his shoulders, finally, although reluctantly, he consented.

The police boat was drawn up beside the steps, and I, first in my eagerness, clambered on to the roof of the cabin, from there sprang to the decaying stone-

178

work of the balustrade and climbed to the top. Balancing somewhat hazardously and reaching up, I found that I could just grasp the ornamental ironwork which I had pointed out.

"Give me a lift," I directed Stocco, who stood beside me.

He did so. The boat rocked, but he succeeded in lifting me high enough to enable me to release my left hand and to grasp the upper railing. The rest was easy.

Colonel Correnti, as Stocco in turn was hoisted up beside me, cried out some order.

"We are to go," said the detective, "down to the main door, open it if possible and admit the chief."

I put my shoulder to the broken lattice, and it burst open immediately. Out of silvery moonlight I stepped into complete darkness. My companion produced a flashlamp.

I found myself in a room which at some time had been a bedroom. It was quite denuded of furniture, but here and there remained fragments of mouldy tapestry. And on the once-polished floor I detected marks to show where an old-fashioned four-poster bed had rested.

"Let us hope the doors are not locked," said Stocco.

However, this one at least was not.

"Upstairs first!" I said eagerly, as we stepped out on to the landing.

Looking over a heavily carved handrail, in the light of the flashlamp directed downwards I saw the sweep of a marble staircase lost in Gothic gloom. A great shadowy hall lay below, with ghostly pillars amid which our slightest movement echoed eerily. There was a damp, musty smell in the place which I found unpleasantly tomb-like. But we paused here for scarcely a moment. We went hurrying upstairs, our footsteps rattling uncannily upon marble steps. Here for a moment we hesitated on a higher landing, flashing the light of the lamp about.

"This is the room," I said, and indicated a closed door.

Stocco tried the handle; the door opened. Right ahead of me across the room beyond I saw a half-opened lattice. A moment later I was on the balcony from which the mysterious woman ·had dropped the rose to Rudolf Adlon.

"This is where she stood!"

The detective shone a light all about us. The room was choicely panelled in some light wood and possessed what had once been a painted ceiling, now no more than a series of damp blotches where minute fungus grew.

"Shine the light down here," I ordered excitedly.

On the heavy dust of a parquet floor were slight but unmistakable marks of high-heeled shoes!

"God's mercy, you were right!" Stocco exclaimed.

Yes, I was right. This house was a tomb. Rudolf Adlon had made an appointment with a creature of another world, a *zombie,* a human corpse brought to life! And here indeed was a fitting abode for such a creature!

No doubt the place was partly responsible, but as I stood there staring at my companion, and remembered how Nayland Smith had been smuggled out of life by the master magician called Dr. Fu Manchu, I was prepared to believe that a dead woman moved among the living.

Chapter 31

PALAZZO MORI

We admitted the chief of police by the main door. It was heavily bolted but not locked. He was at least as nonplussed as I when the marks of little heels were pointed out to him in the room above.

"This," he said, "is supernatural."

Although disposed to agree with him I was determined to leave no stone unturned in my efforts to solve the mystery. Discounting her sorcerous origin for the moment and therefore her magical powers, how had Dr. Fu Manchu's accomplice got into this place, and how had she got out?

"Merely supernormal perhaps," I suggested. "Everything has an explanation, after all." I was trying desperately to restore my own self-confidence. "You know the history of these old buildings better than I do. Have you any explanation to offer of how a person could enter and leave the Palazzo Mori as undoubtedly someone entered and left it tonight?"

"I have no explanation to offer, Mr. Kerrigan," said Colonel Correnti. His expression was almost pathetic. "None whatever."

The second detective began to speak urgently and rapidly, and as a result:

"This officer tells me," the colonel continued, "that at one time, but very, very long ago, there was an entrance to this old palace from the other side of the canal—I mean the Rio Mori, from which we entered."

"I don't think I follow you."

"A passage—they were not uncommon in old days—under the Rio Mori, which of course is quite shallow. It seems that the boathouse of the family was on the opposite bank in those days, and for the convenience of the gondoliers this passage was made. It has been blocked up for at least a century."

"That hardly seems to help us!"

"No, not at all. I think I know the place—an old stone shed." He spoke rapidly to his subordinate who replied with equal rapidity. "It was used, I am told, as a store by a house decorator for a time but is now empty again. No, my friend, this is useless. We must seek elsewhere for the solution of our mystery."

Of our search of the old palace it is unnecessary that I give any account. It yielded nothing. Apart from those footprints in the upper room there was no evidence whatever to show that anyone had entered the building for many years. Certainly below the grand salon, where patches on the walls from which paintings had been removed, pathetically told of decayed grandeur, there were locked rooms.

To these we were unable to gain access, and it seemed pointless to attempt it. Examination of the locks clearly indicated that they had not been recently used. At this stage of the search I had given up hope.

We returned to police headquarters. There was no news. I turned aside to hide my despair. An officer who had remained in constant touch with the detectives in the Palazzo da Rosa reported that "Major Baden" had joined the guests for half an hour and had then excused himself on the grounds of urgent business, and had retired again to his own apartment.

"You see?" Colonel Correnti shrugged his shoulders. "We can do nothing."

I tried to control my voice when I spoke:

"Do you really understand what is at stake? An excommissioner of Scotland Yard has been kidnapped, probably murdered. He is one of the highest officials of the British Secret Service. The most prominent figure in European politics, and I do not except Pietro Monaghani, is, beyond any shadow of doubt, in deadly peril. Are you sure, Colonel, that every available man is straining himself to the utmost, that every possible place has been searched, every suspect interrogated?"

"I assure you, Mr. Kerrigan, that every available man in Venice is either searching or watching tonight. I can do no more. . . ."

I think during the next hour I must have plumbed the uttermost deeps of despair. I wandered about the gay streets of Venice like a ghost at a banquet, staring at lighted windows, into the faces of the passers-by, until I began to feel that I was attracting public attention. I returned to the hotel, went to my room and sat down on that settee where Ardatha had bewitched me with kisses.

How I cursed every moment of that stolen happiness! No contempt I had ever known for a fellow being could approach that which I had for myself. I conjured up a picture of Nayland Smith; almost in my state of distraction I seemed to hear his voice. He was trying to tell me something, trying to direct me, to awaken in my dull brain some spark of enlightenment.

Had our cases been reversed what would *he* have done?

This idea seemed to give me a new coolness. Yes! what would he have done? I sat there, head buried in my hands, striving to think calmly.

That the dark woman had entered and left that ruined palace was a fact. Whoever or whatever she might be, of her presence there we had unassailable evidence. Our search had revealed no explanation of the mystery. But there were doors we had failed to open—

This would not have been Nayland Smith's way!

He would never have been satisfied to leave the Palazzo Mori until those lower rooms had been examined. Nor would he have been content with the assertion of the chief of police that the ancient passage under the canal was blocked. . . .

I sprang up.

This was the line of inquiry which Smith would have followed! I was sure of it. This should be my objective. A dishevelled figure (I had not been undressed for thirty-six hours), once more I set out.

2

The ancient house of the gondoliers was easy to locate. It was solidly built of stone with three windows on the land side and a heavy, padlocked door at the end. The narrow lane by which one approached it was dark and deserted. I had brought an electric torch, and I shot a beam through one of the broken windows. It showed a quantity of litter: fragments of wall paper, mortar boards and numerous empty paint cans. I inspected the padlock.

This bore evidence of use: it had recently been oiled!

But it was fast.

Greatly excited, I returned to the broken window and looked in again. The litter had not been disturbed, I could have sworn, for a considerable time—yet the door had recently been used.

My excitement grew. I thought that from some place, in this world or beyond, Nayland Smith had succeeded in inspiring me with something of his old genius for investigation. A great task lay to my hand. I determined to do it well.

I studied the padlock. I had no means of picking it, nor indeed any knowledge of that art. To crash a pane in one of the windows would have been useless, for they were of a kind not made to open, and the panes were too narrow to allow entrance had the glass been entirely removed. I walked around to the other side. Here was evidence of a landing stage long demolished. There were three windows and a walled-up door. Inspection was carried out from a narrow ledge which overhung the canal.

Baffled again, I was about to return—when I heard footsteps coming down the lane!

I stayed where I was. Directly opposite, the narrow canal glittering between, rose a wall of the deserted Palazzo Mori. I could see that stone balustrade up which I had scrambled, the irony balcony to which I had clung. Nearer and nearer the footsteps approached, and now I heard a woman's voice:

"Wait, just a moment! . . . I have the key."

185

It was a soothing, a caressing voice, and I longed for a glimpse of the speaker, but dared not move.

I heard the rattling of the padlock, opening of the door.

"Please wait! Not yet! We may be seen!"

Light suddenly illuminated the interior of the building. I crouched low, my heart beating fast, and cautiously from one corner of a window, peered in.

What I saw made my heart beat faster yet. It strengthened my resolution to do what Nayland Smith would have done. . . .

Rudolf Adlon, wearing a half mask, and a cloak over his evening dress, stood hands clasped behind him, watching a woman who knelt in a corner of the floor!

His eyes were ardent; he tore the mask off—and I saw a man enslaved. The woman wore a loose fur wrap; her arms resembled dull ivory. She was slender, almost serpentine; jet-black hair lay close to her shapely head. And as I looked and recognised her, she stood upright.

A trap had been opened, a section of floor with its impedimenta of pots and litter had been slid aside! She turned—and for the first time I saw her eyes. . . .

Her eyes—long, narrow, dark-lashed eyes—were emerald green! I had thought that there were no eyes in the world like these except the eyes of Dr. Fu Manchu.

She made a gesture of triumph. She smiled as perhaps long ago Calypso smiled.

"Be patient! This is the only way—come!"

The words reached me clearly through the broken window. Pulling her wrap over her bare shoulders, she beckoned and began to descend steps below the trap. I saw that she carried a flashlamp.

Rudolf Adlon obeyed. The light below shone up into his dark, eager face as he stooped to follow.

And then came darkness.

Chapter 32

THE ZOMBIE

Rudolf Adlon, dictator of a great European nation, was going to his death!

I thought rapidly, trying to envisage the situation from what I believed would have been Nayland Smith's point of view.

Probably I could reach police headquarters in ten minutes. A call box was of no avail, owing to my ignorance of the language, so that this meant ten minutes wasted. Before the police arrived, Adlon might have disappeared as Nayland Smith had disappeared. That the passage led to the Palazzo Mori I had good reason to suppose. But unless it had been planned to assassinate the chancellor in that deserted building and hide his body, where were they going?

My experience of the methods of the Si-Fan inclined me to believe that Adlon would be given a final opportunity to accept the Council's orders. My decision was soon made. I would follow; and when I had found out where the woman was leading the dictator, return and bring a party large enough to surround the place.

The door I knew to be unfastened. I groped my way to where a dim oblong of light indicated the position of the trap. I saw stone steps. I descended cautiously. The place in which I found myself had a foul reek; the filthy water of the Rio Mori dripped through its roof in places. It was an ancient stone passage, slimy and repellent. A vague moving light at the further end was that of the flashlamp carried by the woman.

Adlon's infatuation had blinded him to his danger. But putting myself in his place and substituting Ardatha for the woman of death, I knew that I, too, would have followed to the very gates of hell.

Fixing my eyes on that guiding light, I proceeded. The light disappeared, but I discovered ascending steps. A spear in the darkness led me up to a door ajar. I heard a voice and recognised it. It was the voice of Adlon.

"Where are you leading me, Mona Lisa?"

In the exquisite face of this ghoul who hunted human souls for Dr. Fu Manchu he had discovered a resemblance to that famous painting. The resemblance was not perceptible to me. . . .

Along an arched cellar, silhouettes against the light of the moving lamp which cast grotesque shadows, I saw the pair ahead: the slender figure of the woman, the cloaked form of the doomed man. There was a great squat pillar in this forgotten crypt and I crept behind it until they had come to the top of the open stair and vanished into a Gothic archway.

Complete darkness had come when I crept forward and followed, feeling my way to the foot of the stair.

The sound of footsteps ceased. I stood stockstill. I heard the woman's laughter, low-pitched, haunting. It ended abruptly. There came thickly muttered words in a man's voice. He had her in his arms . . . Then the footsteps continued.

A key was placed in a lock and I heard the creaking of a door. It echoed, phantomesque, as though in a cavern; it warned me of what I should find. I waited until those sounds, mockingly repeated by the ghosts of the place, grew faint. Advancing, I found myself in the tomblike entrance hall of the Palazzo Mori.

The light carried by the woman was now a mere speck. However, using extreme caution, I followed it. As I crossed that haunted place, the shades of men trapped, poisoned, murdered there, seemed to move around me in a satanic dance. Tortured spirits of medieval Venice formed up at my back, barring the road to safety. Yet I pressed on, for I knew that the great outer door was open, that even if my way through the foul tunnel be cut off, here was another sally port although it meant a plunge into the Grand Canal.

The light faded out entirely, but a hollow ringing of footsteps assured me that I had further to go. One of those doors which the police party had found closed, was open! (The ancient lock had been wedged. It was fitted with a new, hidden lock.) And beyond that door Rudolf Adlon went to destruction.

Down five steps I groped, and knew that I was below water level again.

Far along a tunnel similar to that which led under the Rio Mori, I saw the two figures. The man's arm was around the woman; his head was close to hers. I knew that I could never be detected in the darkness of this ancient catacomb unless my own movements betrayed me; and when the silhouettes became blurred and then disappeared altogether I divined the presence of ascending steps at the end of the passage.

One fact of importance I noted: this damp and noisome burrow ran parallel to the Grand Canal. I must be a long way from my starting point.

And now it had grown so black that I had no alternative but to use my torch. I used it cautiously, shining its ray directly before my feet. The floor was clammily repulsive, but I proceeded until I reached the steps. I switched off the torch.

A streak of light told me that a door had been left ajar at the top.

Gently I pushed it open and found myself in an empty wine cellar. One unshaded electric light swung from the vaulted roof. An open stone stair of four steps led up to an arch.

I questioned the wisdom of further advance. But I fear the spirit of Nayland Smith deserted me, that hereditary madness ruled my next move, for I crept up, found a massive, nail-studded door open, and peered out into a carpeted passage!

Emerging from that subterranean chill, the change of atmosphere was remarkable. Rudolf Adlon's voice reached me. He spoke happily, passionately. Then the speaker's tone rose to a high note — a cry . . . and ceased abruptly!

They had him — it was over! Inspired by a furious indignation I stole forward and peered around the edge of a half-opened door into a room beyond. It was a small room having parquet flooring of a peculiar pattern: a plain border of black wood

some three feet wide, the center designed to represent a lotus in bloom. Its walls were panelled, and
the place appeared to be empty until, venturing
unwisely to protrude my head, I saw watching me
with a cold smile the woman of death!

2

I suppose she was exceptionally beautiful, this
creature who, according to Nayland Smith, should
long since have been dust; but the aura surrounding her, my knowledge, now definite, of her murderous work, combined to make her a thing of
horror.

She had discarded her wrap; it was draped over
her arm. I saw a slenderly perfect figure, small
delicately chiselled features. Hers was a beauty so
imperious that it awakened a memory which presently came fully to life. She might have posed for
that portrait of Queen Nefertiti found in the tomb
of Tutankhamen. An Arab necklace of crudely
stamped gold heightened the resemblance. I was to
learn later of others who had detected this.

But it was her eyes, fixed immovably upon me,
which awakened ancient superstitions. The strange
word *zombie* throbbed in my brain; for those eyes,
green as emeralds, were long and narrow; their
gaze was hard to sustain . . . and they were like
the eyes of Dr. Fu Manchu!

"Well" — she spoke calmly — "who are you, and
why have you followed me?"

Conscious of my dishevelled condition, of the

fact that I had no backing, I hesitated.

"I followed you," I said at last, "because it was my duty to follow you."

"Your duty — why?"

She stood there, removed from me by the length of the room, and the regard of those strange, narrowed eyes never left my face.

"Because you had someone with you."

"You are wrong; I am alone."

I watched her, this suave, evil beauty. And for the first time I became aware of a heavy perfume resembling that of hawthorn.

"Where has he gone?"

"To whom do you refer?"

"To Rudolf Adlon."

She laughed. I saw her teeth gleam and thought of a vampire. It was the laugh I had heard down there in the cellars, deep, taunting.

"You dream, my friend — whoever you are — you dream."

"You know quite well who I am."

"Oh!" she raised delicate eyebrows mockingly. "You are famous then?"

What should I do? My instinct was to turn and run for it. Something told me that if I did so, I should be trapped.

"If you were advised by me you would go back. You trespass in someone's house — I do not advise you to be found here."

"You advise me to go back?"

"Yes. It is kind of me."

And now although common sense whispered that to go would mean ambush in that echoing tomb which was the Palazzo Mori, I was sorely tempted to chance it. There was something wildly disturbing in this woman's presence, in the steady glance of her luminous eyes. In short, I was afraid of her — afraid of the silent house about me, of the noisome passages below — of all the bloodthirsty pageant of medieval Venice to which her sheath frock, her ivory shoulders, seem inevitably to belong.

But I wondered why she temporised, why she stood there watching me with that mocking smile. Although I could hear no sound surely it must be a matter of merely raising her voice to summon assistance.

Forcing down this insidious fear which threatened to betray me, I rapidly calculated my chances.

The room was no more than twelve feet long. I could be upon her in three bounds. Better still — why had I forgotten it? I suppose because she was a woman . . .

In a flash I had her covered with my automatic.

She did not stir. There was something uncanny in her coolness, something which again reminded me of the dreadful Dr. Fu Manchu. Her lips alone quivered in that slight, contemptuous smile.

"Don't move your hands!" I said, and the urgency of my case put real menace into the words. "I know this is a desperate game — you know it too. Step forward. I will return as you suggest, but you will go ahead of me."

"And suppose I refuse to step forward?"

"I shall come and fetch you!"

Still there was no sound save that of our low-pitched voices, nothing to indicate the presence of another human being.

"You would be mad to attempt such a thing. My advice was sincere. You dare not shoot me unless also you propose to commit suicide, and I warn you that one step in my direction will mean your death."

I watched her intently—although now an attack from the rear was what I feared, having good reason to remember the efficiency of Fu Manchu's Thugs. Perhaps one of them was creeping up behind me. Yet I dared not glance aside.

"Go back! I shall not warn you again."

Whereupon, realising that now or never I must force the issue, I leapt forward. . . . That heavy odour of hawthorn became suddenly acute—overpowering—and stifling a scream, I knew too late what had happened.

The woman stood upon the black border, where I, too, had been standing. The whole of the center of the floor was simply an inverted "star trap."

It opened silently as I stepped upon it, and I fell from life into a sickly void of hawthorn blossom and oblivion. . . .

Chapter 33

ANCIENT TORTURES

"Glad to see that you are feeling yourself again, Kerrigan."

I stared about me in stupefaction. This of course was a grotesque dream induced by the drug which had made me unconscious — the drug which smelled like hawthorn blossom. For (a curious fact which even at this moment I appreciated) my memories were sharpcut, up to the very instant of my fall through the trap in the lotus floor. I knew that I had dropped into some place impregnated with poison gas of an unfamiliar kind. Now came this singularly vivid dream . . .

A dungeon with a low, arched roof: the only light that which came though a barred window in one of the stone walls; and in this place I sat upon a massive chair attached to the paved floor. My hands and arms were free, but my ankles were chained to the front legs of the chair by means of gyves evidently of great age and also of great strength. On my left was a squat pillar some four feet in diameter, and in the shadows behind it I discerned a number of strange and terrifying implements: braziers, tongs and other equipment of a torture chamber.

Almost directly facing me and close beside the barred window, attached to a similar chair, sat Nayland Smith!

This dream my conscious mind told me must be due to thoughts I had been thinking at the moment that unconsciousness came. I had imagined Smith in the power of the Chinese doctor; I had seemed to feel all about me uneasy spirits of men who had suffered and had died in those old palaces which lie along the Grand Canal.

There came a low moaning sound, which rose and fell — rose and fell — and faded away. . . .

"I know you think you are dreaming, Kerrigan!" Smith's voice had lost none of its snap. "I thought so myself, until I found it impossible to wake up. But I assure you we are both here and both awake."

Tentatively I tried to move the chair. Stooping, I touched the iron bands about my ankles. Then I stared wanly across at my fellow captive. . . . I knew I was awake.

"Thank God you're alive, Smith!"

"Alive, as you say, but not, I fear, for long!"

He laughed. It was not a mirthful laugh. The sound of our voices in that horrible musty place was muted, toneless, as the voices of those who speak in a crypt. I had never seen Smith otherwise than well groomed, but now, growing accustomed to the gloom, I saw that there was stubble on his chin. His hair was of that crisp, wavy sort which never seems to be disordered. But this growth of beard deepened the shadows beneath his cheekbones, and the quick gleam of his small even teeth as he laughed seemed to accentuate the haggardness of his appearance.

"I left in rather a hurry, Kerrigan; I forgot my pipe. It's been damnable here, waiting for . . . whatever he intends to do to me. You will find that the chains are long enough to enable you to reach that recess on your right, where, very courteously, the designer of this apartment has placed certain toilet facilities for the use of one confined here during any considerable time. I am similarly equipped. A Thug of hideous aspect, whom I recognise as an old servant of Doctor Fu Manchu, has waited upon me excellently."

He indicated the remains of a meal on a ledge in the niche beside him.

"Knowing the doctor's penchant for experiments in toxicology, frankly, my appetite has not been good."

I stood up and moved cautiously forward, dragging the chains behind me.

"No, no!" Smith smiled grimly. "It is well thought out, Kerrigan. We cannot get within six feet of one another."

I stood there at the full length of my tether watching him where he sat.

"What I was about to ask is: do you happen to have any cigarettes?"

I clapped a hand to my pocket. My automatic, my clasp knife, these were gone—but not my cigarettes!

"Yes, the case is full."

"Do you mind tossing one across to me? I have a lighter."

I did as he suggested, and he lighted a cigarette. Returning to the immovable chair I followed his example; and as I drew the smoke between my lips I asked myself the question: Am I sane? Is it a fact that I and Nayland Smith are confined in a cell belonging to the Middle Ages?

That gruesome moaning arose again—and died away.

"What is it, Smith?"

"I don't know. I have been wondering for some time."

"You don't think it's some wretched—"

"It isn't a human sound, Kerrigan. It seems to be growing louder. . . . However—how did you fall into this?"

I told him—and I was perfectly frank. I told him of Ardatha's visit, of the sounds which I had heard out on the canal side, of all that had followed right to the time that I had fallen into the trap prepared for me.

"There would seem to be a point, Kerrigan, where courage becomes folly."

I laughed.

"What of yourself, Smith? I have yet to learn how *you* come to be here."

"Oddly enough, our stories are not dissimilar. As you know, I did not turn in when you left me, but I put out the lights and stared from the window. The room was not ideal in view of the peril in which I knew myself to be. But I noted with gratitude a moored gondola in which a stout policeman was seated, apparently watching my window. It occurred to me that the sitting-room windows were equally accessible and, quietly, for I assumed you had gone to bed, I went in to look.

"I found that one was wide open and as I moved across to close it, I heard voices in your room. My first instinct was to dash in, but I waited for a moment because I detected a woman's voice. Then I realised what had happened. Ardatha had paid you a secret visit!

"Knowing your sentiments about this girl, I was by no means easy in my mind. However, I determined not to disturb you or to bring you into the matter in any way. But here was a chance not to be missed.

"Dropping out of the sitting-room window (which the man in the gondola could not see) I tripped and fell. The sound of my fall must have attracted your attention. I discovered a half-gate which shut me off from the courtyard directly below your room. I tried it very gently. It was not locked. Knowing that Ardatha must have approached from the other end, I crept past your window and concealed myself in a patch of shadow near the small bridge which crosses the canal at that point.

"When Ardatha came out (I recognised her from your description) I followed; and my experiences from this point are uncommonly like your own. She entered the old stone storehouse facing the Palazzo Mori; and I, too, performed that clammy journey through the tunnels. I lost her at the top of the steps leading out of the wine cellar. But having learned all I hoped to learn I was about to return when something prompted me to look into the room with the lotus floor."

He paused.

"Now, I want to make it quite clear, Kerrigan: I have no evidence to show that Ardatha suspected she was being followed. The presence of the woman whom I found in that room may have been accidental, but as I looked in I saw her . . ."

"You saw whom?"

"The *zombie*!"

"Good God!"

"My theories regarding her identity were confirmed. I had been right. Failing the presence of Doctor Fu Manchu in the case, she could only be a spirit, a creature of another world. For myself, I had seen her consigned to a horrible death. But woman or spirit, I knew now that she had to be silenced. I sprang forward to seize her—"

"I know!" I groaned.

"At that moment, Kerrigan, my usefulness to the world ended."

He stared down at the smoke arising from the tip of his cigarette.

"You say you recognised her. Who is she?"

"She is Doctor Fu Manchu's daughter."

"What!"

"Unchanged from the first moment I set eyes upon her. She is a living miracle, a corpse moving among the living. But—here we are! And frankly, I confess here we deserve to be!"

He paused for a moment as if listening—perhaps for that awesome moaning. But I could detect no sound save a faint drip-drip of water.

"Of course you realise, Smith," I said in a dull voice, "that Rudolf Adlon is in the hands of Doctor Fu Manchu?"

"I realise it fully. I may add that I doubt if he is alive."

Why I should have felt so about one who was something of a storm centre in Europe I cannot say, but momentarily forgetting my own peril I was chilled by the thought that Rudolf Adlon no longer lived, that the power which swayed a nation had ceased to be. We were silent for a long time, sitting there smoking and staring vacantly at each other. At last:

"As I see it," said Nayland Smith, "we have just one chance."

"What is that?"

"Ardatha!"

"Why do you think so?"

"Now that I know her Oriental origin, which all along I had suspected, I think if she learns that you are here she will try to save you."

I shook my head.

"Even if you are right I doubt if she would have the power . . . and I am sorry to say that I believe her to be utterly evil."

"Let us pray that she is not. She risked perhaps more than you understand to save you once before. If she fails to try again . . ."

That unendurable moaning arose, as if to tell us that Ardatha would fail—that all would fail.

2

I don't know how long I had been sitting there in hopeless dejection when I heard a slow, soft foot-step approaching. I glanced across at Nayland Smith. His face was set, expressionless.

A rattling of keys came, and the heavy door swung open. At the same moment a light set some-where behind that squat pillar sprang up, and I saw as I had suspected a fully equipped torture chamber. Nocturnal insects rustled to cover.

Dr. Fu Manchu came in. . . .

He wore a plain yellow robe having long sleeves, and upon his feet I saw thick-soled slippers. His phenomenal skull was hidden by a mandarin's cap, perhaps that which I had found in a hut on the Essex marshes.

I am unable to record my emotions at this moment, for I cannot recall that I had any. When on a previous occasion I had found myself in the power of the Chinese doctor, I had been fortified by the knowledge that Nayland Smith was free, that there was a chance of his coming to my aid. Now we were fellow captives. I was numbly resigned to whatever was to be.

Seated on Dr. Fu Manchu's left shoulder I saw a tiny, wizened marmoset. I thought that it peered at me inquisitively. Fu Manchu crossed nearly to the centre of the cell—he had a queer, catlike gait. There, standing midway between us, he looked long and searchingly, first at Nayland Smith and then at me. I tried to sustain the gaze of his half-closed eyes. I was mortified when I found that I could not do it.

"So you have decided to join me, Sir Denis?" He spoke softly and raising one hand caressed the marmoset. "At last the Si-Fan is to enjoy the benefit of your great ability."

Nayland Smith said nothing. He watched and listened.

"Later I shall make arrangements for your transport to my temporary headquarters. I shall employ you to save civilisation from the madmen who seek to ruin it."

The meaning of these strange words was not entirely clear to me, but I noted, and drew my own conclusions, that Dr. Fu Manchu seemed to have forgotten my presence.

"Tonight, a man who threatens the peace of the world will make a far-reaching decision. To me his life or death are matters of no importance, but I am determined that there shall be peace; the assumption of the West that older races can benefit by your ridiculous culture must be corrected. Your culture!"

His voice sank contemptuously on a guttural note.

"What has it done? What have your aeroplanes—those toys of a childish people—accomplished? Beyond bringing every man's home into the firing line—nothing! Napoleon had no bombers, no high explosives, nor any other of your modern boons. He conquered a great part of Europe without them. Poor infants, who transfer your prayers from angels to aeroplanes!"

He ceased for a moment and the silence was uncanny. From my point of view in the low wooden chair, Dr. Fu Manchu appeared abnormally tall. He possessed a physical repose which was terrifying, because in some way it made more manifest the volcanic activity of his brain. He was like a pylon supporting a blinding light.

The silence was broken by shrill chattering from the marmoset. With a tiny hand it patted the cheek of its master.

Dr. Fu Manchu glanced aside at the wizened

little creature.

"You have met my marmoset before, Sir Denis, and I think I have mentioned that he is of great age. I shall not tell you his age since you might be tempted to doubt my word, which I could not tolerate." There was mockery in his voice. "My earliest experiments in arresting senility were carried out on my faithful Peko. As you see, they were successful."

He removed the marmoset from his shoulder and couched it in a yellow fold covering his left arm. Nayland Smith's face remained completely expressionless. I counted the paces between the chair in which I sat and the spot upon which Dr. Fu Manchu stood.

He was just beyond my reach.

"You have genius, Sir Denis, but it is marred by a streak of that bulldog breed of which the British are so proud. In striving to bolster up the ridiculous pretensions of those who misdirect the West, you have inevitably found yourself opposed to me. Consider what it is that you would preserve, what contentment it has brought in its train. Look around at the happy homes of Europe and America, the labourers singing in your vineyards, the peace and prosperity which your 'progress' has showered on mankind."

His voice rose. I detected a note of repressed but feverish excitement.

"But no matter. There will be ample time in future to direct your philosophy into more suitable channels. I will gratify your natural curiosity regarding my presence in the world, which continues even after my unpleasant experience at Niagara Falls. . . ."

Nayland Smith's hands closed tightly.

"You recovered the body of that brilliant maniac, Professor Morgenstahl, I understand, and also the wreckage of the motorboat. One of my most devoted servants was driving the boat. He was not killed as you supposed and his body lost. He was temporarily stunned in the struggle with Morgenstahl—whom I overcame, however. He recovered in time to deal with the emergency. He succeeded in running the boat against a rock near the head of a rapid. In this he was aided by a Very light contributed by an airman flying over us. This fellow of mine—a sea Dyak—is a magnificent surf swimmer. Carrying a line he swam from point to point and finally reached the Canadian shore."

Dr. Fu Manchu stroked the marmoset reflectively.

"Unaided by this line and the strength of my servant, I doubt if I could have crossed to the bank. The crossing seriously exhausted me—and the boat became dislodged no more than a few seconds after I had taken the plunge. . . ."

Nayland Smith neither spoke nor moved. His hands remained clenched, his face expressionless.

"You have observed," Fu Manchu continued, "that my daughter is again acting in my interests. She is unaware, however, of her former identity: Fah lo Suee is dead. I have reincarnated her as Koreani, an Oriental dancer whose popularity is useful. This is her punishment. . . ."

The marmoset uttered a whistling sound. It was

uncannily derisive.

"Later you will experience this form of amnesia, yourself. The ordeal by fire to which I once submitted Koreani in your presence was salutary, but the furnace contained no fuel. It was one which I had prepared for *you*, Sir Denis. I had designed it as a gateway to your new life in China."

Mentally I seemed to remain numb. Some of the Chinese doctor's statements I failed to follow. Others were all too horribly clear. At times there came a note almost of exultation, severely repressed but perceptible, into the speaker's voice. He had the majesty which belongs to great genius, or, and there was a new horror in the afterthought, to insanity. He was perhaps a brilliant madman!

"I am satisfied to observe," he continued, "that my new anesthetic, a preparation of *crataegus*, the common hawthorn, serves its purpose so admirably. Anesthesia is immediate and complete. There are no distressing after-symptoms. I foresee that it will supplant my mimosa mixture with which, Sir Denis, you have been familiar in the past."

Slowly he extended a gaunt hand in the direction of the torture room:

"Medieval devices designed to stimulate reluctant memories."

He stepped aside and took up a pair of long-handled tongs.

"Forceps used to tear sinews."

He spoke softly, then dropped those instruments of agony. The clang of their fall make my soul sick.

"Primitive and clumsy. China has done better. No doubt you recall the Seven Gates? However, these forms of question are no longer necessary. I can learn all that I wish to know by the mere exercise of that neglected implement, the human will. I recently discovered in this way that Ardatha—hitherto a staunch ally—is not to be trusted where Mr. Kerrigan is concerned."

I ceased to breathe as he spoke those words. . . .

"Accordingly I have taken steps to ensure her noninterference. . . . You are silent, Sir Denis?"

"Why should I speak?" Smith's voice was flatly unemotional. "I allowed myself to fall into a trap which a schoolboy would have distrusted. I have nothing to say."

"You refer to the lotus floor no doubt? Yes, ingenious in its way. That room with others giving access to the cellars and dungeons had been walled up for several generations. I recently had them reopened, but confess I did not foresee it would be for the accommodation of so distinguished a guest. In a dungeon adjoining this I came across two skeletons, those of a man and a woman. Irregularities in certain of the small bones suggested that they had not died happily—"

He turned as if to go.

"I look forward to further conversation in the future, Sir Denis, but now I must leave you. A matter of the gravest urgency demands my attention."

As he moved towards the door, the marmoset sprang from his arm to his shoulder, and turning its tiny head, gibed at us. . . . The light went out. . . . I heard the key turned in the lock—I heard those padding, catlike steps receding in the stone-paved passage. . . .

I was drenched in perspiration.

Chapter 34

THE TONGS

The silence which followed Dr. Fu Manchu's departure was broken by that awful moaning as of some lost soul who had died horribly in one of the dungeons. It rose and fell, rose and fell . . . and faded away.

"Kerrigan!" Smith snapped, and I admired the vigour of his manner. "Was the wind rising out there?"

"Yes, in gusts . . . What do you think he meant about—"

"The wind was from the sea?"

"Yes. Oh my God! Is she alive?"

Again that awful moaning arose—and now to it was added a ghostly metallic clanking.

"What ever is it, Smith?"

"I have been wondering for some time . . . Yes, she's alive, Kerrigan, but we can't count on her! . . . Now that you tell me a breeze has risen, I know what it is. There's a window or a ventilator outside in the passage. What we hear is wind howling through a narrow opening."

"But that awful clanking!"

"Irritatingly significant."

"Why?"

"It was not there before the doctor's visit! It means that he has left the key in the lock with other keys attached to it. The draught of air—I can feel it blowing on the top of my head now through these bars—is swinging the attached keys to and fro."

Across the darkened cell he watched me.

"Among those keys, Kerrigan, in all probability, are the keys to our manacles!"

I thought for some time. A tumult had arisen in my brain.

"Surely *he* was never guilty of carelessness. Why should he have left the key?"

"According to my experience"—Smith stared down at his wrist watch—"the yellow-faced horror who attends to my requirements is due in about five minutes. The key was left in the lock for his convenience no doubt. And although Ardatha is alive—oh! I have learned to read Fu Manchu's hidden meanings—she will not come to our aid tonight. Someone else is alive also!"

"Adlon!"

"But I fear that his hours are numbered."

He stood up on the seat of the massive chair and stared out through the bars. Over his shoulder:

"I have carefully examined this passage no less than six times," he said. "It is no more than three feet wide. The end from which a current of air blows is invisible from here. But that is where the ventilator must be situated. The light is away to my right, the direction from which visitors always approach."

He stepped down and stood staring at me. His eyes were feverishly bright.

"I was wondering," he mused. "Could you toss me another cigarette?"

He lighted it, and apparently unconscious of the length of chain attached to his ankles, began to pace up and down the narrow compass of floor allowed to him, drawing on the cigarette with the vigour of a pipe smoker, so that clouds issued from his lips.

Hope began to dawn in my hitherto hopeless mind.

"Oh for the brain of a Houdini!" he murmured. "The problem is this, Kerrigan: The keys are hanging less than a foot below this grating behind me, but two feet wide of it. If you will glance at the position of the door you will see that I am right. It is clearly impossible for me to reach them. By no possible contortion could I get within a foot of the keyhole from which they are hanging. You follow me?"

"Perfectly."

"Very well. What is urgently required—for my jailer will almost certainly take the keys away—is an idea; namely, how to reach those keys and detach them from the lock. There must be a way!"

Following a long silence interrupted only by the clanking of Nayland Smith's leg irons, periodical moaning of the wind through that unseen opening and the chink of the pendant keys:

"It is not only how to reach them," I said, "but how to turn the lock in order to detach them."

"I agree. Yet there *must* be a way."

He stood still—in fact, seemed almost to become rigid. I saw where his gaze was set.

The sinew-tearing pincers to which Dr. Fu Manchu had drawn our attention lay not at the spot from which he had taken them up, but beside the pillar. . . .

"Smith!" I whispered, "can you reach them?"

With never a word or glance he walked forward to the extreme limit of the chain, went down upon his hands and crept forward with a stoat-like movement.

Fully extended, his right hand outstretched to the utmost, he was six inches short of his objective!

Even as I heard him utter a sound like a groan:

"Come back, Smith!"

My voice shook ridiculously. He got back onto his feet, turned and looked at me.

Although robbed of my automatic, my clasp knife and anything else resembling a lethal weapon, a small piece of string no more than a foot long which I had carefully untied from some package recently received and, a habit, had neatly looped and placed in my pocket proved still to be there. I held it up triumphantly.

Nayland Smith's expression changed.

"May I inquire what earthly use you can suggest for a piece of string?"

"Tie one end to the handle of that metal pitcher on the ledge beside you, then crawl forward again and toss the pitcher into the open arms of the tongs. You can draw them across the floor."

For a moment Smith's stare was disconcerting, and then:

"Top marks, Kerrigan," he said quietly. "Toss the string across. . . ."

Many attempts he made which were unsuccessful, but at last he lodged the pitcher between the iron arms of the pincers. Breathlessly I watched him as he began to pull. . . .

The pitcher toppled forward: the pincers did not move.

"We are done," he panted. "It isn't going to work!"

And at that moment — as though they had been treading on my heart — I heard footsteps approaching.

Chapter 35

KORÊANI

Those soft footsteps halted outside the door. There followed a provocative rattle of keys, the sound of a lock being turned; then the door opened, light sprang up . . .

Dr. Fu Manchu's daughter came in.

She was dressed as I remembered her in the room with the lotus floor. Her frock was a sheath, clinging to her lithe figure as perfectly as scales to a fish. She wore no jewelry save the Arab necklace. As she entered the cell and looked about her I grasped the fact immediately that she was looking, not for me, but for Nayland Smith.

When her long, narrow eyes met my glance their expression conveyed no more than the slightest interest; but as, turning aside, she looked at Smith I saw them open widely. There was a new light in their depths. I thought that they glittered like emeralds.

She stood there watching him. There was something yearning in her expression, yet something almost hopeless. I remembered Dr. Fu Manchu's words. I believed that this woman was struggling to revive a buried memory.

"So you are going to join us," she said.

Fu Manchu had used a similar expression. There was some mystery here which no doubt Smith would

214

explain, for the devil doctor had said also, "Fah lo Suee is dead. I have reincarnated her as Korêani. . . ."

The spoken English of Korêani was less perfect than that of Ardatha, but she had a medium note in her voice, a soft, caressing note, which to my ears sounded menacing as the purr of one of the great cats—a puma or a tigress.

There was no reply.

"I am glad—but please tell me something."

"What do you want me to tell you?" Nayland Smith's tones were coldly indifferent. "Of what interest can my life or death be to you?"

She moved more closely to his side, always watching him.

"There is something I must know. Do you remember me?"

"Perfectly."

"Where did we meet?"

Smith and I had stood up with that automatic courtesy which prompts a man when a woman enters a room. And now she was so near to him that easily he could have grasped her. Watching his grim face into which a new expression had come, I wondered what he contemplated.

"It was a long time ago," he replied quietly.

"But how could it be so long ago? If I remember you how can I have forgotten our meeting?"

"Perhaps you have forgotten your name?"

"That is stupid! My name is Korêani."

"No, no." He smiled and shook his head. "Your real name I never knew, but the name given to you in childhood, the name by which I did know you, was Fah lo Suee."

215

She drew down her brows in an effort of recollection.

"Fah lo Suee," she murmured. "But this is a silly name. It means a perfume, a sweet scent. It is childish!"

"You were a child when it was given to you."

"Ah!" She smiled—and her smile was so alluring that I knew how this woman must have played upon the emotions of those she had lured into the net of Dr. Fu Manchu. "You have known me a long time? I thought so, but I cannot remember your name."

For Korêani I had no existence. She had forgotten my presence. I meant no more to her than one of the dreadful furnishings of the place.

"My name has always been Nayland Smith. How long it will remain so I don't know."

"What does a name matter when one belongs to the Si-Fan?"

"I don't want to forget as you have forgotten—Korêani."

"What have I forgotten?"

"You have forgotten Nayland Smith. Even now you do not recognise my name."

Again she frowned in that puzzled way and took a step nearer to the speaker.

"Perhaps you mean something which I do not understand. Why are you afraid to forget? Has your life been so happy?"

"Perhaps," said Smith, "I don't want to forget you as you have forgotten me."

He extended his hands; she was standing directly before him. And as I watched, unable to believe what I saw, he unfastened the gold necklace, held it for a moment, and then dropped it into his pocket!

"Why do you do that?" She was very close to him now. "Do you think it will help you to remember?"

"Perhaps. May I keep it?"

"It is nothing—I give it to you." Her voice, every line of her swaying body, was an invitation. "It is the Takbîr, the Moslem prayer. It means there is no god but God."

"That is why I thank you for it, Korêani."

A long time she waited, watching him—watching him. But he did not stir. She moved slowly away.

"I must go. No one must find me here. But I had to come!" Still she hesitated. "I am glad I came."

"*I* am glad you came."

She turned, flashed a glance at me, and stepped to the open door. There she paused and glanced back over her shoulder.

"Soon we shall meet again."

She went out, closed the door and extinguished the light. I heard a jingle of keys, then the sound of her footsteps as she went along the passage.

"For God's sake, Smith," I said in a low voice, "what has come over you?"

He raised a warning finger.

2

As I watched uncomprehendingly, Nayland Smith held up the gold necklace. It was primitive bazaar work, tiny coins hanging from gold chains, each stamped with an Arab letter. I saw that it was secured by means of a ring and a clumsy gold hook. Quickly but coolly he removed the string from the handle of the pitcher and tied it to the ring.

Now, I grasped the purpose of that strange episode which in its enactment had staggered me. Once more he dropped onto the stone floor and crept forward until he could throw the hook of the necklace into the angle of the pincers. Twice he failed to anchor the hook; the third time he succeeded.

Gently he drew the heavy iron implement towards him — until he could grasp it in his hand.

"Kerrigan, if I never worked fast in my life before I must work fast now!"

His eyes shone feverishly. He rattled out the words in a series of staccato syllables. In a trice he was onto the chair and straining through the iron bars, the heavy instrument designed to tear human tendons held firmly in his hand. By the tenseness of his attitude, his quick, short breathing, I knew how difficult he found his task.

"Can you reach it, Smith?"

That mournful howling arose, followed by a faint metallic rattling. . . . The rattling ceased.

"Yes, I have touched them! But getting the key out is the difficulty."

More rattling followed. I clenched my hands, held my breath. Smith now extended his left arm through the bars. Stooping down, he began slowly to withdraw his right. I was afraid to speak, until with more confidence he pulled the iron pincers back into the cell — and I saw that they gripped a bunch of keys!

He stepped down, dropped keys and forceps on the floor, and closing his eyes, sat still for a moment. . . .

"Splendid!" I said. "One mistake would have been

fatal."

"I know!" He looked up. "It was a hell of a strain, Kerrigan. But what helped me was—she had forgotten to lock the door. The key slipped out quite easily!"

That short interval over, he was coolly efficient again.

Picking up the bunch, he examined each key closely, presently selected one and tried it on the lock of the band encircling his left ankle.

"Wrong!"

He tried another. I heard a dull grating sound.

"Right!"

In a moment his legs were free.

"Quick, Kerrigan! Come right forward. I will slide them across the floor to you. The one I have separated fits my leg iron; it probably fits yours."

In a moment I had the bunch in my hand. Fifteen seconds later I, too, was free.

"Now the keys! Be quick!"

I tossed them back. He caught them, stood upon the chair, looked out through the iron grating . . . and threw them onto the floor of the passage!

"Smith! Smith!" I whispered.

He jumped down and turned to face me.

"What?"

"We were free! Why have you thrown the keys back?"

Silently he pointed to the door.

I stared. There was no keyhole!

"Even if we had the key it would be useless to us. There is no means of opening this door from the inside! We must wait. Tuck your feet and the manacles well under your chair. I shall do the same. Soon the yellow jailer will be here. If he crosses first to you I will spring on his back. If he comes to me you attack him."

"He may cry out."

Smith smiled grimly. He picked up the iron forceps. "Will you have them, or shall I? It's a fifty-fifty chance."

"Keep them, Smith; you will get an opportunity in any event."

And scarcely had we disposed ourselves in a manner to suggest that the leg irons were still in place, when I heard quick footsteps approaching along the passage.

"Good! he's here. Remember the routine, Kerrigan."

There was a pause outside the door and I heard muttering. Then came a jangle as the man stooped to pick up the keys. Their having fallen from the lock clearly had made him suspicious. When presently he opened the door and stepped in he glanced from side to side, doubt written upon one of the most villainous faces I had ever beheld.

He wore a shirt with open collar, gray flannel trousers, and those sort of corded sandals which are rarely seen in Europe. By reason of his build, his glossy black hair and the cast of his features, I knew him for one of Dr. Fu Manchu's Thugs. Indeed, as I looked, I saw the brand of Kâli on his forehead. His yellow face was scarred in such a way that one eye remained permanently closed, and the effect of the wound which reached the upper lip was to produce a perpetual leer.

His doubts were not easily allayed, for he stood staring about him for some time, his poise giving me the impression of a boxer on tiptoes. He had replaced the key in the door with the pendant bunch and now going out again, he returned with a tray upon which was something under a cover, a bowl of fruit and a pitcher. For yet another long moment before he crossed towards Nayland Smith he hesitated and glanced aside at me.

Then, walking over to the alcove, he was about to set the tray upon the ledge when I sprang.

I caught him at a disadvantage, collared his legs and threw him forward, head first. The tray and its contents crashed to the floor. But even as he fell I recognised the type of character with whom I had to deal.

He twisted sideways, took the fall on his left shoulder, and lashing out with his feet, kicked my legs from under me! It was a marvellous trick, perfectly executed. I fell half on top of him, but reached for a hold as I did so.

It was unnecessary. . . . .

As the Thug forced his trunk upward on powerful arms Smith brought the forceps down upon the glossy skull! Against this second attack the yellow man had no defence. There was a sickening thud. He dropped flat on his face and lay still.

Chapter 36

BEHIND THE ARRAS

"We are safe for an hour," snapped Smith. "Come on!"

"Some sort of weapon would be a good idea," I said, bruised and still breathless from my fall.

"Quite useless! Brains, not brawn, alone can save us now."

As we stepped out into the passage came that ghastly moaning and a draught of cold air. It tricked me into a momentary panic, but Nayland Smith turned and examined a narrow grille set near the top of the end of the passage; for here was a cul-de-sac.

"There's an air shaft above that," he said. "Judging from the look of this place, we are down below water level. The fact that the actual ventilator above evidently faces towards the sea conveys nothing."

The passage was about thirty feet long. A bulkhead light was roughly attached to one of the stone walls. It was reflection from this which had shone through the iron bars of our prison. We hurried along. There were other doors with similar grilles on one side, doubtlessly indicating the presence of more cells. At the end was a heavy door, but it was open.

"Caution," said Smith.

A flight of stone steps confronted us. We mounted them, I close behind Smith. I saw ahead a continuation of the passage which we had just left, but one walls was wood panelled. This passage also was lighted by one dim lamp.

Creeping to the end, we found similar corridors opening right and left.

Speaking very close to my ear:

"Let's try right," Smith whispered.

We stole softly along. Here, again, there was one dim light to guide us, but we passed it without finding any way out of the place. We came to a second door which proved to be unlocked. Very cautiously Nayland Smith pushed it open.

We were in a maze . . . beyond stretched yet another passage! But peering ahead I observed a difference.

The floor was thickly carpeted with felt. There was no lamp, but points of light shone upon the ancient stonework of one wall, apparently coming from apertures in the panels which formed the other. Only by a grasp of his hand did Smith enjoin special caution as we pushed forward to a point where two of these openings appeared close together.

We looked through.

I recognised a remarkable fact. That rough and ancient woodwork which extended along the whole of the right-hand wall was no more than a framework or stretcher upon which tapestry was supported.

We were in a passage behind the arras of a large apartment.

Something seemed to obscure my vision. Presently I realised what it was: At certain points the tapestry had been cut away and replaced by gauze, painted on the outside, so that to those in the room the opening would be invisible.

I saw a chamber furnished with all the splendour of old Venice, but it was decaying splendour. The carved chairs richly upholstered in royal purple were damaged and faded; a mosaic-topped table was cracked; the patterned floor was filmed with ancient dust. Tapestry (through one section of which I peered) covered all the walls. Upon it were depicted scenes from the maritime history of the Queen of the Adriatic. But it was mouldy with age.

Four magnificent wrought-iron candelabra, each supporting six red candles, gave light, and a fine Persian carpet was spread before a sort of dais upon which was set a carven ebony chair resembling a throne. Dr. Fu Manchu, yellow robed, the mandarin's cap upon his head, sat there — his long ivory hands gripping the arms of the chair, his face immobile, his eyes like polished jade.

Standing before him, one foot resting on the dais, was a defiant figure: a man wearing evening dress, a man whose straight black hair and black moustache, his pose, must have revealed his identity to almost anyone in the civilised world.

It was Rudolf Adlon!

2

There had been silence as we had crept along the felt-padded floor behind the tapestry; a false step would have betrayed us. This silence remained unbroken, but the clash of those two imperious characters stirred my spirit as no rhetoric could have stirred me —

and my conception of the destiny of the world became changed. . . .

Then Adlon spoke. He spoke in German. Although my Italian is negligible I have a fair knowledge of German. Therefore, I could follow the conversation.

"I have been tricked, trapped, drugged!" The suppressed violence in the orator's voice startled me. "I find myself here—I realise now that I am not dreaming—and I have listened (patiently, I think) to perhaps the most preposterous statements which any man has ever made. I have one thing to say, and one only: Instantly"—he beat a clenched fist into his palm—"I demand to be set free! Instantly! And I warn you—I will not temporise—that for this outrage you shall suffer!"

He glanced about him swiftly, and as his face which I had always thought to lack natural beauty was turned in my direction, something in those blazing eyes, in the defiant set of his chin, won an admiration which I believed I could never have felt for him.

But Dr. Fu Manchu did not move. He might have been not a man, but a graven image. The he spoke in German. I had not heard that language spoken so perfectly otherwise than by a native of Germany.

"Excellency is naturally annoyed. I have sought a personal interview for one reason only. I could have removed you from office and from life without so much formality. I wished to see you, to talk to you. I believed that as one used to giving but not to receiving orders, the instructions of the Council of Seven of the Si-Fan might have seemed to be inacceptable."

"Inacceptable?" Rudolf Adlon bent forward threateningly. "Inacceptable! You fool! The Si-Fan! I have had more than enough of this nonsense! My time is too valuable to be wasted upon Chinese conjurers. Let this farce end or I shall be reduced to the extremity of a personal attack."

Fists clenched, nostrils dilated, he seemed about to spring upon that impassive figure enthroned in the ebony chair. Knowing from my own experience what he must be suffering at this moment, of humiliation, ignorance of his whereabouts, a bewilderment complete as that which belongs to an evil dream, I thought that Rudolf Adlon was a very splendid figure.

And in that moment I understood why a great, intellectual nation had accepted him as its leader. Whatever his failings, this man was fearless.

But Dr. Fu Manchu never stirred. The twenty-four red candles burned steadily. There was no breath of air in that decaying, deadly room. And the gaze of those still eyes checked the chancellor.

"Dictators"—the guttural voice compassed that germanic word perfectly—"hitherto have served their appointed purpose. Their schemes of expansion I have been called upon to check. The Si-Fan has intervened in Abyssinia. We are now turning our attention to Morocco and Syria. China, my China, can take care of herself. She will always absorb the fools who intrude upon her surface as the pitcher plant absorbs flies. To some small extent I have forwarded this process."

And Rudolf Adlon remained silent.

"I opened the floodgates of the Yellow River"—that note of exultation, of fanaticism, came now into the strange voice. "I called upon those elemental spirits in whom you do not believe to aid me. The children of China do not desire war. They are content to live on

226

their peaceful rivers, in their rice fields, in those white valleys where the opium poppy grows. They are content to die. . . . The people of *your* country do not desire war—"

And Adlon still remained silent, enthralled against his will. . . .

"My agents inform me that a great majority desires peace. There are no more than twelve men living today who can cause war. You are one of them. Your ideals cross mine. You would dispense with Christ, with Mohammed, with Buddha, with Moses. But not one of these ancient trees shall be destroyed. They have a purpose: they are of use—to me. You have been ordered by the Council of Seven not to meet Pietro Monaghani—yet you are here!"

Some spiritual battle the dictator was fighting—a battle which I had fought and lost against the power in those wonderful, evil eyes. . . .

"I forbid this meeting. I speak for the Council of which I am the president. A European conflict would be inimical to my plans. If any radical change take place in the world's map, my own draughtsmen will make it."

Adlon had won that inner conflict. In one bound he was upon the dais, looking down quiveringly upon the seated figure.

"I give you the time in which I can count ten! We are man to man. You are mad and I am sane. But I warn you—I am the stronger."

I was so tensed up, so fired to action, that I suppose some movement on my part warned Nayland Smith, for he set a sudden grip upon my wrist which made me wince: it brought me to my senses. I think I had contemplated tearing a way through the tapestry to take my place beside Rudolf Adlon.

"From several loopholes," Dr. Fu Manchu continued, his voice now soft and sibilant, "you are covered by my servants. I have explained to you patiently and at some length that I could have brought about your assassination twenty times within the past three months. Because I recognise in your character much which is admirable I have adopted those means which have brought us face to face. You have received the final notice of the Council; you have one hour in which to choose. Leave Venice tonight within that hour and I guarantee your safety. Refuse, and the world will know you no more. . . ."

Chapter 37

THE LOTUS FLOOR

Nayland Smith was urging me back in the direction we had come. Having passed the door which we softly opened and closed:

"Why this way?" I whispered.

"You heard Fu Manchu's words. He was covered by his servants from several loopholes—"

"Probably a lie—he has nerves of steel."

"That he has nerves of steel, I agree, Kerrigan, but I have never known him to lie. No, this is our way."

We groped back along those dimly lighted passages until we came to the point at which of two ways we had selected that to the right. We now tried the left. And dimly in the darkness, for there was no light here, I saw a flight of wooden steps. Smith leading, we mounted to the top. Another door was there on the landing and it was ajar. Light shone through the opening.

"I expect this is the way my jailer came," whispered Smith.

Beyond, as we gently pushed the door open, was a narrow lobby. Complete silence reigned. . . . But at the very moment of our entrance this silence was interrupted.

Unmistakable sounds of approaching footsteps

came from beyond a curtained opening. The footsteps ceased. There came a faint shuffling, and then—unmistakably again—the sound of someone retreating.

"Run for it!" Smith snapped, "or we are trapped!"

Dashing blindly across, I pulled up sharply on the threshold of a room. It was, I think, a horribly familiar perfume which checked me—that of hawthorn blossom! I clutched at Nayland Smith, staring, staring at what I saw. . . .

It was the room with the lotus floor!

We had entered it from the other side, and at that door through which I had stepped into oblivion, Ardatha stood, her eyes widely open, her face pale!

"Mercy of God!" she said, "but how did you get here? Don't move. Stay where you are."

No word came from Nayland Smith. For a moment I could hear his hard breathing, then:

"Go round it, Kerrigan," he said. "Stick to the black border. Don't be afraid, Ardatha, you had nothing to do with this."

As I reached the other side of the room and stood beside her:

"Ardatha!" I threw my arm about her shoulders. "Come with me! I can't bear it!"

"No!" She freed herself, her face remained very pale. "Not yet!"

"Go ahead, Kerrigan." Smith was making his way around the room. "Leave Ardatha to me; she's in safe hands."

With one last look into the amethyst eyes, I

hurried on — but at the top of the steps which led to the wine cellar paused, stepped back and:

"It's unnecessary to go the whole way," I said. "The door of the Palazzo Mori is not locked. For God's sake, don't linger, Smith."

He was standing looking down at her; she made no attempt to retreat. . . .

My flashlamp had gone the way of my automatic, but a box of matches for some obscure reason had been left in my pocket. With the aid of these I groped my way through to that noisome passage which led to the old palace. Along I went, moving very slowly and working my way match by match. I wondered why Smith delayed, what he had in mind. Some quibble of conscience, I thought, for clearly it was his duty to arrest Ardatha.

My plan was to learn if the exit by way of the water gate were still practicable. I knew it must be very late, and I wondered if it would be possible to attract the attention of a passing gondolier. Otherwise we should have to swim for it.

The door remained unfastened as the police had left it. Outside the wind howled through a dark night. The surface of the Grand Canal was like a miniature ocean. I could see no sign of any craft.

I confess that that second tunnel which led under the canal presented terrors from which I shrank.

Propping the great door open so that some dim light penetrated to the tomb-like hall, I began to retrace my steps. Approaching me, a ghostly figure, I saw Nayland Smith groping his way by the aid of a tiny torch — none other than his lighter!

He was alone. . . .

As we stood together on the steps, buffeted by that keen breeze, and still at the mercy of the enemy should we be attacked from the rear:

"Smith," I said, for the thought was uppermost in my mind, "what became of her?"

"She had a second set of keys—God knows where she had found them—and was on her way to release us. . . . I hadn't the heart to arrest her."

2

We stood there in the stormy night for three, four, five minutes, but no sort of craft was abroad.

"Nothing else to it," snapped Smith. "We must go through the tunnel. To delay longer would be madness."

"But the door at this end may be locked!"

"It is—but I have the key."

"You got it from Ardatha?"

"Yes."

"What of the padlock at the other end?"

"That is unfastened."

"Which means—someone is expected to go out tonight?"

"Exactly. I leave the identity of that someone to your imagination."

We groped across the clammy, echoing hall. With the key Ardatha had given him, Smith opened the door to the last gruesome tunnel. He locked it behind him.

"That was stipulated," he explained drily. "It also protects us from the rear."

We hurried as fast as we could through the foetid passage and up the steps at the end. The trap was open.

As we came out into that black and narrow lane which led to freedom:

"You must be worn to death, Smith," I said.

"I confess to a certain weariness, Kerrigan. But since frankly I had accepted the fact that I must lose my identity and be transported to some point selected by Doctor Fu Manchu to carry out the duties of another life, this freedom is glorious! But remember: Rudolf Adlon!"

"He had an hour— —"

"We have less . . . if we are to save him."

Chapter 38

IN THE PALAZZO BRIONI

Colonel Correnti sprang up like a man who sees a ghost. Even the diplomatic poise of Sir George Herbert had deserted him. These were the small hours of the morning, but police headquarters hummed with the feverish activity of a hive disturbed.

"The good God be praised!" Correnti cried, and the points of his gray moustache seemed to quiver. "It is Sir Denis Nayland Smith and Mr. Kerrigan!"

"Glad to see you, Smith," said Sir George drily.

"Quick!" Smith looked from face to face. "The latest news of Adlon?"

The chief of police dropped back into his chair and extended his palms eloquently.

"Tragedy!"

"What? Tell me quickly!"

"He disappeared from the suite allotted to him at the palace — it has a private exit — some time during the night. No one can say when. It was certainly a love tryst — for Mr. Kerrigan saw the appointment made. But, he has not returned!"

"He will never return," said Nayland Smith grimly, "if we waste a moment. I want a party — at least twenty men."

"You know where he is?" Sir George Herbert was the speaker.

The chief of police sprang up, his eyes mad with excitement.

"I know where he *was*!"

"But where? Tell me!"

"In a room in the Palazzo Brioni—"

"But Palazzo Brioni belongs to Mr. Brownlow Wilton, the American!"

"No matter. Rudolf Adlon was there less than half an hour ago."

As the necessary men were assembled Smith began to issue rapid orders. One party under a Carabinieri captain hurried off to the old stone boathouse. A second party proceeded to the water gate of the Palazzo Mori, a third covered both palaces from the land side. Ourselves, with the main party and the chief of police, set out for the Palazzo Brioni.

It was not clear to me how Smith had determined that this was the scene of our recent horrible adventure, but:

"I counted my paces as I went—and returned—along the passage," he explained. "There is no shadow of doubt. The room in which we saw Doctor Fu Manchu and Rudolf Adlon is in the Palazzo Brioni. . . ."

Against that keen breeze which shrieked eerily along the Grand Canal, the black police launch headed for the palace. As we slowed up against the water steps, no light showed anywhere; the great door was closed. Persistent ringing and knocking, however, presently resulted in a light springing up in the hallway.

When at last, preceded by the shooting of several bolts, the door opened, I saw a half-clad and very frightened manservant staring out.

"I represent the police," said Nayland Smith rapidly. "I must speak immediately to Mr. James Brownlow Wilton. Be good enough to inform him."

We all crowded into the hallway, a beautiful old place in which I had glimpses of fine pictures, statuary and furniture, every item of which I recognised to be museum pieces. The man, pulling his dressing gown about him, stared pathetically from face to face.

"But, please, I don't understand," he said. He was Italian, but spoke fair English. "What is this? What has happened?"

In that dimly lighted hall as we stood about him, wind howling at the open door, I could well believe that his bewilderment was not assumed.

"First, who are you?" Smith demanded.

"I am the butler here, sir. My name is Paulo."

"Mr. Wilton is your employer?"

"Yes sir."

"Where is he?"

"He left tonight, sir."

"What! Left for where?"

"For his yacht Silver Heels in the lagoon."

"But what of his guests?"

"They have all gone too."

"You mean that the house is empty?"

"Except for myself and the staff, sir, yes."

One of the party said urgently to the chief of police: "Silver Heels has sailed."

"Silver Heels must be overtaken!" snapped Smith. "Send someone to make the necessary arrangements. I leave it to you. But I must be one of the party."

A man, following rapid instructions from Colonel Correnti, went doubling off.

Turning again to the frightened butler:

"How long have you worked here?"

"Only for two weeks, sir. I was engaged by Mr. Wilton's secretary. But I have worked here before for others who have leased the palace."

"Lead the way to the tapestry room lighted by four iron candelabra."

The man stared in almost a horrified manner.

"That room, sir, is part of what is called the Old Palace. It has been long been locked up. I have no key."

"Nor to the room with the lotus floor?"

Nayland Smith was watching him keenly, his unshaven face very grim.

"The room with the lotus floor!" Paulo's expression grew even more wild. "I have heard of it, sir, but it is also part of the Old Palace. I have never seen it. Those rooms have a very unpleasant reputation, you understand. No one would lease the palace if they knew of them. The doors have not been unlocked for twenty years."

"Then one must be broken down. Do you know where they are?"

"I know of two."

"Go ahead."

As Paulo turned to obey I heard a sound of distant voices.

"What is that?" snapped Smith.

"Some of the other sevants, sir, who have been aroused!"

Smith glanced at Colonel Correnti.

"Have this looked into, Colonel," he said. "You, Paulo, lead on."

Our party was broken up again, Smith, myself, the chief of police, Detective Stocco and two Carabinieri following the butler. He led us to a doorway set in an arched recess. A magnificent cabinet—a rare piece of violet lacquer—stood in front of the arch.

"Behind here, sir, is one of the doors, but I have no key to open it."

"Get this thing out of the way."

In a few minutes the men had set the cabinet aside. Smith stepped forward and examined an ancient iron lock. He was soon satisfied. He turned and shook his head.

"This is not the door in use. You say you know of another?"

"Yes sir, if you will come this way."

Aside to me:

"The fellow is honest," Smith muttered. "This is a very deep plot." He glanced at his wrist watch as we crossed a deserted dining room. "Our chance of saving Adlon grows less and less, but there is someone else in danger."

"Who is that?"

"James Brownlow Wilton! He is notorious throughout the United States for his Nazi sympathies. The full extent of this scheme is only just beginning to dawn upon me, Kerrigan."

In a room overluxuriously furnished as a study, Paulo opened a satinwood door inlaid with ivory and mother-of-pearl to reveal an empty cupboard.

"At the back of this cupboard, sir," he said, "you see there are very ancient panels. I have always understood it is an entrance to the Old Palace. . . ."

"This door has been used recently. . . . It has a new lock!"

Smith's eyes glittered feverishly.

"I don't think so, sir. Mr. Wilton used the room, and I am sure he did not know of the door. I have always been careful to avoid mentioning to tenants who came anything about those locked rooms."

"Carbines!" Smith cried on a high note of excitement. "Those two men forward. Blow the lock out. The fate of a nation hangs on it!"

The sound of muffled shots reverberated insanely in that lavishly furnished study. I heard cries—racing footsteps. The other police party dashed to join us. . . . The lock was shattered, the door flung open.

"Follow me, Kerrigan!"

Nayland Smith, shining a ray of light ahead, stepped into the dark cavity. I went next, Colonel Correnti close at my heels.

"You see, Kerrigan! You see!"

Descending four stone steps we found ourselves in one of those narrow passages which surrounded the rooms of the Old Palace. I took a rapid bearing.

"This way, Smith, I think!"

"You're right!" he cried. "Ah! what's this?"

A door was thrown open, we crowded in, and flashlamps flooded the tapestry room in which I had seen Rudolf Adlon confronting Dr. Fu Manchu!

The red candles in the candelabra were extinguished, and in the light of our lamps I saw that the tapestry was so decayed as to be in places dropping from the wall. The ebony chair on the dais was there, but save for the extinguished candles, one of which

Smith examined, there was nothing to show that this sinister apartment had been occupied for a generation. . . .

During the next hour we explored some of the strangest rooms I had ever entered. We even penetrated to the cellar below the lotus floor. The place still reeked of hawthorn, but that unknown gas was no longer present in anesthetic quantity. A net was hung below the trap. . . .

We had a glimpse in those evil catacombs of the Venice in which men had disappeared never to be heard of again.

But not a soul did we find anywhere!

None of the other police parties had anything to report. Rudolf Adlon, whose slightest words disturbed Europe, had vanished as completely as in the days of the doges when prominent citizens of Venice had vanished!

It was a fact so amazing that I found it hard to accept. No member of that household had ever entered these locked rooms and cellars. All that I had heard, all that I had seen there, might have been figments of a dream! Saving the presence and the evidence of Nayland Smith I should have been tempted to suppose it so.

Yet again, like an evil cloud out of which lightning strikes destruction, Dr. Fu Manchu had gone with the breeze, to leave no trace behind!

And Ardatha?

Chapter 39

SILVER HEELS

"Are you ready, Kerrigan?"

Nayland Smith burst into my room at the hotel. A bath and a badly needed shave had renewed the man. He lived on his nerves. To me he was a constant source of amazement.

"Yes, Smith, I'm ready. Is there any more news?"

He dropped down on the side of my bed and began to fill his pipe. Wind howled through the shutters, and this was the darkest hour of the night.

"Silver Heels has answered the radio and is waiting for us."

"What do you think it all means, Smith? To me it still seems like a dream that you and I were confined there in that vile place. Granting Paulo's statement to be true, that Brownlow Wilton and his guests had left before my arrival, it's still incredible. That scene between Fu Manchu and Rudlof Adlon . . . Now at this moment I cannot believe it ever happened!"

"Think," snapped Smith. "The Palazzo Brioni was leased on behalf of Brownlow Wilton by his secretary and a staff assembled. Neither the secretary, one assumes, nor Brownlow Wilton, had the remotest idea of the history of the place. It contained a series of rooms belonging to what is known apparently as the Old Palace which, for good reasons, were shut off—never entered."

"So far, I agree."

His pipe satisfactorily filled, Nayland Smith struck a match. While he lighted the tobacco, he continued:

"Only one member of the household, Paulo, the butler who has served there before, knows anything about those hidden rooms. Very well. A genius of evil who *does* know about them, seizes this opportunity. Wilton, who had upheld to his peril the Nazi banner in the United States, is in a position to entertain Rudolf Adlon. Fu Manchu knows that Rudolf Adlon is coming incognito to Venice. An invitation to a luncheon party on the millionaire's yacht is arranged. There are servants of Fu Manchu on board."

He paused, pushed down the smouldering tobacco with his thumb and lighted a second match.

"At that party, Rudolf Adlon meets the woman known as Korêani. He is attracted. She makes it her business to see that he *shall* be attracted; and of this art, Kerrigan, she is a past mistress. She promises him an appointment, but stresses the danger and difficulty in order to prepare Adlon for the journey through those filthy passages. . . . No doubt she posed as an unhappily married woman."

"It's logical enough."

"Adlon, now enslaved, slips away from the Palazzo da Rosa and goes to the spot at which she has promised to confirm their meeting. In the interval

242

she has consulted Doctor Fu Manchu and the nature of Adlon's reception has been arranged. Luckily, you saw the message delivered. Adlon keeps the appointment . . . We know what happened."

His pipe now well alight, he began to walk across and across the floor.

"But, Smith," I said, watching him fascinatedly, for his succinct summing up of the fact revealed again the clarity of his mind, "you mean that Brownlow Wilton has been ignorant of this from first to last?"

He paused for a moment, surrounding himself with clouds of smoke, and then:

"Hard to believe, I agree," he snapped, "but at the moment there is no other solution. Wilton, as you probably know, is an eccentric and a chronic invalid—in fact a dying man. Although he entertains lavishly, he often secludes himself from his guests. We have found out that his decision to leave for Villefranche was made suddenly, but the party was a small one. Two, I think, we have identified."

I nodded.

There was little doubt that Ardatha had been one of Brownlow Wilton's guests, according to the account of a police officer who had been on board. His description of the only other female member of the party made it clear that this was Korêani. Paulo's account of the women tallied.

"It had been most cunningly arranged," Smith went on, speaking rapidly and resuming his restless promenade. "No doubt Brownlow Wilton met them under circumstances which prompted the invitation. After all, they are both charming women!"

"You think they flew from Paris and joined the yacht party?"

"Undoubtedly. They were under Si-Fan orders, but Brownlow Wilton did not know it. Where he met them no doubt we shall learn. But the facts are obvious, I think."

"They cannot possibly have sailed in Silver Heels?"

"No—evidently Doctor Fu Manchu had other plans for them and for himself. But I know, in my very bones I know, that Wilton is in danger. He may even be running away from that danger now. . . ."

2

The Adriatic was behaving badly from the point of view of a naval cutter, when presently we cleared the land and set out to overtake Silver Heels. I thought that the chief of police was not easy as our small craft rolled and pitched in a moderately heavy sea.

However, the storm was subsiding, and a coy moon began to peep through breaking clouds. For my own part I welcomed the storm, for neither the flashes of lightning nor rumbling of distant thunder were out of keeping with my mood.

Unknown to most of its inhabitants, Venice tonight was being combed for one of Europe's outstanding figures. Reserves of police had been called in from neighbouring towns. No representative of a great power was in his bed.

Rudolf Adlon had been smuggled out of life.

I think that high-speed dash through angry seas in some way calmed my spirit. Lightning flashed again, and:

"There she is!" came the hail of a lookout.

But from where we sat in the cabin, all of us, I suppose, had seen Silver Heels, bathed in that sudden radiance, a fairy ship, riding a sea bewitched, a white and beautiful thing.

A ladder was down when we drew alongside, but it was no easy matter to get aboard. At last, however, our party assembled on deck. We were received by Brownlow Wilton and the captain of the yacht.

My first glimpse of Brownlow Wilton provoked a vague memory to which I found myself unable to give definite shape.

He wore a beret and a blue rainproof overcoat with the collar turned up, a wizened little man as I saw him in the deck lights, with the sallow complexion of a southerner, peering at us through black-rimmed spectacles.

The captain, whose name was Farazan, had all the appearance of a Portuguese. He, too, was a sallow type; he wore oilskins. The astonishment of the American owner was manifest in his manner and in his eyes, magnified by the lenses of his spectacles.

"Although it is a very great pleasure to have you gentlemen aboard," he said in a weak, piping voice, "it is also a great surprise. I don't pretend that I have got the hang of it, but you are very welcome. Let's all step down to the saloon."

We descended to a spacious saloon to find a lighted table and a black-browned steward in attendance. I saw a cold buffet, the necks of wine bottles peeping from an ice bucket.

"I thought," said Wilton, peeling off his coat and his beret, "that on a night like this and at this hour, you might probably be feeling peckish. Just make yourselves comfortable, gentlemen. I was hauled out of bed myself by the radio message, and I guess a snack won't do any of us any harm."

Silver Heels was riding the swell with an easy and soothing movement, but the chief of police stared at the cold fare as a doomed man might stare at the black cap.

"I think, perhaps," he said, "that a brandy and soda might do me good."

The attendant steward quietly executed the order, and Brownlow Wilton, seated at the head of the table, dispensed an eager hospitality.

"It was all unexpected," he explained. "But I feel like a snack myself and I guess all of us could do no better than reinforce."

He had simple charm, I thought, this man who directed a great chain of newspapers and controlled the United States' biggest armament works. I had expected nothing so seemingly ingenuous. His reputation, his palace on the Grand Canal, his sea-going yacht, had prepared me, I confess, to meet someone quite different. Only in respect to his state of health did he conform to my expectations. He was a sick man. Despite his protestations, he ate nothing and merely sipped some beverage which looked like barley water.

"A little early in the morning," said Nayland Smith, "for Kerrigan and myself"—when the efficient but saturnine steward proffered refreshments.

He glanced at me smilingly, but I read in his glance that he meant me to refuse.

"I turned in directly we sailed," said Wilton; "and when a man has just fallen asleep and then is called up suddenly, I always find it takes him a little while to readjust his poise. But now, Sir Denis Nayland Smith"—he peered across the table in his short-sighted way—"I can ask you a question: What is this all about?"

Nayland Smith glanced around the saloon, in shadow save for that lighted table at which we were seated.

"It is rather difficult," he replied, "to explain. But, to begin: where are your guests?"

"My guests!" Brownlow Wilton's magnified eyes opened widely. "I have no guests, sir."

"What!"

"Those I had staying on board—there were four only—returned by the late express to Paris. I was unexpectedly compelled to break up the party. I am alone with my crew."

The storm was dying away over the sea, but distant rumbles of thunder reached us from time to time.

"I understand," said Nayland Smith, "that your four guests were Count and Countess Boratov, Mr. van Dee and Miss Murano."

"That's correct."

Wilton looked surprised.

"Who is Mr. van Dee?"

"A well-known Philadelphia businessman. We have been friends for years."

"I see. And Miss Murano?"

"A schoolmate of Countess Boratov, very attractive and young. She has lived much in Africa where her family have met with serious misfortune. She has unusually beautiful titian hair."

I grew hotly unhappy, for I knew that he was describing Ardatha!

"And where did you make this lady's acquaintance?"

"In London four weeks back."

"Through the Boratovs I suppose?"

"Surely. I asked her to join us here (she was with the countess in London) and she consented."

"How long have you known the Boratovs, Mr. Wilton?"

Brownlow Wilton's sallow face grew lined and stern. As he glanced at Colonel Correnti, that elfin memory peeped out, and then eluded me again. Silver Heels rolled uneasily. Dimly, I heard thunder.

"I appreciate the fact, gentlemen, that you are acting with full authority; but not knowing why I have been favoured with your company, perhaps I may ask in what way my friends are of interest?"

"No doubt I have been over-brusque, Mr. Wilton," said Smith. "But your own future is at stake. A crime which may change the history of Europe was committed at the Palazzo Brioni earlier tonight—"

"What's that?"

Brownlow Wilson bent forward over the table.

"I have no time for details now. I merely ask for your co-operation. Where did you meet the Boratovs?"

"When they visited America, in the fall of last year."

"Could you describe the countess?"

"A very lovely woman, sir." A note of unmistakable admiration had entered the speaker's high-pitched voice. "Tall, slender, with fascinating eyes: they are brilliantly green—"

Nayland Smith nodded grimly.

"And the count?"

"A distinguished Russian aristocrat, once in the Imperial Guard."

"And they all left by the Paris express, you say?"

"All of them, yes."

"You remained alone for some time then at the palace?"

"No sir. We dined here on board. News from England had come which meant I had to get back. Captain Farazan got busy. He secured the necessary clearance papers and we sailed immediately. My guests made the train and are now on their way to Paris."

Nayland Smith stared hard at James Brownlow Wilton, and then:

"Excuse me," came a discreet voice.

The steward (his name was Lopez), who had gone out, stood now at Wilton's elbow, extending a message on a salver. Wilton took it, nodded his apologies, and read the message. The saturnine

Lopez went out again.

"Ah! — a personal matter, gentlemen — of no importance."

But his expression belied his words. Nayland Smith's face offered me a perplexing study. As Wilton crumpled the scrap of paper in his hand:

"May I ask," said Smith, "if you used the small study in Palazzo Brioni? I refer to the one distinguished by a very beautiful figure of the Virgin."

Brownlow Wilton stared hard through his powerful spectacles. I thought he was striving for composure.

"I looked after all my correspondence there, sir. I have always been attracted to that room."

"Were you aware, or did the agent who negotiated the deal inform you, that there is a disused wing which has been locked for years?"

"I never heard that. This is news to me."

"I understand that you have a secretary who takes care of most of these details. I am told that he put Silver Heels into commission in Monaco and also came over to Venice to arrange a suitable household for your arrival. What is this gentleman's name?"

"You mean Hemsley? He has been with me for years. I sent him ahead to London. I am due back there myself, but I want to put the yacht into dry dock before I go. There's something radically wrong with her engines."

"He engaged the present crew, I believe?"

"He did — and by and large, very efficient they are."

"Have any of them worked for you before?"

"Not one. Hemsley believes in a clean slate. The same applies to the staff in Venice. Never saw one of them in my life before."

Chapter 40

SILVER HEELS (CONTINUED)

Silver Heels rode the swell uneasily. The chief of police continued to look unhappy. He glanced at me from time to time. I could hear the tramping of feet on the deck above, and I knew that the police were going about their work inspecting the papers of the crew. Peering into the shadows at the darkened end of the saloon, I had a momentary impression that someone had been standing there . . . and had disappeared.

The creaking of the ship in a silence which had fallen became to my ears a sinister sound. Nayland Smith's eyes were fixed intently upon the face of the American owner. For some reason I was glad when he spoke:

"You entertained Rudolf Adlon to lunch on board?"

"I did. I had introductions to him from Pietro Monaghani with whom I am well acquainted."

"I suggest that Rudolf Adlon was much attracted by the countess?"

Brownlow Wilton smiled uneasily, then leaning forward selected a cigar from a box which lay upon the table. As he tore the label:

"Maybe you're right," he replied, "and I am not blaming him. But he is a man who makes no attempt to hide his feelings."

"Herr Adlon returned after luncheon to the Palazzo

da Rosa?"

"I had two! I got a third while Adlon was on board. "Yes — and I won't say I was sorry."

"Did you go ashore to the palace during the afternoon?"

"No, I stayed on board, but most of the party went ashore. They had odd jobs to do, you understand, before leaving for Paris."

"Did you see them off?"

"No sir. They said good-bye on the yacht and went ashore in the launch. You see, I'm not as active as I used to be. I had a conference with the chief engineer. I wanted to find out if she could make Villefranche under her own steam."

"So that was the last you saw of your guests?"

"It was. But we are all meeting again in London in three days."

Again that uncomfortable silence fell, and then:

"You are quite sure, Mr. Wilton, that your reason for breaking up the party was purely engine trouble? I mean you have not, by any chance, received a notice from the Si-Fan?"

At those words, Wilton's face changed completely. He laid down the cigar which he had just lighted, and the effect was as though he had discarded a mask. His large, dark eyes, magnified by spectacles, gleamed almost feverishly as he glared at Nayland Smith.

"How can you know that?" he asked and clutched the edge of the table. "How can you know that?"

"It may be my business to know, Mr. Wilton."

"Yes, I admit it. I was running away. Now you have the truth."

Nayland Smith nodded.

"I thought as much. You control a great American newspaper, Mr. Wilton. Its sympathies are rather pointedly with Adlon and Monaghani. Am I right?"

"Maybe you are."

"Also, may I suggest that your armament works do a large trade with the governments represented by these gentlemen?"

"You seem to know a lot, sir. But, as you say, maybe it's your business."

"How long does the third notice give you?"

"Until noon tomorrow."

"What are you to do?"

"I was ordered to come here to Venice." His glance now as he looked about him was that of a hunted man. "And I was ordered to give that lunch on board to Adlon. Now I am told to beat it as fast as I can get away. This whole journey has been in obedience to those orders. I will admit it: I am a badly frightened man. I once spent some years in the Orient, and I know enough about the Si-Fan to have done what I have done."

Nayland Smith looked hard at me.

"You are noting these facts, no doubt, Kerrigan? You see how Mr. Wilton has been used for a dreadful purpose, a purpose which I fear has succeeded."

For some time past, faintly, I had heard the crackling of radio, and now came hurrying footsteps. A police officer ran in carrying a message which he handed to the chief.

Colonel Correnti adjusted a powerful monocle and read it. Then he looked up, his hitherto pale face flushed with excitement.

"It is from headquarters," he exclaimed. . . . "A

body has been found in the canal!"

"What!"

Smith sprang to his feet.

"They cannot be certain but they think—"

"Merciful heaven! this is terrible! What does it mean?"

Wilton, also, had stood up and was staring at the colonel's pale face.

"It means, Mr. Wilton," snapped Smith, "that something intended to avert war has happened tonight which, instead, may lead to it."

"Why should we be silent," the colonel cried, "about that which the world must know tomorrow! Mr. Wilton, a terrible thing has happened in Venice. Rudolf Adlon, a short time after he left this yacht, disappeared completely!"

"What do you say?"

Wilton dropped back into his chair.

"Those are the facts," said Nayland Smith sternly. "You were used to bring together Adlon and the woman known to you as Countess Boratov under circumstances which would enable them to meet again secretly. This meeting took place—you have heard the result."

"But there may be a mistake! I find myself quite unable to believe it!"

2

"Catch him, Kerrigan—he has collapsed!"

Just as he stepped out onto the deck, we both saw Wilton stagger and clutch blindly for support. . . . I

255

caught him as he fell. In the deck light his face appeared ghastly.

"This murderous farce"—he spoke in a mere whisper—"has taken more out of me than I realised. Now I know why it was planned, the thing that has happened—I guess I'm through!"

Colonel Correnti was already on board the cutter, although it had proved no simple task to transfer his portly form from the moving ladder. I could see him staring up through a cabin window. We had all planned to return immediately, leaving the crew to bring Silver Heels back to port with two police on board.

Now I realised that our plans would have to be changed.

"My cabin is just forward," Brownlow Wilton muttered. "If I may lean on you I think I can make it."

Smith and I took him forward to his cabin. It was commodious, with up-to-date equipment, and having laid him on the bed:

"My small medical knowledge does not entitle me to prescribe," said Nayland Smith, "but would some stimulant—"

Lopez, the steward, appeared in the doorway. Behind him I saw the Carabinieri uniforms of the two men detailed to remain on board. In light shining out of the cabin, I disliked the steward's appearance more than ever.

"If you will leave Mr. Wilton to me, gentlemen," he said, "I think I can take care of him."

Brownlow Wilton's face was now contorted; he appeared to be in agony.

"What is it?" I asked aside.

"Angina pectoris, sir. The excitement. I am afraid he is in for another attack. There are some tablets . . ."

"God God! don't you travel with a doctor?"

"No sir. Mr. Wilton has a regular physician in Venice, but I don't think he felt any symptoms of any attack until this present moment."

Nayland Smith was staring down at the sick man, and somehow from his expression I deduced what he was thinking. Dr. Fu Manchu, he had told me on one occasion, could reproduce the symptoms of nearly every disease known to medical science. . . .

"I will take no drugs—"

The sick man had forced himself upright—Smith sprang forward to assist him.

"Is this wise, Mr. Wilton?"

"Be so good as to give me your arm—as far as that chair. Lopez! I have found that a small glass of old Bourbon whisky never does any harm at these times. If you abstemious gentlemen would join me, why that would hasten the cure!"

His pluck was so admirable that to refuse would have been churlish. Lopez went to find the old Bourbon and Nayland Smith, going out on deck, hailed the cutter.

"Head for port! Don't delay. I am remaining on board. Silver Heels will put about and follow. . . ."

At the small cabin table I presently found myself seated, the invalid on my left and Nayland Smith, too restless to relax, leaning against an elaborate washbowl with which the room was equipped. Behind me Lopez poured out the drinks.

"Pardon," Smith muttered, and turning, began to wash his hands. "Grimy from the journey."

When he turned to take the glass which Lopez handed to him, I had a glimpse of Smith's face in the mirror which positively startled me. His eyes shone like steel; his jaws were clenched. Almost, I doubted my senses—for as he fronted us again he was smiling!

Lopez withdrew quietly, leaving the cabin door open. I could hear the cutter moving off. There were shouted orders, and now I detected vibration. Silver Heels was being put about.

"To the future, gentlemen!"

Brownlow Wilton raised his glass, when:

"Good God! Look! *Doctor Fu Manchu!*"

Nayland Smith snapped out the words and glared across the cabin!

Brownlow Wilton, setting his glass unsteadily on the table (I had not touched mine), shot up from his chair with astounding agility and we both stared at the open door. I was up, too.

The deck outside was empty!

I turned with a feeling of dismay to Smith. He was draining his glass. He set it down.

"Forgive me, Mr. Wilton"—he spoke with a nervousness I had never before detected in him—"that bogey is beginning to haunt me! It was only the shadow of a cloud."

"Well"—Wilton's high voice quavered—"you certainly startled me—although I don't know whom you thought you saw."

"Forget it, Mr. Wilton. I'm afraid the strain is telling. But that whisky has done me good. Finish your drink, Kerrigan. Perhaps I might rest awhile, if there's an available cabin?"

"Why, certainly!" Brownlow Wilton pressed a bell.

"Your very good health, gentlemen!"

He drank his Bourbon like a man who needed it, and as Lopez came in silently I finished mine.

"Lopez—show Sir Denis Nayland Smith and Mr. Kerrigan to cabin A. It is at your disposal, gentlemen. We have an hour's sailing ahead of . . ."

I glanced swiftly at Smith. The shock of his strange outcry had provoked another spasm of Wilton's dread ailment. His features were convulsed. He lay back limply in his chair!

"All right, sir!" said Lopez as I stooped and raised the frail body. "If he lies down I hope he will recover—"

I laid the sick man on his bed. His eyes were staring past me at Lopez. He tried to speak—but not a word came.

"Here's your next patient, Kerrigan," Nayland Smith spoke thickly . . . he was swaying!

I ran to him.

"This way, sir."

Lopez remained imperturbable. As I clutched Smith's arm and the steward led us along the deck, I cannot even attempt to depict my frame of mind. . . .

What ailed Nayland Smith?

Lightning flickered far away over the sea; thunder sounded like rolling drums. . . . The police cutter was already out of sight. Silver Heels swung slowly about.

As Smith reeled along the deserted deck:

"Take your cue from me!" he whispered in my ear. "When I lie on the bed drop down beside me in a chair—anywhere—but as near as you can! Begin to stagger. . . ."

The steward opened a door and illuminated a commodious cabin, similar to that occupied by Brownlow

259

Wilton.

"In here, sir."

"Always . . . poor sailor, I fear," Smith muttered thickly. "Lie down awhile . . ."

I assisted him on to one of the two beds, while Lopez removed the coverlet. He lay there with closed eyes, seeming to be trying to speak. An armchair stood near by, and distrusting my acting I slumped suddenly into it. I had ceased trying to think, but trusted Nayland Smith, for he could see where I was blind.

As the steward solicitously removed the coverlet from the neighbouring bed and spread it over me:

"Sorry . . . whacked!" I muttered and closed my eyes.

The steward went out and shut the cabin door.

"Don't speak—don't move!" It was a mere murmur. "Roll over so that you face me, and wait."

I rolled over on my side and lay still. Now I could see Smith clearly. His eyes, though half-closed, were questing about the cabin, particularly watching the door and the two ports which gave upon the deck. Over the creaking and groaning of the ship I heard those distant drums. Something told me to lie still— that we were being watched.

"Speak softly," said Nayland Smith; "the man Lopez has gone to report. Do you realise what has happened?"

"Not in the least."

"We have fallen into a trap!"

"What!"

"Lie still. Someone is probably watching us. . . . I foresaw the danger but still walked into it. I suppose I had no right to bring you with me."

260

"I don't even know what you mean."

The manoeuvre of turning the ship about had been clumsily accomplished, and I realised that we were now headed back for Venice. There was less creaking and groaning and the sound of thunder drums grew fainter.

"I suspect Fu Manchu's plan to be that we shall never return."

"Good heavens!"

"Ssh! Quiet! Someone at the porthole."

I lay perfectly still; so did Nayland Smith. Only by the prompting of that extra sense which comes to us in hours of danger did I realise that someone was indeed peering into the cabin. My brain, tired by a whirl of grotesque experiences, obstinately refused to deal with this new problem. Why should we both be overcome? And what were we waiting for?

"All clear again," Smith reported in a low voice. "Even if the door is locked, which I doubt, those deck ports are wide enough to enable us to get out."

"But Smith, what to you suspect?"

"It isn't a suspicion, Kerrigan; it's a fact. This yacht is in the hands of servants of Doctor Fu Manchu from the commander downwards."

"Good God! Are you sure?"

"Quite sure."

"But Wilton . . ."

"In Europe our concern is concentrated upon kings and dictators, but Wilton in the United States wields almost as much power as, shall we say, Goebbels in Germany. His political sympathies are well known, his interests widespread."

"But Wilton is a dying man."

"I think you would be nearer the mark, Kerrigan, if you said 'Wilton is a dead man'!"

Only the sound of the propellers broke the silence now. I knew instinctively that Nayland Smith was thinking hard, and presently:

"Can you hear me, Kerrigan?" he asked in a low voice. "I dare not speak louder."

"Yes."

Those words "Wilton is a dead man" haunted me. I wondered what he meant.

"We should probably be well-advised to make a dash for it; grab those life belts and jump over the side. But there's a fairly heavy swell and I don't entirely fancy the prospect."

"I don't fancy it at all!"

"Perhaps we can afford to wait until we are rather nearer land. Our great risk at the moment is that they discover we are not insensible."

"Insensible! But why should we be insensible?"

Of all the strange and horrible memories which I have of this battle to prevent Dr. Fu Manchu from readjusting the balance of world power, there is none more strange, I think, than this muttered interlude, lying there in the cabin of Silver Heels.

"For the simple reason," the quiet, low voice continued, "that the drinks we shared with Wilton were drugged. Bourbon whisky was insisted upon for that reason: its marked flavour evidently conceals whatever drug was in it."

"But, Smith—"

"I switched them, Kerrigan, having created a brief distraction! My own, if you remember, I apparently drained at a draught. It went into the washbowl at my elbow."

"But mine?"

"There was no alternative in the time at my disposal. Wilton had yours—*you* had Wilton's."

"Good God! Do you mean you think he is lying dead there in his cabin?"

"Ssh! Remember we are through if they once suspect us. I mean that he is dead, yes—but not lying in his cabin. . . ."

He lay silent for a while, and I divined the fact that he was listening. I listened also, puzzling my brain at the same time for a clue to the meaning of his words. Then:

"I am wondering why the two police have not—"

My sentence was cut short. I heard a sudden scuffling of feet, a wild cry—and then came silence again, except that very far away I detected a dull rumbling of thunder.

"Smith! Good God, can we do nothing!"

"The murderous swine! It's too late! I was playing for time—trying to make a plan"—there was an agony of remorse in his low-pitched voice. "Hello!"

The lights went out!

"Now we can move," snapped Smith, and as he spoke the engines ceased to move. Silver Heels lay rolling idly on the swell.

"This is where we jump to it! Quick, Kerrigan! Have your gun handy!"

I rolled off the bed and made for the door. I was

nearer to it than Smith.

"Damnation!" I exclaimed.

The door was locked!

Dimly I could see Smith trying one of the big rectangular ports which opened onto the starboard deck.

"Hullo! This is more serious than I thought! These are locked, too!"

We stood there for a moment listening to increasing sounds about us.

"They're getting the launch away," I muttered, for I had noted that the yacht carried a motor launch. "What does that mean?"

"It means they're going to sink Silver Heels—with ourselves on board!"

Chapter 41

SILVER HEELS (CONCLUDED)

"Listen, Kerrigan, listen!"

To the sound of voices, running feet, creaking of davits and wheezy turning of chocks, a suggestive silence had succeeded, broken only by the cracking and groaning of the ship's fabric. If Nayland Smith's conclusions were true, and he was rarely wrong, we were trapped like rats, and like rats must drown.

I listened intently.

"You hear it, Kerrigan?"

"Yes. It's in some adjoining cabin."

It was a moaning sound; but unlike that which had horrified me in the cellars of Palazzo Brioni, this certainly was human. Even as I listened and wondered what I heard, Nayland Smith had a wardrobe door open. The wardrobe was empty, but in the dim light I saw that he had his ear pressed to the woodwork.

"It's behind here!" he said. "We daren't use a torch yet. Noise we must risk. The ship's noises may drown it, but this boarding has to be stripped. Hello!"

As I joined him I saw that there was a ventilator at the back of the wardrobe.

"No time and no means to unscrew it," he muttered, and I saw that he had succeeded in wedging his fingers between two of the bars. "Let's hope it doesn't make too much row!"

He wrenched it bodily from the light wood in which it was set. Speaking very close to the gap thus created:

"Anyone there?" he called softly.

A stifled muttering responded.

"Come on, Kerrigan! This is our only chance!"

So far as I could make out, every living soul on board, other than ourselves or whoever might be in the next cabin, had joined the launch. We attacked that job like demons, stripping three-ply woodwork from the back of the wardrobe. Every crack of the shattered fragments sounded in my ears like the shot of a pistol. We made a considerable gap—and no one hindered us.

"If anybody comes in," snapped Smith, "shoot him down."

There was a second partition behind, and now that stifled cry reached us more urgently.

"Stand behind me," said Smith.

He flashed a momentary beam upon this new obstacle.

"Matchboarding," I muttered. "These rooms once communicated."

Not awaiting his reply, I hurled myself against it.

I crashed through into a small cabin, as fitful moonlight from a porthole told me. On the floor the two men of the Carabinieri lay bound—bandages tied over their mouths! One was struggling furiously; the other lay still.

"This one first."

Quickly we released the struggling man. He spoke a little English and the situation was soon explained. He had been struck down from behind as he patrolled the deck, and had recovered consciousness to find himself bound in the cabin. His opposite number, when we released him in turn, proved to be insensible, but alive.

"Now," snapped Smith. "Yes or no . . ."

The cabin was locked.

"This is awful!" I groaned. "But we could blow the lock out."

"Yes—fortunately we're armed, for these men's carbines have gone. But wait—"

He sprang to the porthole, worked feverishly for a few seconds and then:

"A different fitting," he gasped. "I have it open!"

I climbed through onto the deck . . . and the key was in the cabin door. We were on the starboard side of Silver Heels; the launch lay at the port ladder. And from the ladder-head at this moment sounds of disturbance arose. Facing us a small lifeboat hung at the davits; forward, just abaft the bridge, an alleyway connected the two decks.

"Do you know anything about boats?" Smith snapped.

"Not much."

"Do you?" to the police officer.

"Yes sir. I was at sea before I joined the Carabinieri."

"Right! Kerrigan, steal through that alleyway and watch what is going on. You"—to the ex-seaman—"lend a hand with your friend."

They began to haul the insensible man across the deck. I turned and crept along the alleyway. Soon I had a view of the ladder-head. The portside was in shadow, relieved only by the light of a solitary hurricane lantern.

One man stood there. He was tapping his foot impatiently upon the deck and watching a door which I thought led to the engine room. It was Lopez. Heralded by a rattling of feet on iron rungs, a man wearing dungarees burst into view.

"You have set it?"

"Yes."

"Down quickly! — not a moment to waste!"

"But Doctor Chang! Where is the doctor? I have not seen him."

"His orders were to join the launch immediately she was swung out."

"Doctor Chang is not on board," came a voice from the foot of the ladder.

"How long have we?"

"Three minutes."

Silver Heels, her wheel abandoned, creaked and groaned: it became difficult to hear the speakers.

"I shall not sacrifice myself for the doctor!" Lopez spoke furiously. "Already he has taxed my patience. . . . Hoy!" — he hailed — "Doctor!"

"Doctor Chang!"

Other voices joined in the cry.

But Dr. Chang — whoever Dr. Chang may have been — did not appear.

At the head of the ladder the man in dungarees hesitated, looking back over his shoulder, whereupon:

"Down, I say!" cried Lopez, a note of cold authority in his voice. "Who is in charge here? Always the doctor was mad. If he wishes to be destroyed who cares? There is not a moment to spare! Everyone for himself!"

Nayland Smith and the police officer had succeeded in lowering away the ship's boat with the insensible Carabinier on board, for when I got back to the starboard rail it was already riding an oily swell, fended off by the man in uniform. Smith, bathed in perspiration as I could see, was watching for my return.

"Well?"

"They've gone. The ship will blow up in two minutes! But Wilton—"

"Come on! The ladder is down."

"But—"

"There are not 'buts.' Come on!"

Although I have said that the swell was subsiding, boarding that boat was no easy matter. We accomplished it, however, so that I am in a position to testify to the fact that some prayers are answered.

As dimly we heard the launch racing away from Silver Heels, we began furiously to pull around the stern of the vessel. We rowed as though our lives depended upon our efforts.

And this indeed was the case.

I was too excited at the time, too exhausted, to be competent to say now how far from Silver Heels we lay when it happened . . . but the effect was as though a volcano had belched up from the sea.

A shattering explosion came—and the graceful yacht seemed to split in the middle. Minor explosions followed. Flames roared up as if to lick the clouds.

Her end, I think, was a matter of minutes. . . .

I can hear myself now as that deafening explosion

came, and Silver heels disappeared below the waves, creating a maelstrom which wildly rocked the boat:

"Smith! I don't understand! . . . Why did we desert Brownlow Wilton? He died a terrible death, and we—"

"He deserved it. God knows how or when the *real* Wilton died! The staff engaged in Venice had never seen Wilton. It was a plot to trap Adlon. The man who died on Silver Heels was a double, a servant of Doctor Fu Manchu!"

"Good heavens, Smith! A memory has come back!"

"Dictators have no monopoly of doubles. Doctor Fu Manchu employs them with notable success."

"Those fellows were crying out for someone called Doctor Chang, who was missing—"

"Wilton's impersonator, no doubt! I suspected a Mongolian streak. He lay drugged—by his own hand! I saw it all in the mirror, Kerrigan, hence my remarkable behaviour! The man, Lopez, was directing; he is senior to the other in the Si-Fan. But 'doctor' is significant. Probably Doctor Chang, apart from his resemblance to Brownlow Wilton, is a poison specialist—"

"I know he is, Smith—I know it! He is the man who came to your rooms and fixed the Green Death to the telephone!"

"Poor devil! You mean he *was* the man. . . ."

Chapter 42

THE MAN IN THE PARK

The wheels seemed to turn very swiftly in those strange days and nights during which I found myself beside Nayland Smith in his battle to hold the world safe from Dr. Fu Manchu.

Throughout the week that followed our escape from Silver Heels so many things happened that I find it difficult to select a point from which to carry on my story, since I realise that this story, almost against my will, from the first has wound itself insidiously about the figure of Ardatha.

First had come what Smith called "the great hushup."

Since Rudolf Adlon's double had been reviewing troops at the time when the real Adlon had been at Palazzo da Rosa, it was impossible for his government to divulge the fact that he had died (or disappeared) in Venice. When it became necessary to admit his death to a public which had looked up to him as to a god, they were told that he had died in his bed. The double, Rudolf Adlon No. 2, ceased to exist. It was done adroitly: the newspapers were muzzled. Patriotic physicians issued fictitious bulletins, then the final news for which a breathless Europe waited.

Mourning millions filed past a guarded dummy lying in state. . . .

Next came the retirement from public life of the ruler of Turkey, "a bloodless victory for Fu Manchu" was Nayland Smith's comment. (Pietro Monaghani, I should mention, had failed to keep the appointment with Adlon in Venice. He had accepted the orders of the Si-Fan.)

When an astonishing fact became undeniable—the fact that Fu Manchu with all his people, including Ardatha, had vanished from Venice as though they had never entered the City of the Lagoons, I remember that I advocated a secret departure to some base unsuspected by the Chinese doctor.

"Will you never realise, Kerrigan," Nayland Smith had said, "that from the point of view of the organisation controlled by Fu Manchu, there is no such thing as a secret base. He knew that Adlon was going to be in Venice before the combined intelligence services of Europe knew it. He brought a crew of highly trained criminal specialists to deal with the situation and dispersed them into thin air when their work was done, as a conjurer vanishes a bowl of goldfish. And think of the pack of cutthroats who left Silver Heels in the murder launch. The explosion was heard for miles—we were picked up ten minutes later; but what of the launch? It hasn't been traced to this day, nor anybody on board!"

And so on one never-to-be-forgotten evening I found myself back at my flat in Bayswater Road.

I stared from my window across the park as dusk gathered and pedestrians moved in the direction of the gates. I had not seen Nayland Smith since the forenoon. At this time, frankly, I was terrified whenever he was out of my sight. That he continued to live while the awful hand of Fu Manchu was extended against him became every hour a miracle more worshipful.

Presently the behaviour of a man who had just reached the gate nearly opposite my window began to intrigue me.

He was a tall, rather shabby-looking man, bearded and bespectacled. His wide-brimmed hat suggested a colonial visitor, and he walked with a stoop, leaning heavily upon an ash stick. Under one arm he carried a bulky portfolio. He was accompanied by a park-keeper and a policeman who assisted his every step. But it was something else which had arrested my attention.

He was staring up intently at my window!

Now as I drew the curtain aside and peered out, he raised his stick and lowered it, pointing to the front door!

That he was directing me to go down and admit him was an unmistakable fact, for I saw during a halt in the traffic that he was being shepherded across. I delayed only long enough to slip an automatic into my pocket and then went out and began to descend.

Mrs. Merton, my daily help, had gone, for I was not dining at home. As the flat below remained unoccupied and my upstairs neighbour was away, I confess that my steps to the front door were not unfearful. But I knew that this growing dread of the demoniac Dr. Fu Manchu was something I must combat with all my strength. Fear was his weapon.

I threw the door open and stood looking out at the man who waited there.

With a terse nod to his two supporters, he stepped in.

273

"Shut the door," he snapped.

It was Nayland Smith!

2

"Smith," I said reproachfully, "you promised me you would never go about alone!"

"I was *not* alone!"

He removed the wide-brimmed hat, the glasses, and straightened bent shoulders.

"I cannot complete the transformation in the best stage tradition," he said, with a grim smile. "False whiskers, if they are to sustain close scrutiny, must be attached with some care."

"But, Smith, I don't understand!"

"My dramatic appearance, Kerrigan, is easily explained. I was in a flying squad car with Gallaho. Nearly at the top of Sloane Street, just before one reaches Knightsbridge, there is a narrow turning on the right. Out of this at the very moment that we were about to pass, a lorry shot — I use the word advisedly — for the acceleration pointed to an amazing engine. It struck the bonnet of our car, turned us completely around. We capsized — and before the lorry driver could check his mad career, it resulted in the destruction of a taxi-cab, and, I fear, of the taximan!"

"But, Smith, do you mean—"

"That it was deliberate? Of course!" The pipe and pouch came from the pocket of his shabby coat. "Gallaho was knocked out, and I am afraid our driver was badly injured. As you see"— he indicated the side of his skull — "I did not escape entirely."

I saw a jagged gash which was still bleeding.

"Some iodine, Smith?"

"Later. A scratch."

"What happened then? How do you come to be here?"

"What happened was this: In spite of my disguise I had been recognised. This was a planned attempt to recover something which I had in my possession! In the tremendous disturbance which followed I climbed out of the window of the overturned car and lost myself in the crowd which began to collect. The casualties were receiving attention. My business was to slip away."

He paused, stuffing tobacco into the briar bowl and staring at me, familiar grey eyes in that unfamiliar bearded face leaving an odd impression."

"I always carry the badge of a king's messenger." He pulled back the lapel of his coat and I saw the silver greyhound. "It ensures prompt official assistance in an emergency without long explanations. I grabbed a constable, told him to come along, and made straight across the park. Here I roped in a park-keeper. Even so, I kept as much as possible to open spaces and checked up on anybody walking in the same direction."

He stared through the window across to the darkening park.

"What should you have done if I had not been looking out or if I had not replied?"

"I should have been compelled to ring the bell, meaning delay—which I feared. But I knew you would be at home for I had promised to communicate."

As I crossed to the dining room for refreshments he dropped into an armchair and began to light his pipe. The big portfolio he set upon the floor beside him. On my return:

"The full facts of the Venice plot are now to hand," he said bitterly. "Our pursuit of Silver Heels may or may not have been foreseen, but in any event it is certain that they meant to destroy the vessel."

"Why?"

"The story of engine trouble had been circulated. She was, as you know, a Diesel engine ship. By the simple device of blowing her up at sea, everybody on board having first slipped away on the motor launch, the death of James Brownlow Wilton would be satisfactorily explained. I think we may take it for granted that the launch did not make for land. I am postulating, though I may never be able to prove it, some other craft in the neighbourhood by which they were picked up."

"But . . . James Brownlow Wilton?"

"I have the facts—all of them, but the details are unimportant, Kerrigan. James Brownlow Wilton travelled by the Blue Train from London to Monte Carlo to join the yacht—I mean the *real* James Brownlow Wilton. At some time during the night (the French police think at Avignon) he was smuggled off the train. His double took his place. . . ."

"It's too appalling to think about!"

"His retiring habits made the job a comparatively easy one. He avoided—refused to see—those to whom the real Wilton was well known, and joining the yacht, sailed for Venice. The same procedure was followed there. Rudolf Adlon was dealt with, and saving our presence, the death of the millionaire at sea would have concluded the episode."

"That conclusion has been generally accepted,

Smith. The newspapers are full of it."

"I know. Those who are aware of the real facts have been instructed to remain silent . . . as in the case of Rudolf Adlon."

"Good God! What a ghastly farce!"

He took the glass I handed to him, and holding it up to the light, stared through it as though inspiration might reside in the bubbles.

"A farce indeed! But any government such as the Adlon government, which consistently hoodwinks the public, must be prepared to face such an emergency. One must admit that they have faced it well. General Diesler, Adlon's successor, acted with promptitude and vision. The figure lying in state was in the true tradition of Cesare Borgia. The bulletins of the medical men were worthy of Machiavelli. And now, today, an empty shell has reverently been set in place, and a monument will be raised above it!"

My phone rang.

"Careful, Kerrigan!" snapped Smith. "Remember that Doctor Fu Manchu employs mimics. Don't say I'm here unless you are absolutely sure to whom you are speaking. But it may be news of poor Gallaho."

I picked up the receiver.

"Hello," came a typically English voice. "Is that Mr. Bart Kerrigan's flat?"

"Yes."

"I have been told by Sir Denis Nayland Smith's man that Sir Denis may be with you. This is Egerton of the Foreign Office speaking."

I turned to Smith, and without uttering the words, framed with my lips: "Egerton, F.O.!"

Close to my ear Smith whispered:

"Say you will communicate with me if he will give you Fey's number."

"If you will give me Fey's number," I said (wondering what Fey's number might be), "I will endeavour to communicate with Sir Denis."

"Seven six nine four," came the reply.

"Seven six nine four," I mouthed.

Nayland Smith took up the receiver.

"That you, Egerton? Yes . . . precautions are necessary I am afraid. We have had an unexpected scoop today. Be good enough to mention to *no one* that I am here. . . . Yes . . . What's that? . . ."

He seemed to grow rigid. The grey eyes in that bearded face shone feverishly as he listened. Only once he interpolated a query:

"The mob killed him, you say? Is that certain?"

He listened again, nodding grimly. And at last:

"We knew he had had the notices," he said in a dull voice, "but he was even more obstinate than Adlon. In fact I am disposed to believe, Egerton, that he distrusted me. You know I was refused admission to the country?"

I heard the voice of the unseen Egerton talking for a while longer, and then:

"You may count upon me. I will communicate at once," said Smith and hung up the receiver.

He turned, and his expression warned me: Dr. Fu Manchu had scored again.

"Yes," he nodded, "the work of the Si-Fan carries on."

"What has happened, Smith?"

"Something even more spectacular," he replied bitterly, than the published facts relating to Rudolf

Adlon. The newspapers and news bulletins will have it tonight. All the world must know, for this is something which cannot be suppressed, nor edited. Standing on a black-draped balcony before no less than two hundred thousand people, General Diesler was delivering a funeral oration over the draped shell which does *not* contain the body of Rudolf Adlon. He said, so Egerton informs me: 'We have all suffered an irreparable loss. There is a fiendish enemy, by you unsuspected, an enemy in our very midst. . . .' Those, roughly, were his words. . . ."

"Well, what happened?"

"They were his last words, Kerrigan."

"What!"

"He stopped, clutched at his breast and fell. The sound of a distant, a very distant report, was heard. He had been shot through the heart."

"But, Smith, on such an occasion every place within range would have been emptied, held by the police or the military!"

"Every place within range — I agree, Kerrigan — that is, within ordinary range. This shot was fired from the top of the cathedral spire — thirty-five hundred yards away!"

"I don't understand!"

"A body of police who happened to be marching through the cathedral close by heard the report from the top of the steeple. They rushed in and caught a man who was hurrying down those hundreds of steps. It was none other than Baron Trenck, the millionaire publisher, ruined and exiled by Adlon, but acknowledged to be one of the three finest big-game shots in Europe!"

"But, Smith—"

"The rifle which he carried was fitted with telescopic sights . . . and a Jasper vacuum charger!"

"Good God!"

"You see, the doctor has already made use of that valuable invention, thanks to the work of his daughter, Korêani! In spite of the efforts of the police who endeavoured to escort the baron under arrest, fanatical Adlonites"—he paused for a moment—"I gather that he was practically torn to pieces."

3

"I am now going to make a curious request, Kerrigan."

"What is it?"

Let me confess that I had not yet recovered from the shock of that dreadful news.

"I am going to ask you to look out of the window while I select a hiding place somewhere in your rooms for this portfolio!"

"A hiding place?"

"Let me explain. It was to recover this portfolio which I was taking to Scotland Yard that that mad attack was made upon me in Sloane Street. A flying squad car will be here in a few minutes—I authorised the constable to phone for one—in which I propose to leave."

"And I to come with you."

"Not at all!"

"What!"

"Another attempt, although probably not of the

same character, is to be expected. I shall be well guarded. Your presence could not save me. But this time the attempt might succeed. Therefore, I am going to hide this valuable thing in your rooms."

"Why hide it?"

"Because if you knew where to find it, Fu Manchu might discover a means of forcing you to tell him!"

"But why leave it here at all?"

"For a very good reason. Be so kind as to do as I ask, Kerrigan."

I stared out of the window, thinking into what a mad maze my footsteps had blundered since that first evening when Nayland Smith had rung my bell. I could hear him walking about in an adjoining room, and then he returned. I saw a police car pull up at the door. The bell rang.

"I shall be in good hands until I see you again," snapped Smith. "Later I will communicate when I have made arrangements for the safe transfer of the portfolio to a spot where I propose to place its contents before a committee which I must assemble for the purpose."

"But what is it, Smith?"

"Forgive me, Kerrigan, but I don't want to tell you. You will know in good time. One thing only I ask — and you will serve me best by doing exactly as I direct. Don't leave your flat tonight until you hear from me, and distrust visitors as I distrust every inch of my route from here to Scotland Yard!"

When he was gone (and I went down to the front door to satisfy myself that the car really belonged to the flying squad) I sat at my desk for some time endeavouring to get my notes in order, to transfer to paper something of the recent amazing developments in this campaign of the Si-Fan against dictatorship. It was a story hard to believe, harder to tell; yet one that some day must be told, and one well worth the telling.

A phone call interrupted me. It was from Scotland Yard, and I knew the speaker: Chief Inspector Leighton of the special branch. News of Gallaho. He had escaped with cuts and contusions. The doctors despaired of the life of the driver; and among other casualties great and small occasioned by the apparently insane behaviour of the truckman, was that of this person himself. His neck had been broken in the collision.

"He was some kind of Asiatic," said Inspector Leighton. "Sir Denis may be able to recognise him. The firm to whom the lorry belonged know nothing of the matter. . . ."

I was still thinking over his words when again my phone rang. I took up the receiver.

"Hello!"

"Yes," said a voice, "is that Bart Kerrigan?"

The speaker was Ardatha!

Chapter 43

MY DOORBELL RINGS

By dint of a mighty effort I replied calmly:

"Yes, Ardatha. How did you find my number? It isn't in the book."

"You should know now"—how I loved her quaint accent—"that private numbers mean nothing to the people I belong to."

There was a moment of almost timorous hesitancy.

"I hate to hear you say that, Ardatha. I am desperately unhappy about you. Thank God you called me! Why did you call me?"

"Because I had to."

"What do you mean?"

"I cannot possibly speak to you long from here. I must see you tonight. This is urgent!"

I continued the effort to control my voice, to bid my thumping heart behave normally.

"Yes, Ardatha, you must know I am longing to see you. But—"

"But what?"

"I cannot go out tonight."

"I do not ask you to go out tonight. I will come to you."

"Oh, my dear, it's wonderful! But every time you take such risks for my sake—"

"This is a risk I must take, or there will be no you,

no Nayland Smith!"

"When shall I expect you?"

"In five minutes. But, listen. I know the house where you live. You cannot believe how well I know it! Fasten open the catch of the front door, so that I do not have to wait out in the street. I will come up and ring your bell. Please do not look out of the window or do anything to show that you expect anyone. Will you promise?"

"Of course."

Silence.

I hung up the receiver as a man in a daze. Ardatha was real after all. Nayland Smith was wiser than I, for always he had acted as her counsel when in my despair I had condemned her as a Delilah.

Then, as if to banish the wild happiness with which my spirit was intoxicated, came a logical thought. . . .

That mysterious portfolio—so valuable that Smith had been afraid to take it with him even in a flying squad car! It was here. . . . The Si-Fan knew. Ardatha was coming to find it!

My hand on the door, I paused, chilled, doubting, questioning.

Were my instincts betraying me? I could not recall that I had ever proved myself easily glamoured by that which was worthless. If the soul of Ardatha be not a brave and a splendid soul but a hollow, mocking thing, I told myself, then the years of my maturity have been wasted. I am indeed no philosopher.

In any event, now was the acid test. For if she came with a hidden purpose I should learn it. And whatever the wrench—it would be the finish.

For the rest I had nothing to fear unless I were

overpowered and the flat ransacked. There was no information which I could give, even under torture, for I did not know where Nayland Smith had concealed the portfolio.

I went downstairs. The lights were on in the little glass arcade which led to the porch. I opened the door and fixed the catch so that a push from outside would give access; then, in that frame of mind which every man in such circumstances has known, I returned to my flat.

The interval, though short, seemed interminable. . . .

My doorbell rang I walked from the study along the short passage. I was trying to frame words with which I should greet Ardatha, trying to school myself to control hot impulses, and yet not to seem too cold.

I opened the door . . . and there on the landing, wearing a French cape and a black soft-brimmed hat, stood Dr. Fu Manchu!

Chapter 44

"ALWAYS I AM JUST"

When I say that horror, disillusionment, abject misery robbed me of speech, movement, almost of thought, I do not exaggerate the facts. My beliefs, my philosophy, my world, crumbled around me.

"Mr. Kerrigan"—my dreadful visitor spoke softly— "do not hesitate to accept any order I may give."

His right elbow rested upon his hip, his long yellow fingers held an object which resembled a silver fountain pen. I wrenched my glance away from those baleful eyes and stared at this thing.

"Death in the form of disintegration I hold in my hand," he continued. "Step back. I will follow you."

The little silver tube he pointed in my direction. I walked slowly along to the study. I heard Dr. Fu Manchu close the front door and follow me in. I stood in front of the table, and turning, faced him. I avoided his eyes, but watched the long silver object which he held in his hand.

I despised myself completely. This man—I judged him to be not less than seventy years of age—held no weapon other than a small tube, yet had me cowed. I was afraid to attack him, afraid to defend myself—for behind this thing which he held I saw all the deadly armament of his genius.

But my weakness of spirit was not due entirely to

cowardice, to fear of the dreadful Chinese doctor. It was due in great part to sudden recognition of the frightful duplicity of Ardatha! She, she whom I longed to worship, she had tricked me into opening my door to this awful being!

"Do not misjudge Ardatha."

Those words had something of the effect of a flash of lightning. In the first place, they answered my unspoken thought (which alone was terrifying), and in the second place, they brought hope to a mind filled with black despair.

"Tonight," that strange impressive voice continued, "Ardatha lives or Ardatha dies. One of my purposes is to be present at your interview, for I know that this interview is to take place."

Love of a woman goes deep in a man as I learnt at that moment; for, clutching this slender thread of promise—a thread strengthened by Nayland Smith's assurance that Dr. Fu Manchu never lied—I found a new strength and a new courage. I raised my eyes.

"Make no fatal mistake, Mr. Kerrigan," he said coldy, precisely. "You are weighing your weight against mine, youth against age. But consider this device which I hold in my hand. From a thing which once demanded heavy cables and arc lamps, it is now, as you see"—always pointing it in my direction—"a small tube. I dislike that which is cumbersome. The apparatus with which I project those visible and audible images of which you have had experience can be contained in a suitcase. There are no masts, no busy engine rooms, no dynamos."

I watched him but did not move.

287

"This is Ericksen's Ray, in its infancy at the so-called death of its inventor, Doctor Sven Ericksen—rather before your time, I think—but now, perfected. Allow me to demonstrate its powers."

He pointed the thing, which I now decided resembled a hypodermic syringe, towards a vase which Mrs. Merton had filled that morning with flowers.

"Do you value that vase, Mr. Kerrigan?"

"Not particularly. Why?"

"Because I propose to use it as a demonstration. Watch."

He appeared to press a button at the end of the silver tube. There was no sound, no light, but where the vase of flowers had been there appeared a momentary cloud, a patch of darkness. I became aware of an acrid smell. . . .

Vase and flowers had disappeared!

"Ericksen is a genius. You will observe that I say 'is.' For although dead to the world, he lives—to work for me. You will realise now why I said that I held death in my hands. Ardatha is coming to see you. She loves you; and when any of my women becomes thus infatuated with one who does not belong to me, I deal with her as I see fit. If she has betrayed me she shall die. . . . Stand still! If she merely loves, which is fallible but human, I may spare her. I am come in person, Mr. Kerrigan, not for this purpose alone, but for that of recovering from you the letter of instruction signed by every member of the Council of Seven, which Sir Denis Nayland Smith—I have always recognised his qualities—secured this afternoon from a house in Surrey."

I did not speak; I continued to watch the tube.

"Love so transforms a woman that even my powers of plumbing human nature may be defeated. I am uncertain how low Ardatha has fallen in disloyalty to the Si-Fan where *you* have been concerned. I shall learn this tonight. But first, where is the document?"

I glanced into brilliant green eyes and quickly glanced aside.

"I don't know."

He was silent. That deadly tube remained pointed directly at my breast.

"No. I recognise the truth. He brought it here but left without it. He had concealed it. He was afraid that my agents would intercept him on the way. He was afraid of *you*. No matter. Answer me. He left it here?"

I stared dazedly at the tube. The hand of Dr. Fu Manchu might have been carved of ivory: it was motionless.

"Look at me — answer!"

I raised my eyes. Dr. Fu Manchu spoke softly:

"He left it. I thought so. I shall find it."

My doorbell rang.

"This is Ardatha." The voice became guttural, a voice of doom. "You have a fine mushrabîyeh screen here, Mr. Kerrigan, which I believe you brought from Arabia when you went there on behalf of your newspaper last autumn. I shall stand behind this screen, and you will admit Ardatha. She has been followed; she is covered. Any attempt to leave the building would be futile. Do not dare to warn her of my presence. Bring her into this room and let her say what she has come to say. I shall be listening. Upon her words rest life or death. Always I am just."

Fists clenched, bathed in clammy perspiration, I turned and walked to the door.

"No word, no hint of warning — or I shall not spare you!"

I opened the door. Ardatha stood on the landing.

"My dear!" I exclaimed.

God knows how I looked, how wild my eyes must have been, but she crept into my extended arms as into a haven.

"Darling! I cannot bear it any longer! I had to come to save you!"

I thought that our embrace would never end, except in death.

Chapter 45

THE MUSHRABÎYEH SCREEN

Ardatha, perhaps with the very next word which she uttered, was about to betray himself to the master of the Si-Fan!

My inclination was to take her up and race downstairs to the street. But Fu Manchu's servants were watching; he had said so, and he never lied. On the other hand, few human brains could hold a secret long from those blazing green eyes. If I tried to warn her, if I failed to return, I was convinced deep within me that it would be the end of us. I thought of that gleaming tube like a hypodermic syringe of which Dr. Fu Manchu had said:

"I hold death in my hand."

No, I must return to the study, must allow Ardatha to say what she was there to say — and abide by the consequences.

Her manner was strangely disturbed: I had felt her trembling during those bitter-sweet moments when I had held her in my arms. Remembering her composure on the occasion of that secret visit in Venice, I knew that tonight marked some crisis in her affairs — in mine — perhaps in the history of the world.

I led her towards the study. At the doorway she looked up at me. I tried to tell her silently with my eyes (but knew how hopelessly I failed) that behind the mushrabîyeh screen Dr. Fu Manchu was hidden.

"Sit down, dear, and let me get you a drink."

I forced myself to speak casually, but:

"No, no, please don't go!" she said. "I want nothing. I had to see you, but I have only a few moments in which to tell you — oh, so many things! Please listen." The amethyst eyes were wide open as she raised them to me. "Every second is of value. Just stay where you are and listen!"

Looking down at her, I stood there. She wore a very simple frock and her adorable creamy arms were bare. The red gleam of her wind-blown hair filled me with an insane longing to plunge my fingers in its living waves. I watched her. I tried to tell her. . . .

"Although the affair of Venice was successful in its main purpose," she went on swiftly, "it failed in some other ways. High officials of the French police know that James Brownlow Wilton was stolen away from the Blue Train, that it was not James Brownlow Wilton who died on the yacht. Sir Denis — yes? — he knows all about it too. And Baron Trenck, who silenced General Diesler, he was not given safe protection. . . . All these things are charged against the president."

She spoke those words with awe — the president! And watching her, watching her intently, I tried to say without moving my lips: "The president is here!"

But as a telepathist I found myself a failure, for she continued:

"I betray no Si-Fan secrets in what I tell you, because I tell you only what you know already. I am one of them — and all the wrong I have ever done has been to try to save you. Because I am a woman I cannot help myself. But now what I am here to say to

292

you — and when I have said it I must go — is this: A new president is to be elected!"

"What!"

"By him all the power of the Si-Fan — you cannot even guess what that power is — will be turned upon Sir Denis and — you."

She clasped her hands and stood up.

"Please, please! if you value my happiness a little bit I beseech you from my soul, when that notice comes, make him obey it! Force him to obey it! Imprison him if you like! — for I tell you, if you fail in this, nothing, nothing on earth can save him — nor you! Come to the door with me, but no further. I must go."

"But not yet, Ardatha!"

Dr. Fu Manchu stepped from behind the screen.

It was a situation so appalling that it seemed to dull my sensibilities. Such a weakling and traitor did I stand in my own regard that I would have welcomed complete oblivion.

Ardatha drew back from that tall cloaked figure — back and back — until she came to the wall behind her; and there, arms outstretched, she stood. The colour was draining from her cheeks, her expression was one of utter despair.

"Look at me, Ardatha" — Dr. Fu Manchu spoke softly.

As she raised her eyes to the majestic evil of his face I thought of a hare and a cobra. . . .

"I am satisfied" — his voice was little more than a whisper — "that your motives have been as you say, but I can no longer employ you in my personal service. Mr. Kerrigan" — it was a harsh command. He raised the Ericksen tube — "be good enough to look out of

293

your window and to report to me what you see."

Without hesitation I obeyed, stepping forward to the window so that Dr. Fu Manchu stood behind me.

"Draw the curtain aside."

I did so. Immediately I recognised the fact that the house was invested by the forces of the Si-Fan!

Two men over by the closed park gate unmistakably were watching the windows. Two others lingered in conversation near the door below. A big car was drawn up on the corner, and another pair were engaged in peering under the bonnet.

"Be good enough, Mr. Kerrigan, to raise your hand. The signal will be understood."

Automatically, I was about to obey . . . when a number of strange things happened.

A car coming from the direction of Marble Arch swung out sharply against oncoming traffic. It was pulled up by a skillful driver almost directly at my door. Another, approaching from the opposite direction, stopped with a great shrieking of brakes almost at the park gate. A third, which apparently had been following the first, checked dead on the corner of Porchester Terrace.

In a matter of seconds twelve or fifteen men were disgorged into Bayswater Road. . . . Without a moment's hesitation they hurled themselves upon the loiterers!

My heart leapt madly. It was the flying squad!

One warning came, and one only—a weird, minor, wailing cry—but I knew that it was meant for Dr. Fu Manchu. Its effect was immediate. From behind me he spoke in a changed voice, harsh, guttural:

"What has occurred? Answer."

"The police, I think. Three cars."

"Stay where you are. Don't stir. Ardatha—with me."

I stood still, fists clenched, watching the melée below.

"Bart! Bart!" Ardatha cried my name despairingly.

"Be silent! Precede me."

I heard them hurrying along the passage. But he had said "Don't stir," and I did not stir. I made no move until the opening and closing of the door told me that they were gone. Then I sprang around.

Footsteps were bounding up the stairs. I could hear excited voices—and an amazing, an all but unbelievable fact dawned upon me:

Dr. Fu Manchu was trapped!

Chapter 46

PURSUING A SHADOW

"Kerrigan! Kerrigan!"

Nayland Smith was banging on the door.

I ran to open it. He sprang in, his eyes gleaming excitedly. He had removed the synthetic beard but still wore his shabby suit. Beside him was Inspector Gallaho, head bandaged beneath a soft hat which took the place of his usual tight-fitting bowler. Four or five plainclothes police came crowding up behind.

"Where is he?"

"Gone! He went at the moment that I heard you on the stair!"

"What!"

"That's not possible," growled Gallaho, staring at me in a questioning way. "No one passed us, that I'll swear."

"Lights on that upper stair!" snapped Smith. "Stay where you are, Gallaho—you men, also."

He examined me intently.

"I know what you're thinking, Smith," I said, "but I am quite myself. Ardatha and Fu Manchu were here two minutes ago. He held me up with a thing which disintegrates whatever it touches."

"Ericksen's Ray?"

"Yes. How did you know?"

"Good God! But it's a cumbersome affair!"

"No larger than a fountain pen, Smith! He has perfected it, so he says. But—where *is* he?"

Nayland Smith tugged at the lobe of his ear.

"You say the girl went with him?"

"Yes."

"Who lives above?"

"A young musician, Basil Acton—but he's abroad at present."

"Sure?"

He began to run upstairs, crying out over his shoulder:

"Gallaho and two men! The others stand by where they are."

We reached the top landing and paused before my neighbour's closed door.

Gallaho rang the bell, but there was no response.

"Hello!"

Smith stooped.

I had switched on the landing light, and now I saw what had attracted his attention. Also I became aware of a queer acrid smell.

Where a Yale lock had been there was nothing but a hole, some two inches in diameter, drilled clean through the door!

"It's bolted inside," said Gallaho.

"But they are trapped!" I cried excitedly. "There is no other way out!"

"Unfortunately," growled Gallaho, "there is no other way *in*. Down to the tool chest, somebody."

There came a rush of footsteps on the stair, an interval during which Gallaho tried to peer through the hole in the door and Nayland Smith, ear pressed to a panel, listened but evidently heard nothing. To the high landing window which overlooked Bayswater Road arose sounds of excited voices from the street below.

"Seven black beauties roped in there," said Gallaho grimly, "but it remains to be seen if we've got anything on them."

One of the flying squad men returned with the necessary implements, it was a matter of only a few minutes to break the door down. I had been in my neighbour's flat on one or two occasions, and when we entered I switched the lights up, for we found it in darkness.

"Is there anyone here?" called Gallaho.

There was no reply.

We entered the big, untidy apartment which, sometimes to my sorrow, I knew that Acton used as a music room. It had something of the appearance of a studio. Bundles of music were littered on chairs and settees. The grand piano was open. An atmosphere stale as that inside a pyramid told of closed windows. Knowing his careless ways, I doubted if Acton had made arrangements to have his flat cleaned or aired during his absence. There was no one there.

"How many rooms, Kerrigan?" Smith snapped.

"Four, and a kitchenette."

"Three men stay on the landing!" shouted Gallaho.

We explored every foot of the place, and the only evidence we found to show that Dr. Fu Manchu and Ardatha had entered was the hole drilled through the front door, until:

"What's this?" cried one of the searchers.

We hurried into the kitchenette which bore traces of a meal prepared at some time but not cleared up. The man had opened a big cupboard in which I saw an ascending ladder.

"The cisterns are up there," I explained. "This is an old house converted."

"At last!" Smith's eyes glinted. "That's where he is hiding!"

Before I could restrain him he had started up the ladder, shining the light of a flashlamp ahead. Gallaho followed and I came next.

We found ourselves under the sloping roof in an attic containing several large tanks, unventilated, and oppressively stuffy.

There was no one there.

"Doctor Fu Manchu is a man of genius," said Smith, "but not a spirit. He must be somewhere in this building."

"Not so certain, sir!" came a cry.

One of the Scotland Yard men was directing light upon lath and plaster at that side of the attic furthest from the door. It revealed a ragged hole—and now we all detected a smell of charred wood.

"What's beyond there?" Gallaho demanded.

"The adjoining house, at the moment in the hands of renovators. It is being converted into modern flats."

But already Smith, stooping, was making his way through the aperture—and we all followed.

We found ourselves in an attic similar to that which we had quitted. We crossed it and climbed down a ladder. At the bottom was a room smelling strongly of fresh paint, cluttered up with decorators' materials, in fact almost impassable. We forced a way through onto the landing, to discover planks stretched across a staircase, scaffolding, buckets of whitewash. . . .

Nayland Smith ran down the stairs like a man demented, and even now in memory I can recapture the thud of our hammering feet as we followed him. It drummed around that empty, echoing house; the lights of our lamps danced weirdly on stripped walls, bare boards and half-painted woodwork. We came to the lobby. Smith flung open the front door.

It opened not on Bayswater Road as in the case of the adjoining house, but a side street, Porchester Terrace. He raced down three steps and stood there looking to right and left.

Dr. Fu Manchu had escaped. . . .

2

"The biggest failure of my life, Kerrigan."

Nayland Smith was pacing up and down my study; he had even forgotten to light his pipe. His face was wan—lined.

"I don't think I follow, Smith. It's amazing that you arrived here in the nick of time. His escape is something no one could have anticipated. He has supernormal equipment. This disintegrating ray which he carried defeats locks, bolts and bars. How could any man have foreseen it?"

"Yet I *should* have foreseen it," he snapped angrily. "My arrival in the nick of time had been planned."

"What!"

"Oh, I didn't know Ardatha was coming. For this I had not provided. But my visit to you earlier in the evening, my leaving here, or pretending to leave, the most vital piece of evidence on which I have ever laid my hands, was a leaf torn from Doctor Fu Manchu's own book!"

"What do you mean?"

"I was laying a trail. I was doing what *he* has done so often. He knew that I had those incriminating signatures; he knew that failing their recovery, the break-up of the Council of Seven was at least in sight. You are aware of how closely I was covered, how narrowly I escaped death. What I didn't tell you at the time was this: In spite of my disguise, I had been followed from Sloane Street right to the door of your flat."

"Are you sure?"

"I made sure. I intended to be followed."

"Good heavens!"

"I had not hoped, I confess, for so big a fish as the doctor in person, but that you would be raided by important members of the Si-Fan shortly after my departure was moderately certain. They were watching. I saw them as I left in the Yard car. I gave them every opportunity to note that although I had arrived with a bulky portfolio, I was leaving without it!"

"But, Smith, you might have given me your confidence!"

Anger, mortification, both were in my tones, but instantly Nayland Smith had his hands on my shoulders. His steady eyes sobered me.

"Remember the Green Death, Kerrigan. Oh, I'm not reproaching you! But Doctor Fu Manchu can read a man's soul as you and I read a newspaper. I had men posted in the park (closed at that time), and I had a key of your front door—"

"Smith!"

"You were well protected. The arrival of Ardatha

presented a new problem. I had not counted on Ardatha—"

"Nor had I!"

"But when no fewer than seven suspicious characters were massed in front of the house, and a tall thin man wearing a cloak was reported as having entered—(your front door, apparently being open)—I gave the signal. You know what followed."

"I understand now, Smith, how crushing the disappointment must be."

"Crushing indeed! I had King Shark in my net—and he bit his way out of it!"

"But the Ericksen Ray?"

"He had held the secret of the Ericken Ray for many years. Doctor Ericksen, its inventor, died or is reported to have died in 1914. As a matter of fact, he (with God knows how many other men of genius) has been working in Doctor Fu Manchu's laboratories probably up to the present moment!"

"But this is incredible! You have hinted at it before, but I have never been able to follow your meaning."

Automatically Nayland Smith's hand went to the pocket of his dilapidated coat and out came the briar and the big pouch.

"He can induce synthetic catalepsy, Kerrigan. I was afraid when I found you in Whitehall the other day that for some reason he had practised this art upon *you*. Except in cases where I have been notified, these wretched victims have been buried alive."

"Good God!"

"Later, at leisure, his experts disinter them, and they are smuggled away to work for the Si-Fan!"

"And to where are they smuggled?"

"I have no idea. Once his base was in Honan. It is no longer there. He has had others, some as near home as the French Riviera. His present headquarters are unknown to me. His genius lies not only in his own phenomenal brain, but in his astonishing plan of accumulating great intellects and making them his slaves. This is the source of his power. He wastes nothing. You see already, as General Diesler's death proves, he is employing the Jasper vacuum charger. I think we both know the name of the man who invented the television apparatus which you have seen in action. But probably we don't want to talk about it. . . ."

Up and down the carpet he paced, up and down, restless, overtensed, and stared out of the window.

"There lies London," he said, "in darkness, unsuspecting the presence in its midst of a man more than humanly equipped, a man who is almost a phantom — who is served by phantoms!"

A second later I sprang madly to his side.

Heralded by no other sound, there came a staccato crash of glass . . . then I was drenched in fragments of plaster!

A bullet had come through the window and had buried itself in the wall. . . .

"Smith! Smith!"

He had not moved, but he turned now and looked at me. I saw blood and was overcome by a sudden, dreadful nausea. I suppose I grew pale, for he shook his head and grasped my shoulder.

"No, Kerrigan. It was the top of my ear. Good shooting. The whizz of the bullet was deafening."

"But there was no sound of a shot!"

He moved away from the window.

"Diesler was killed at a range of three thousand odd yards," he said. "You remember we were talking about the Jasper vacuum charger?"

3

"I am disposed to believe that what Ardatha told you was true," said Nayland Smith.

He was standing staring down reflectively at something resting in his extended palm: the bullet which had made a hole in my wall. The cut in his ear had bled furiously, but now had succumbed to treatment and was decorated with a strip of surgical plaster.

"This attempt, for instance"—he held up the bullet—"somehow does not seem to be in the doctor's handwriting. In spite of its success I doubt if the 'silencing' of General Diesler was directed by Fu Manchu. If there is really trouble in the Council of Seven it may mean salvation. Assuming that I live to see it, I think I shall know, without other evidence, when Doctor Fu Manchu is deposed."

"In what way?" I asked curiously.

"Remind me to tell you if it occurs, Kerrigan. Ah! may I put the light out?"

"Certainly."

He did so, then glanced from my study window.

"Here are our escorting cars, I think. Yes! I can see Gallaho below."

He turned and began to reload his pipe.

"Tonight's near-triumph, Kerrigan, was made possible by the remarkable efficiency of Chief Detective Inspector Gallaho. Gallaho will go far. He obtained evidence to show that none other than Lord Weimer, the international banker, is a member of the Si-Fan. . . ."

"What!"

I cried the word incredulously.

"Yes — astounding, I admit. In fact, it almost appears that his house in Surrey is the temporary headquarters of Si-Fan representatives at present in England. I obtained a search warrant, paid a surprise visit during Weimer's absence in the city, and went over the place with a microscope. I experienced little difficulty — such a violent procedure had not been foreseen. Nevertheless, although the staff was kept under observation, news of the raid reached Weimer. . . . He has disappeared."

"But, Lord Weimer — a member of the Si-Fan!"

"He is. And a document involving even greater names was there as well. Even as I held it in my hand (I had time for no more than a glance) I wondered if I should ever get through alive with such evidence in my possession. I was not there in my proper person. You know what I looked like when I returned. The proceedings, officially, were in charge of Gallaho, but I adopted a precautionary measure."

His pipe filled, he now lighted it with care. I saw a grim smile upon his face:

"I sent Detective Sergeant Cromer back to Scotland Yard. He travelled in a Green Line bus, accompanied by one other police officer — and between them they carried evidence to upset the chancelleries of Europe! One idea led to another. I took it for granted that I should be followed, that attempts would be made to intercept me. I led the trail to your door, hoping for a big haul. I had one. But there was a hole in the net."

"What do we do now?"

"We are going to Number 10 Downing Street."

"What!"

"This discovery means an international situation. The Prime Minister has returned from Chequers and is meeting us there. The commissioner is bringing the documents from Scotland Yard, in person. Here is something for your notes, Kerrigan. I promised you a bigger story than any you had ever had. Come on!"

Indeed I had never expected to be one of such a gathering. There were three cars, one leading, then that in which I travelled with Nayland Smith, and a third bringing up the rear. The leading car, belonging to the flying squad, was driven at terrific speed through the streets. Under the circumstances I confess I was not surprised that we arrived at our destination without any attempt being made upon us. So vast were the issues at stake that even my fear of Ardatha was numbed.

Despairingly, I had come to the conclusion that I should never see her again. . . .

In a room made familiar by many published photographs I found the Premier and some other members of the Cabinet. Sir James Clare, the home secretary whom I had met before, was there and two ambassadors representing foreign powers. An air of deadful apprehension seemed common to all. Somewhat awed by the company, I looked at Nayland Smith.

He was pacing up and down in his usual restless manner, glancing at his wrist watch.

"Sir William Bard is late," murmured the Prime Minister.

Nayland Smith nodded. Sir William Bard, commissioner of metropolitan police, of all those summoned to this meeting was the only one who had not appeared.

"Until his arrival, sir," said Smith, "we can do nothing."

But even as he spoke came a rap on the door, and a voice announced:

"Sir William Bard."

Chapter 47

WHAT HAPPENED IN DOWNING STREET

"A trifle late, Sir William," said the Prime Minister genially.

"Yes sir — I must offer my apologies." The commissioner bowed perfunctorily to everyone present. "I think the circumstances will explain my delay."

A slightly built, alert man with a short jet-black moustache, he had a precision of manner and intonation which suggested, as was the fact, that his training, like that of the home secretary, had been for the legal profession. He laid a bulging portfolio upon the table. The Premier continued to watch him coldly but genially. Everyone else in the room became very restless, as Bard continued:

"Just as my car was about to turn out of Whitehall, a girl, a lady from her dress and bearing I judged, stepped out almost under my front wheel, and as my chauffeur braked furiously, sprang back again, but tripped and fell on the pavement."

"In these circumstances," said the home secretary, one eye on the rugged brow of the Prime Minister, "your delay is of course explained."

"Exactly," Sir William continued. "I pulled up, of course, and hurried back. Quite a crowd gathered, as always occurs, among them, fortunately, a doctor. The only injury was a sprained ankle. The lady, although one must confess it was her own fault, proved to live in Buckingham Gate, and naturally I gave her a lift home, Doctor Atkin accompanying her to that address. However, sir"—turning to the Prime Minister—"I trust I am excused?"

"Certainly, Bard, certainly. Anyone would have done the same."

Now quite restored, we sat down around the big table, the commissioner produced his keys and glanced at Nayland Smith.

"A strange attire for so formal an occasion, Smith!" he commented. "But it may be forgiven, I think, in view"—he tapped the portfolio—"of the information which is here. I had had time merely to glance over it, but I may say"—looking solemnly about him—"that in dealing with the facts revealed, the astonishingly unpleasant facts, our united efforts will be called for. And even when we have done our best . . ."

He shrugged his shoulders. He appeared to find some difficulty in fitting the key to the lock. We were all on tiptoes and all very impatient. I saw a sudden shadow creep over Sir William Bard's face as he glanced at his own initials stamped on the leather. He shrugged and persevered with the key.

There was no result.

"Might I suggest," snapped Nayland Smith, beginning to tug at his ear but desisting when he detected the presence of the plaster, "that you borrow a pair of stout scissors and force the catch, Sir William?"

"Always impatient, Smith!" The commissioner looked up, but his expression was not easy. "I don't understand this."

He tried again and then made an angry gesture. "I locked it myself before I left Scotland Yard." "Since time is our enemy," said the Prime Minister drily, "I think Sir Denis Nayland Smith's suggestion is a good one."

He rang a bell, and to a man who entered gave curt orders. . . .

The lock proved to be more obstinate than we had anticipated, but with the aid of a pair of office scissors and the expenditure of considerable force, ultimately it was snapped open. The man withdrew. We were all standing up, surrounding the commissioner. He opened the portfolio.

I heard a loud cry. For a moment I could not believe Sir William Bard had uttered it. Yet indeed it was he who had cried out . . .

The portfolio was stuffed with neatly folded copies of *The Times*!

One by one with shaking fingers he drew them out and laid them upon the table. Last of all he discovered a square envelope, and from it he drew a single sheet of paper.

There had been such a silence during this time that I could hear nothing but the breathing of the man next to me, a portly representative of a friendly power.

Sir William Bard cast his glance over the sheet which the envelope had contained, and then, his face grown suddenly pallid, laid it before the Prime Minister.

I glanced swiftly at Nayland Smith, and found myself unable to read his expression.

The statesman, imperturbable even in face of this

situation, adjusted his spectacles and read; then clearing his throat, he read again, this time aloud:

"The Council of Seven of the Si-Fan is determined to preserve peace in Europe. Some to whom this message is addressed share these views — some do not. The latter would be well advised to reconsider their policies, and to confine their attentions to their proper occasions.

PRESIDENT OF THE COUNCIL"

Chapter 48

"FIRST NOTICE"

"Smith! I am a ruined man!"

Sir William Bard sat in an armchair behind a huge desk laden with official documents, his head sunk in his hands. In that quiet room which was the heart of Scotland Yard, the menace represented by Dr. Fu Manchu presented itself more urgently to my tired mind that had been possible in the official sanctum of the British government.

Out of the charivari which had arisen when we had realised that documents calculated to cast down those in high places had been stolen from none other than the commissioner of metropolitan police, only one phrase recurred to me: the Premier's inquiry:

"Do you consider, Sir Denis, that this is a personal threat?"

Nayland Smith stared at the commissioner, and then, jumping up from his chair: "I don't think," he said, "that I should take the thing so seriously. It may be mere arrogance on my part to say so, but with all my experience (and it has been a long one) the particular genius who tricked you tonight has tricked me many times."

Sir William Bard looked up.

"But how was it done? Who did it?"

"As to how it was done," Smith replied, "it was a

fairly simple example of substitution. As to who did it—Doctor Fu Manchu!"

"I have accepted the existence of Doctor Fu Manchu with great reluctance, as you know, Smith—although I am aware that my immediate predecessor regarded this Chinese criminal with great respect. Are you sure that it was he who was responsible?"

"Perfectly sure," Smith snapped, then glanced swiftly at me.

"Describe the girl who was nearly run down by your car."

"I can do so quite easily, for she was a beauty. She had titian red hair and remarkable eyes of a pansy colour; a slender girl, not English, a fact I detected from her slight accent."

I did not groan audibly: it was my spirit that groaned.

"Quite sufficient!" Smith interrupted. "Kerrigan and I know this lady. And the doctor?"

"A tall man, grey-haired, of distinguished appearance, Doctor Maurice Atkin. I have his card here, and also Miss Pereira's."

"Neither card means anything," said Smith grimly. He turned to me. "This grey-haired aristocrat, Kerrigan, seems to play important parts in Fu Manchu's present drama. I detect a marked resemblance to that Count Boratov who was a guest of Brownlow Wilton, and of course you have recognised Miss Pereira?"

I nodded but did not speak.

"Don't make heavy weather of it, Kerrigan. Ardatha is in the toils—this task was her punishment."

He walked across to the wretched man sunk in the armchair and rested his hand upon his shoulder.

"May I take it that you usually carry the missing portfolio?"

The commissioner nodded.

"From my house to Scotland Yard every day, and to important conferences."

"The Si-Fan had noted this. After all, you are officially their chief enemy in London. I suggest that the duplicate portfolio has been in existence for some time. Tonight an occasion arose for its use. Judging from my own experience, farsighted plans of this character have been made with regard to many notable enemies of the Si-Fan."

Sir William was watching him almost hopefully.

"To illustrate my meaning," Smith went on, "they have duplicate keys of my flat!"

"What!"

"It is a fact," I interpolated; "I have seen the keys used myself."

"Exactly." Smith nodded. "They even succeeded in installing a special radio in my premises. It would not surprise me to learn that they have a key to Number 10 Downing Street. You must appreciate the fact, Bard, that this organisation, once confined to the East, now has its ramifications throughout the West. It is of old standing and has among its members, as the missing documents proved, prominent figures in Europe and the United States. Its financial backing is enormous. Its methods are ruthless. Your car, immediately following the pretended accident, was of course surrounded by a crowd."

"It was."

"Those members nearest to the door from which you jumped were servants of the Si-Fan and one of them carried the duplicate portfolio. He was no doubt an adept in his particular province. The substitution was not difficult. The address to which you took Miss Pereira was a block of flats?"

"Yes."

"Inquiry is useless. She does not live there."

"Smith!" Sir William Bard sprang up. "Your reconstruction of what took place is perfect — except in one particular. I recall the fact clearly now that Doctor Atkin carried a similar portfolio! The substitution was effected during the short drive to Buckingham Gate!"

"H'm!" Smith glanced at me. "Count Boratov would seem to be a distinct asset to the doctor's forces!"

"But what can we *do*?" groaned the commissioner. "Lacking the authority of those damning signatures, we dare not take action."

"I agree."

"We can watch these people whose names we have learnt, but it will be necessary to obtain new evidence against them before we can move a finger in such high places."

"Certainly. But at least we are warned . . . and I may not be too late to save their next victim. We cannot hope to win every point!"

2

We returned to Nayland Smith's flat in a flying squad car and two men were detailed to remain on duty in the lobby. Only by a perceptible tightening of Fey's lips did I recognise the mighty relief which he experienced when he saw us.

He had nothing to report. Smith laughed aloud when he saw me looking at a freshly painted patch on the front door.

"My new lock, Kerrigan!" The merriment in his eyes was good to see. Something of my own burden seemed to be lifted from my shoulders by it. "The lock was fitted under my own supervision, by a locksmith known to me personally. It's a nuisance to open, being somewhat complicated. But once I am in I think I'm safe!"

In the familiar room with photographs of his old friends about him, he relaxed at last, dropping down into an armchair with a sigh of content.

"If there is any place in the civilised world where you would really be safe, a month's rest would do you good, Smith."

He stared at me. Already he was groping for his pipe.

"Can any man rest till his task is finished?" he asked quietly. "I doubt it. Since Doctor Fu Manchu has tricked all the normal laws of life—will my task ever end?"

Fey served drinks and silently retired.

"I had a bad shock tonight, Smith," I said awkwardly. "Ardatha was instrumental in the theft of the commissioner's portfolio."

Smith nodded, busily filling his pipe.

"She had no choice," he snapped. "As I said at the time it was her punishment. At least she was not concerned in a murder, Kerrigan. Probably she had to succeed or die. I wonder if this really remarkable achievement has reinstated the doctor in the eyes of the Council."

"Is it a fact, Smith, that the names of the Council were actually in your possession?"

"Yes. Some I had suspected, nor would their identity convey anything to the public. But three of the Seven are as well known to the world as Bernard Shaw. Even to me those names came as a surprise. But lacking the written evidence, as the commissioner says, we dare not move. Ah well! the doctor has obtained a firm footing in the Western world since he first began operating from Limehouse."

He took up a bundle of letters which Fey had placed on a table near the armchair. He tossed them all aside until presently he came upon one at which he frowned queerly.

"Hello!" he murmured, "what's this?"

He examined the writing, the post office stamp — and finally tore open the envelope. He glanced at the single sheet of paper which it contained. His face remained quite expressionless as he bent forward and passed it to me. . . .

I stared, and my heart missed a beat as I read:

FIRST NOTICE

The Council of Seven of the Si-Fan has decided that you are an obstruction to its policy. Its present purpose being the peace of the world, a purpose to which no sane man can be opposed, you are given a choice of two courses. Remain in London tonight and the Council guarantees your safety and will communicate with you by telephone. We are prepared for an honourable compromise. Leave, and you will receive a second notice.

PRESIDENT OF THE COUNCIL

I don't know why these words written in a square heavy hand, on thick paper embossed with a Chinese hieroglyphic, should so have chilled me, but they did. It was no novelty for Nayland Smith to go in peril of his life, but knowing its record, frankly the dictum of the Council of Seven touched me with an icy hand.

"What do they mean, Smith, about leaving London?" I asked in a hoarse voice. "I suspected some new move when you spoke to the commissioner about saving the next victim."

"Marcel Delibes, the French statesman, has received two warnings. Copies were among the papers I found in Lord Weimer's house!"

"Well?"

"You may also recall that I promised to tell you when Doctor Fu Manchu ceased to be president?"

"Yes."

"He has ceased to be president!"

"How can you possibly know?"

He held up the first notice.

"Doctor Fu Manchu's delicate sense of humour would never permit him to do such a thing! Surely you realise, Kerrigan, that this means I am safe until the second notice arrives?"

"And what are you going to do?"

"I have made arrangements to leave for Paris tonight. Gallaho is coming, and—"

"So am I!"

318

Chapter 49

BLUE CARNATIONS

"This is the sort of atmosphere in which Doctor Fu Manchu finds himself at home!"

We stood in the workroom of Marcel Delibes, the famous French statesman. He had been unavoidably detained but requested us to wait. Two windows opened onto a long balcony which I saw to be overgrown with clematis. It looked down on a pleasant and well-kept garden. Beyond one saw the Bois. The room, religiously neat as that of some Mother Superior, was brightened along its many bookshelves by those attractively light bindings affected by French publishers; and a further note of colour was added by the presence of bowls and vases of carnations.

The perfume of all these flowers was somewhat overpowering, so that the impression I derived during my stay in the apartment was of carnations and of photographs of beautiful women.

There was a nearly full moon; the windows were wide open; and with Smith I examined the balcony outside. Our translation in a Royal Air Force plane from London had been so rapid, so dreamlike, that I was still in a mood to ask myself: Is this really Paris?

Yes, that carnation-scented room, dimly lighted

except for one green-shaded lamp upon the writing desk, with photographs peeping glamorously from its shadows was, as Nayland Smith had said, an ideal atmosphere for Dr. Fu Manchu.

Gallaho was downstairs with Jussac of the Sûreté Générale, and I knew that the house was guarded like a fortress. Even at this hour messengers were coming and going, and a considerable crowd had collected in the Bois outside, invisible and inaudible from the house by reason of its embracing gardens.

That sort of rumour which electrifies a population was creeping about Paris. Delibes, the rumour ran, had planned a political coup which, if it failed in its purpose, would mean that before a new day dawned France would be plunged into war.

"The grounds may be guarded, Smith," I said, looking about me. "But Delibes takes no other precautions."

I indicated the widely opened windows.

Smith nodded grimly.

"We have here, Kerrigan," he replied, "another example of that foolhardy courage which has already brought so many distinguished heads under the axe of Doctor Fu Manchu."

He took up the table telephone and examined it carefully, then shook his head.

"No! He has been warned of the Green Death, a fact of which the Si-Fan is undoubtedly aware. If only the fool would face facts—if only he would give me his confidence! He knows, he has been told, of the fate of his predecessors who have defied the Council of Seven! He is a gallant man in more senses than one"—Smith nodded in the direction of

320

the many photographs. "I must know what he plans to do and I must know what time the Si-Fan has given him in which to change his mind."

"His peril is no greater than yours!"

"Perhaps not—but I don't happen to be the political master of France! You are thinking of the letter which awaited me at the hotel desk?"

"I am."

"Yes"—he nodded—"the second notice!"

"But, Smith—"

"About one thing I am determined, Kerrigan—and I come provided to see it through: M. Delibes must accept my advice. Another Si-Fan assassination would paralyse European statesmanship. It would mean submission to a reign of terror. . . ."

Marcel Delibes came in, handsome, grey-haired; and I noted the dark eyebrows and moustache which had proved such a boon to French caricaturists. He wore a blue carnation in his buttonhole; he was charmingly apologetic.

"Gentlemen," he said, "You come at an hour so vital in the history of France that I think I may be forgiven."

"So I understand, sir," said Nayland Smith curtly. "But what I do not understand is your attitude in regard to the Si-Fan."

Delibes seated himself at his desk, assumed a well-known pose, and smiled.

"You are trying to frighten me, eh? Fortunately for France, I am not easily frightened. You are going to tell me that General Quinto, Rudolf Adlon, Diesler—oh, quite a number of others—died because they refused to accept the order of this secret society! You are going to say that Monaghani has accepted and this is why Monaghani lives! Pouf! a bogey, my friend! A cloud comes, the sky is darkened, when the end of a great life draws near. So much the Romans knew, and the Greeks before them. And this scum, this red-hand gang, which calls itself Si-Fan, obtains spectacular success by sending these absurd notices. . . . But how many have they sent in vain?"

He pulled open a drawer of his desk and tossed three sheets of paper onto the blotting pad. Nayland Smith stepped forward and with no more than a nod of apology picked them up.

"Ah! The final notice!"

"Yes—the final notice!" Delibes had ceased to smile. "To *me*! Could anything be more impudent?"

"It gives you, I see, until half past eleven tonight."

"Exactly. How droll!"

"Yet, Lord Aylwin has seen you, and Railton was sent by the Foreign Office with the special purpose of impressing upon you the fact that the power of the Si-Fan is real. I see, sir, that you are required to lower and then to raise the lights in this room three times, indicating that you have destroyed an order to Marshal Brieux. That distinguished officer is now in your lobby. I had a few words with him as I came in. As a privileged visitor, may I ask you the exact nature of this order?"

"It is here, signed." Delibes opened a folder and drew out an official document. "The whole of France, you see, as these signatures testify, stands behind me in this step which I propose to take tonight. You may read it if you please, for it will be common property tomorrow."

With a courteous inclination of the head he handed the document to Nayland Smith.

Smith's steely eyes moved mechanically as he glanced down the several paragraphs, and then:

"Failing a message from Monaghani before eleven-fifteen," he said, "this document, I gather, will be handed to Marshal Brieux? It calls all Frenchmen to the Colours. This will be construed as an act of war."

"Not necessarily, sir." The Minister drew down his heavy brows. "It will be construed as evidence of the unity of France. It will check those who would become the aggressors. At three minutes before midnight, observe, Paris will be plunged into darkness—and we shall test our air defences under war conditions."

Smith began to pace up and down the thick Persian carpet.

"You are described in the first notice from the Si-Fan," he went on, "as one of seven men in the world in a position to plunge Europe into war. It may interest you to know, sir, that the first warning of this kind with which I became acquainted referred to fifteen men. This fact may be significant?"

Delibes shrugged his shoulders.

"In roulette the colour red may turn up eighteen times," he replied. "Why not a coincidence of eight?"

We were interrupted by the entrance of a secretary.

"No vulgar curiosity prompts my inquiry," said Nayland Smith, as the Minister stared angrily at him. "But you have two photographs in your charming collection of a lady well known to me."

"Indeed, sir?" Delibes stood up. "To which lady do you refer?"

Smith took the two photographs from their place and set them on the desk.

Both were of the woman called Korêani: one was a head and shoulders so fantastically like the bust of Nefertiti as to suggest that this had been one of her earlier incarnations; the other showed her in the revealing dress of a Korean dancer.

Delibes glanced at them and then stared under his brows at Nayland Smith.

"I trust, Sir Denis, that this friendship does not in any way intrude upon your affairs?"

"But certainly not — although I have been acquainted with this lady for some years."

"I met her during the time she was appearing here. She is not an ordinary cabaret artiste, as you are aware. She belongs to an old Korean family and in performing the temple dances, has made herself an exile from her country."

"Indeed," Smith murmured. "Would it surprise you to know that she is also one of the most useful servants of the Si-Fan? . . . That she was personally concerned in the death of General Quinto, and in that of Rudolf Adlon? — to mention but two! Further, would it surprise you to know that she is the daughter of the president of the Council of Seven?"

Delibes sat down again, still staring at the speaker.

"I do not doubt your word—but are you sure of what you say?"

"Quite sure."

"Almost, you alarm me." He smiled again. "She is difficult, this Korêani—but most, most attractive. I saw her only last night. Today, for she knows my penchant, she sent me blue carnations."

"Indeed! *Blue* carnations, you say? Most unusual."

He began looking all about the room.

"Yes, but beautiful—you see them in those three vases."

"I have counted thirty-five," snapped Smith.

"The other, I wear."

Smith sniffed at one cautiously.

"I assume that they came from some florist known to you?"

"But certainly, from Meurice frères."

Smith stood directly in front of the desk, staring down at Delibes, then:

"Regardless of your personal predilection, sir," he said, "I have special knowledge and special facilities. Since the peace of France, perhaps of the world is at stake, may I ask you when these carnations arrived?"

"At some time before I was awake this morning."

"In one box or in several?"

"To this I cannot reply, but I will make inquiries. Your interests are of an odd nature."

Nevertheless, I observed that Delibes was struggling to retain his self-assurance. As he bent aside to press a bell, surreptitiously he removed the blue carnation from his buttonhole and dropped it in a wastebasket. . . .

Delibes' valet appeared: his name was Marbeuf.

"These blue carnations," said Nayland Smith, "you received them from the florist this morning?"

"Yes sir."

Marbeuf's manner was one of masked alarm.

"In one box or in a number of boxes?"

"In a number, sir."

"Have those boxes been destroyed?"

"I believe not, sir."

Smith turned to Delibes.

"I have a small inquiry to make," he said, "but I beg that you will spare me a few minutes when I return."

"As you wish, sir. You bring strange news, but my purpose remains undisturbed. . . ."

We descended with the valet to the domestic quarters of the house. The lobby buzzed with officials; there was an atmosphere of pent-up excitement, but we slipped through unnoticed. I was studying Marbeuf, a blond, clean-shaven fellow with the bland hypocrisy which distinguishes some confidential menservants.

"There are four boxes here," said Smith rapidly and stared at Marbeuf. "You say you received them this morning?"

"Yes sir."

"Here, in this room?"

"Yes."

"What did you do?"

"I placed them on that table, sir, for such presents frequently arrive for Monsieur. Then I sent Jacqueline for vases, and I opened the boxes."

"Who is Jacqueline?"

"The parlourmaid."

"There were then nine carnations in each box?"

"No sir. Twelve in each box, but one box was empty."

"What!"

"I was surprised, also."

"Between the time that these boxes were received from the florist and placed on the table, and the time at which you began to open them, were you out of the room?"

"Yes. I was called to the telephone."

"Ah! By whom?"

"By a lady, but when I told her that Monsieur was still sleeping she refused to leave a message."

"How long were you away?"

"Perhaps, sir, two minutes."

"And then?"

"Then I returned and began to open the boxes."

"And of the four, one contained no carnations?"

"Exactly, sir; one was empty."

"What did you do?"

"I telephoned to Meurice frères, and they assured me that not three, but four dozen carnations had been sent by the lady who ordered them."

Smith examined the four boxes with care but seemed to be dissatisfied. They were cardboard cartons about 18 inches long and 6 inches square, stoutly made and bearing the name of the well-known florist upon them. His expression, however, became very grave, and he did not speak again until we had returned to the study.

As Delibes stood up, concealing his impatience with a smile:

"The time specified for the reply from Monaghani has now elapsed," said Smith. "Am I to take it, sir, that you propose to hand that document to Marshal Brieux?"

"Such is my intention."

"The time allotted to you by the Si-Fan expires in fifteen minutes."

Delibes shrugged his shoulders.

"Forget the Si-Fan," he said. "I trust that your inquiries regarding Korêani's gift were satisfactory?"

"Not entirely. Would it be imposing on your hospitality to suggest that Mr. Kerrigan and myself remain here with you until those fifteen minutes shall have expired?"

"Well" — the Minister stood up, frowned, then smiled. "Since you mention my hospitality, if you would drink a glass of wine with me, and then permit me to leave you for a few moments since I must see Marshal Brieux, it would of course be a pleasure to entertain you."

He was about to press a bell, but changed his mind and went out.

On the instant of his exit Smith did an extraordinary thing. Springing to the door, he depressed a switch — and all the lights went out!

"Smith!"

The lights sprang up again.

"Wanted to know where the switch was! No time to waste."

He began questing about the room like a hound

on a strong scent. Recovering myself, I too began looking behind busts and photographs, but:

"Don't touch anything, Kerrigan!" he snapped. "Some new agent of death has been smuggled into this place by Fu Manchu! God knows what it is! I have no clue, but it's here! It's here!"

He had found nothing when Delibes returned. . . .

The Minister was followed by Marbeuf. The valet carried an ice bucket which contained a bottle of champagne upon a tray with three glasses.

"You see, I know your English taste!" said Delibes. "We shall drink, if you please, to France — and to England."

"In that case," Nayland Smith replied, "if I may ask you to dismiss Marbeuf, I should esteem it a privilege to act as server — for this is a notable occasion."

At a nod from Delibes, Marbeuf, having unwired the bottle, went out. Smith removed the cork and filled three glasses to their brims. With a bow he handed one to the statesman, less ceremoniously a second to me, then, raising his own:

"We drink deep," he said — his eyes glittered strangely, and the words sounded oddly on his lips — "to the peace of France and of England — and so, to the peace of the world."

He drank nearly the whole of the contents of his glass. Delibes, chivalrously, did the same. Never at home with champagne, I endeavoured to follow suit, but was checked — astounded — by the behaviour of Delibes.

Standing upright, a handsome military figure, he

became, it seemed, suddenly rigid! His eyes opened widely as though they were staring from his head. His face changed colour. Naturally pallid, it grew grey. His wineglass fell upon the Persian carpet, the remainder of its contents spilling. He clutched his throat and pitched forward!

Nayland Smith sprang to his side and lowered him gently to the floor.

"Smith! Smith!" I gasped, "he's poisoned! They have got him!"

"Ssh!" Smith stood up. "Not a word, Kerrigan!"

Amazed beyond understanding, I watched. He crossed to the meticulously neat desk, took up the document with those imposing signatures which lay there, and tore it into fragments!

"Smith!"

"Quiet — or we're lost!"

Crossing to the switch beside the door, he put out all the lights. It is mortifying to remember now that at the time I doubted his sanity. He raised them again, put them out. . . .

In the second darkness came comprehension:

He was obeying the order of the Si-Fan!

"Help me, Kerrigan. In here!"

A curtained alcove, luxuriously appointed as the bedroom of a screen star, adjoined the study. We laid Delibes upon a cushioned divan. And as we did so and I raised inquiring eyes, there came a sound from the room outside which made me catch my breath.

It resembled a guttural command, in a tongue unknown to me. It was followed by an odd scuffling not unlike that of a rat. . . . It seemed to flash

330

message to Nayland Smith's brain. With no glance at the insensible man upon the divan he dashed out.

I followed—and all I saw was this:

Some *thing*—I could not otherwise define it, nor can I say if it went on four or upon two legs—merged into the shadow on the balcony!

Smith, pistol in hand, leapt out.

There was a rustling in the clematis below. The rustling ceased.

His face a grim mask in the light of the moon, Smith turned to me.

"There went death to Marcel Delibes!" he said, "but here"—he pointed to the torn-up document on the carpet—"went death to a million Frenchmen."

"But the voice, Smith, the voice! Someone spoke—and there's nobody here!"

"Yes—I heard it. The speaker must have been in the garden below."

"And in heaven's name what was the thing we saw?"

"That, Kerrigan, is beyond me. The garden must be searched, but I doubt if anything will be found."

"But . . ." I stared about me apprehensively. "We must *do* something! Delibes may be dead!"

Nayland Smith shook his head.

"He *would* have been dead if I had not saved him."

"I don't understand at all!"

"Another leaf from the book of Doctor Fu Manchu. Tonight I came prepared for the opposition of Delibes. I had previously wired to my old friend Doctor Petrie in Cairo. He is a modest genius. He cabled a prescription; Lord Moreton endorsed it; and it was made up by the best firm of druggists in

London. A rapidly soluble tablet, Kerrigan. According to Petrie, Delibes will be insensible for eighteen hours but will suffer no unpleasant after-effects — nor will he recall exactly what occurred."

I could think of no reply.

"We will now ring for assistance," Smith continued, "report that the document was torn up in our presence, and express our proper regret for the sudden seizure of M. Delibes."

He poured water from the ice bucket into the glass used by Delibes, and emptied it over the balcony. He then partly refilled the glass.

"Having advised Marshal Brieux that Paris may sleep in peace, we can return to our hotel."

Chapter 50

ARDATHA'S MESSAGE

I think the bizarre drama of those last few minutes in the house of Marcel Delibes did more than anything else I could have accomplished to dull the agony of bereavement which even amid the turmoil of this secret world war shadowed every moment of my life.

Ardatha was lost to me. . . . She belonged to the Si-Fan.

Once too often she had risked everything in order to give me warning. Her punishment was to work henceforth under the eye of the dreadful Dr. Fu Manchu. Perhaps, as Smith believed, he was no longer president. But always while he lived I knew that he must dominate any group of men with whom he might be associated.

Leaving no less than four helpless physicians around the bed of the insensible Minister, we returned to our hotel. Gallaho was with us, and Jussac of the French police. As in London one car drove ahead and another followed.

As we entered the hotel lobby:

"This sudden illness of M. Delibes," said Jussac, "is a dreadful thing. He would be a loss to France. But for myself"—he brushed his short moustache reflectively—"since you tell me that before his seizure he changed his mind, why, if this was due to a rising temperature, I am not sorry!"

Smith was making for the lift, and I was following when something drew my attention to the behaviour of a girl who had been talking to the reception clerk. She was hurrying away, and the man's blank expression told me that she had abruptly broken off the conversation.

Already she was disappearing across a large, partially lighted lounge beyond which lay the entrance from the Rue de Rivoli.

Without a word to my companions I set off in pursuit.

By the swinging doors she turned, glancing back. Seeing me, she made as if to run out, but I leapt forward and threw my arms around her.

"Not this time, Ardatha—darling!"

The amethyst eyes glanced swiftly right and left and then flamed into sudden revolt. But beyond the flame I read a paradox.

"Let me go!"

I did not obey the words, for her eyes were bidding me to hold her fast. I crushed her against me.

"Never again, Ardatha."

"Bart," she whispered close to my ear, "call to your English policeman. . . . Someone is watching us—"

At that, she began to struggle furiously!

"Hullo, Kerrigan! A capture, I see—"

Nayland Smith stood at my elbow.

"Gallaho," he called, "a prisoner for you!"

I glared at him, but:

"Bart!"—I loved the quaint accent with which she pronounced my name—"he is right. I must be arrested—I *want* to be arrested!"

Gallaho hurried up. His brow remained decorated with plaster.

"Who's this?"

"She is known as Ardatha, Inspector," said Smith. "There are several questions which she may be able to answer."

"You are wanted by Scotland Yard"—said Gallaho formally, "to give information regarding certain inquiries. I must ask you to be good enough to come with me."

Smith glanced swiftly around. Jussac joined the party. Two men, their backs to us, stood talking just outside in Rue de Rivoli.

"I won't!" blazed Ardatha, "unless you force me to!"

Gallaho clearly was nonplussed. To Jussac:

"Grab that pair outside the door!" said Smith rapidly. "Lock them up for the night. If I'm wrong I'll face the consequences. Inspector, this lady is in your charge. Bring her upstairs. . . "

Jussac stepped outside and whistled. I did not wait to see what happened. Ardatha, between Inspector Gallaho and Nayland Smith, was walking towards the lift. . . .

Having reached our apartment and switched all lights up:

"Inspector," said Smith, "examine the lobby and the smaller bedroom and bathroom. I will search the others."

In the sitting room he looked hard at Ardatha:

"I am going to have you locked in the end room," he remarked, "as soon as Inspector Gallaho reports that it is a safe place."

He went out. No sooner was the door closed than I

had Ardatha in my arms.

She seemed to search me with her glance: it was the look which a woman gives a man before she stakes all upon her choice.

"I have run away, Bart—to you. I was followed, but they could do nothing while I stood there at the desk. Now they have seen me arrested, and if ever *he* gets me back, perhaps this may save me—"

"No one shall get you back!"

"You do not understand!" She clutched me convulsively. "Shall I never make you understand that unless we can get away from Paris, nothing can save us— *nothing!*" She clenched her hands and stared like a frightened hare as Nayland Smith came in. "It is the order of the Council. I do not know if there is anywhere in the world you can hide from them—but this place you must leave at once!"

"Listen to me, Ardatha," Smith grasped her shoulders. "Have you any knowledge, any whatever, of the Si-Fan plans for tonight?"

She faced him fearlessly; her hands remained clenched.

"If I had, I could not tell you. But I have no knowledge of these plans. As I hope for mercy, it is true. Only I know that you are to die."

"How do you know?"

Ardatha from her handbag took out a square envelope.

"I was ordered to leave this at the desk and not allow myself to be recognised. I waited until I *knew* . . . I had been recognised!"

Nayland Smith passed me the enclosed sheet, and I read:

FINAL NOTICE

Lower and raise the lights in your sitting room slowly twice, to indicate that you are prepared to take instructions. You have until midnight.

PRESIDENT OF THE COUNCIL

Chapter 51

THE THING WITH RED EYES

The apartments faced upon a courtyard. There were a number of police in the hotel under Jussac's orders, and the passports of all residents had been scrutinised. Some of the rooms around the courtyard were empty; the occupants of the others were supposedly above suspicion. But Ardatha's terror-stricken face haunted me. When she had realised that she was to be locked in the end room to await the hour of midnight, a fear so overwhelming had come upon her that my own courage was threatened.

Gallaho was in the lobby outside her door. And now I heard the clocks of Paris chiming. . . .

It was a quarter to twelve.

We had curtained all the windows, although if one excepted opposite rooms, no point commanded them. The atmosphere was stale and oppressive. Paris vibrated with rumours and counterrumours. By some it was believed that France already was at war; another story ran that Delibes was dead. But to the quiet old courtyard none of this penetrated. Instead a more real, a more sinister menace was there. The shadow of Fu Manchu lay upon us.

A hopeless fatalism began to claim me. Already I looked upon Nayland Smith as a dead man.

From Ardatha came no sound. Her eyes had been

unnaturally bright when we had left her. I had seen that splendid composure, that proud fearless spirit, broken. I knew that if she prayed, she prayed for me; and I thought that now she would be in tears—tears of misery, despair—waiting, listening . . . for what?

"Have your gun ready, Kerrigan!"

"What are you going to do?"

"I am going to search every inch of this room."

"What for?"

"I don't know! But you remember the black streak that went over Delibes' balcony? That thing, or another, similar thing, is here!"

I took a grip on failing nerves and stepped up to a walnut cabinet containing many cupboards, but:

"Touch nothing!" Smith snapped. "Leave the search to me. Just stand by."

He began to walk from point to point about the room, sparsely furnished in the manner of a continental hotel. No drawer was left unopened, no nook or cranny unsearched.

But he found nothing.

The electric clock registered seven minutes to midnight. And now came a wild cry, for which I knew that subconsciously I had been waiting.

"Let me out! For God's sake—let me out! I want to be with you—I can't bear it!"

"Go and pacify her, Kerrigan. We dare not have her in here."

"I won't budge!"

"Let me out—let me out—I shall go mad!"

Smith threw the door open.

"Allow her to join you in the lobby, Gallaho. On no account is she to enter this room."

"Very good, Sir Denis."

As Smith released the door, I heard the sound of a lock turned. I heard Ardatha's running footsteps. . . .

"Come out there! Dear God, I beg of you—come out!"

Gallaho's growing tones reached me as he strove to restrain her.

"If you are so sure, Smith"—my voice was not entirely under control—"that the danger is *here*, why should we stay?"

"I have asked you to leave," he replied coldly.

"Not without you."

"It happens to be my business, Kerrigan, to investigate the instruments of murder employed by Doctor Fu Manchu, but it is not yours. I believe some death agent to be concealed in this room, and I am determined to find out what it is."

"Smith! Smith!" I spoke in a hoarse whisper.

"What?"

"For heaven's sake don't move—but look where I am looking. There, under the cornice!"

The apartment had indirect lighting so that there was a sort of recess running around three of the walls directly below the ceiling. From the darkness of a corner where there were no lamps, two tiny fiery eyes—they looked *red*—glared down at us!

"My God!"

"What is it, Smith? In heaven's name, what *is* it?"

Those malignant eyes remained immovable; they possessed a dreadful, evil intelligence. It might have been an imp of hell crouching there, watching. . . . Raising my repeater, I fired, and . . . all the lights went out!

"Drop flat, Kerrigan!"

The urgency of Smith's order booked no denial. I threw myself prone on the carpet. I heard Smith fall nearby. . . .

There came a moaning cry, then a roar from Gallaho:

"What's this game? What's happened?"

The door behind me burst open. I became aware of a pungent odour.

"No lights, Gallaho—and don't come in! Make for the door, Kerrigan!"

I groped my way across the room. The awareness of that unknown thing somewhere in the darkness afforded one of the most terrifying sensations I had ever known. But I got to the door and into the lobby. Gallaho stretched out his hand and grasped my shoulder.

"Where's Sir Denis?"

"I am here."

There were sounds of movement all about, of voices.

"It's the big black-out," came Smith's voice incisively, "ordered by Delibes to take place tonight. Whoever is in charge of the air defences of Paris has received no orders to cancel it. This saved us—for I'm afraid you missed, Kerrigan!"

"Ardatha!" I said shakily, "Ardatha!"

"She fainted, Mr. Kerrigan, when the shot came. . . ."

Chapter 52

THE THING WITH RED EYES
(CONCLUDED)

"Open this door."

We stood before a door bearing the number 36. It was that of a room which adjoined our apartments. Lights had been restored. An alarmed manager obeyed.

"Stand by outside, Gallaho. Come on, Kerrigan."

I found myself in a single bedroom which did not appear to be occupied. There was an acrid smell, and the first object upon which my glance rested was a long, narrow cardboard box labelled: "Meurice frères."

I glanced at an attached tab and read:

Mme Hulbert:
To be placed in number 36 to await Mme Hulbert's arrival.

"Don't touch that thing!" snapped Smith. "I'm not sure, yet — Hullo!"

He was staring up at part of the wall above the wardrobe. There was a jagged hole, perhaps six inches in diameter, which I could only suppose to penetrate to the adjoining apartment.

Smith dragged a chair forward, stood on it and examined the top of the wardrobe.

"Apologise, Kerrigan! You didn't miss after

all. . . . There's blood here!"

Down he came and began questing all about the floor.

"Here's a fresh stain, Smith!"

"Ah! near the window! By gad! I believe it's escaped! I'm going to pull the curtains open. If you see anything move, don't hesitate — shoot!"

Colt in hand I watched him as he dragged the heavy curtains apart. The window was open about four inches at the bottom.

"Stains here, look!"

Standing beside him, I saw on the ledge bloodstains of so strange a character that comment failed me. They were imprints of tiny hands!

"Singular!" murmured Smith.

He stared out right and left and down into the courtyard. The building was faced with ornamental stone blocks.

"Smith —" I began.

"A thing as small as that could climb down such a wall," he rapped, "and into an open window — assuming its wound not to be serious."

"But, Smith — this is the print of a *human* hand!"

"I know!" He ran to the door. "Gallaho! Instruct Jussac to search all rooms opening on this courtyard and to make sure that nothing — not even a small parcel — leaves any of them. Come on, Kerrigan."

Picking up the florist's box, he returned to our locked apartments. Ardatha was in a room near by, in charge of a sympathetic housekeeper. As we entered the sitting room, I pulled up, staring . . .

At the moment of my firing at that thing up under the cornice, Smith, just behind me, had been standing

343

in front of a walnut cabinet.

The top of the cabinet had disappeared!

"Merciful heaven!" I whispered, "you escaped death by a fraction of a second!"

"Yes! Ericksen's Ray! The thing with the red eyes has at least elementary intelligence to be entrusted with such a weapon. This creature, or one like it, had been smuggled into Delibes' house, but made its escape. In the present case the same device of the flower box was used, an adjoining room having been reserved by a mythical Mme. Hulbert. During our absence this evening, by means of the ray, that hole was bored through the wall."

"But the box remains unopened!"

"So do the boxes, apparently, used by stage magicians. I think we may risk it now!"

"Is all well in there, Sir Denis?" came Gallaho's husky voice from the lobby.

"All's well, Inspector."

He cut the string and opened the box.

It was empty.

"Assuming a thinking creature small enough to get into such a box, for it to get out again would be a simple matter: merely necessary to draw these two end flaps and replace them without unfastening the string . . ."

I cannot say, I shall never know, what drew my attention away from the trick box, but I found myself staring fixedly into the shadows beneath the bureau. This bureau stood almost immediately below the hole high up under the cornice. Some dully shining object lay upon the carpet.

As I stepped forward to pick it up, indeed, all but

had my hand upon it, I recognised it for what it was—just such a tube as I had seen in the possession of Dr. Fu Manchu.

And as this recognition came I saw the thing with the red eyes!

"Quick! Grab it for your life, Kerrigan!"

Wounded, the creature had dropped the silver tube in that sudden darkness, had sought to escape, and then for some reason had returned for the ray. It crouched now beside the bureau, a black dwarf no more than fifteen inches high, naked save for a loin-cloth also black: a perfectly formed human being!

Its features, which were Negroid, contorted in animal fury, its red eyes glaring like those of a rabid dog, it sprang upon the tube.

But I snatched it in the nick of time . . .

That which happened next threatens to defeat my powers of description. Smith, who had been manoeuvering for a shot, fired—but as I made that frenzied grab, stumbling onto my knees, my fingers closed upon a sort of trigger in the butt end of the tube.

Smith's bullet buried itself in the wall. I experienced a tingling sensation. The thing with the red eyes which crouched before me, disappeared!

My last recollection is that of the bureau crashing down upon my head.

2

"Bart, dearest, are you better?"

I lay propped on cushions. Ardatha's arms were around me. My head buzzed like a wasps' nest, and a man whom I took to be a surgeon was bathing a painful cut on my brow.

"Yes, he is better," said the surgeon, smiling. "No serious damage." He turned to Nayland Smith who stood watching. "It must have been a heavy blow, nevertheless."

"It was!" Smith assured him. "Fortunately, he has a thick skull."

When the medical man was gone and I felt capable of sitting up and observing my surroundings, I realised that I had been moved to another room.

"Explanation of what had occurred would have been too difficult," Smith declared. "So we brought you in here."

And now came the memory of the black dwarf who had disappeared . . .

"Smith—he was disintegrated!"

"So was a portion of the bureau," Smith replied, "hence your being knocked out. It toppled before I had a chance to get at it. I have the mysterious tube, Kerrigan, Exhibit A, which resolves matter into its particles; but I don't propose to experiment further. We should be grateful for the fact that it was not ourselves who were dispersed!"

Ardatha held my hand tightly, and a swift glad wave of happiness swept over me. The unbelievable had come true. . . .

"I am by no means sure how long this peaceful interlude will last," Smith continued. "My taking forcible means to save Marcel Delibes may be construed, however, as a triumph for the Si-Fan. In this case our interests were identical. Possibly we shall be granted a reprieve!"

"We deserve one!" I was staring at something which lay upon a side table. It resembled a small watch but I knew that I had never seen it before. "What have you there, Smith?"

"Exhibit B!" He smiled. "It must have been in the possession of the dwarf—the smallest and also the most malignant human being I have ever come across. Gallaho found it in the cavity between the two rooms, so that I assume the dwarf intended to return, having recovered the silver tube, and to make his escape by way of the window of number 36. I suspect that this possibility had been provided for."

"But what is it?"

Ardatha's grasp on my hand tightened.

"It is a radiophone," she said. "Sometimes—not often—those carrying out Si-Fan instructions are given one. In this way they are kept directly in contact with whoever is directing them."

I turned my aching head and looked into her eyes.

"Did *you* ever use one, Ardatha?"

"Yes," she answered simply, "when I was sent to get the portfolio of the police commissioner in London!"

"You understand now, Kerrigan," snapped Smith, "that voice which we both heard in the study of M. Delibes? I am going to ask you, Ardatha, to show me how to get 'directly in contact'!"

Ardatha released my hand and stood up. She was supremely graceful in all her movements. Her poise was perfect, and I knew now that that momentary despair had been for *me*. . . .

"I will do so if you wish. Nothing may happen. You can only listen: you cannot reply."

She took the tiny instrument which Smith handed to

her and made some adjustments. We both watched closely. Paris lay about us, not sleeping, but seething with rumours of war. But in that room was silence— silence in which we waited.

It was broken.

A guttural voice spoke rapidly in a tongue unknown to me. It ceased. Ardatha adjusted the instrument.

"To move it to there," she said—but her tones were not steady—"means 'I do not understand.' "

And now (I confess that my heart leapt uncomfortably) that guttural voice spoke in English . . . and I knew that the speaker was Dr. Fu Manchu!

"Can it be Sir Denis who calls me?"

Ardatha's fingers moved.

"Indeed! I rejoice that you live, Sir Denis. I suspect that Ardatha is with you. Any information which she may be able to impart you will find of small value. I assume that one of my three Negritos pygmies is lost. But this is no more than just. Your work in regard to M. Delibes resulted in the cancelling of the grotesque order for your removal. I welcome your co-operation. . . . I regret my dwarf. Such a specimen represents twenty years' culture. Destroy the Ericksen tube: it is dangerous. Those who use it do not live long. The radiophone I commend to you. Waste no time seeking me . . ."

That unique voice faded away. Ardatha was trembling in my arms.

THE BEST IN ADVENTURE FROM ZEBRA

WAR DOGS   (1474, $3.50)
by Nik-Uhernik
Lt. Justin Ross molded his men into a fearsome fighting unit, but
it was their own instincts that kept them out of body bags. Their
secret orders would change the destiny of the Vietnam War, and it
didn't matter that an entire army stood between them and their
objective!

WAR DOGS #2: M-16 JURY   (1539, $2.75)
by Nik-Uhernik
The War Dogs, the most cutthroat band of Vietnam warriors
ever, face their greatest test yet — from an unlikely source. The
traitorous actions of a famous American could lead to the death
of thousands of GIs — and the shattering end of the . . . WAR
DOGS.

GUNSHIPS #1: THE KILLING ZONE   (1130, $2.50)
by Jack Hamilton Teed
Colonel John Hardin of the U.S. Special Forces knew too much
about the dirty side of the Vietnam War — he had to be silenced.
And a hand-picked squad of mongrels and misfits were destined
to die with him in the rotting swamps of . . . THE KILLING
ZONE.

GUNSHIPS #2: FIRE FORCE   (1159, $2.50)
by Jack Hamilton Teed
A few G.I.s, driven crazy by the war-torn hell of Vietnam, had
banded into brutal killing squads who didn't care whom they shot
at. Colonel John Hardin, tapped for the job of wiping out these
squads, had to first forge his own command of misfits into a
fighting FIRE FORCE!

GUNSHIPS #3: COBRA KILL   (1462, $2.50)
by Jack Hamilton Teed
Having taken something from the wreckage of the downed Cobra
gunship, the Cong force melted back into the jungle. Colonel
John Hardin was going to find out what the Cong had taken —
even if it killed him!

*Available wherever paperbacks are sold, or order direct from the
Publisher. Send cover price plus 50¢ per copy for mailing and
handling to Zebra Books, Dept. 1617, 475 Park Avenue South,
New York, N.Y. 10016. DO NOT SEND CASH.*

THE WORLD-AT-WAR SERIES
by Lawrence Cortesi

COUNTDOWN TO PARIS (1548, $3.25)
Having stormed the beaches of Normandy, every GI had one dream: to liberate Paris from the Nazis. Trapping the enemy in the Falaise Pocket, the Allies would shatter the powerful German 7th Army Group, opening the way for the . . . COUNTDOWN TO PARIS.

GATEWAY TO VICTORY (1496, $3.25)
After Leyte, the U.S. Navy was at the threshold of Japan's Pacific Empire. With his legendary cunning, Admiral Halsey devised a brilliant plan to deal a crippling blow in the South China Sea to Japan's military might.

ROMMEL'S LAST STAND (1415, $3.25)
In April of 1943 the Nazis attempted a daring airlift of supplies to a desperate Rommel in North Africa. But the Allies were lying in wait for one of the most astonishing and bloody air victories of the war.

LAST BRIDGE TO VICTORY (1392, $3.25)
Nazi troops had blown every bridge on the Rhine, stalling Eisenhower's drive for victory. In one final blood-soaked battle, the fanatic resistance of the Nazis would test the courage of every American soldier.

PACIFIC SIEGE (1363, $3.25)
If the Allies failed to hold New Guinea, the entire Pacific would fall to the Japanese juggernaut. For six brutal months they drenched the New Guinea jungles with their blood, hoping to live to see the end of the . . . PACIFIC SIEGE.

THE BATTLE FOR MANILA (1334, $3.25)
A Japanese commander's decision—against orders—to defend Manila to the death led to the most brutal combat of the entire Pacific campaign. A living hell that was . . . THE BATTLE FOR MANILA.

Available wherever paperbacks are sold, or order direct from the Publisher. Send cover price plus 50¢ per copy for mailing and handling to Zebra Books, Dept. 1617, 475 Park Avenue South, New York, N.Y. 10016. DO NOT SEND CASH.

NEW ADVENTURES FROM ZEBRA

TRIVIA MANIA
by Xavier Einstein

TRIVIA MANIA has arrived! With enough questions to answer every trivia buff's dreams, TRIVIA MANIA covers it all—from the delightfully obscure to the seemingly obvious. Tickle your fancy, and test your memory!

MOVIES	(1449, $2.50)
TELEVISION	(1450, $2.50)
LITERATURE	(1451, $2.50)
HISTORY AND GEOGRAPHY	(1452, $2.50)
SCIENCE AND NATURE	(1453, $2.50)
SPORTS	(1454, $2.50)
TELEVISION (Vol. II)	(1517, $2.50)
MOVIES (Vol. II)	(1518, $2.50)
COMMERCIALS & ADS	(1519, $2.50)
PEOPLE	(1520, $2.50)
MUSIC	(1521, $2.50)
COMICS & CARTOONS	(1522, $2.50)